MW01688563

THE FAR SECOND OF ETERNITY

NEMO DADE CHRONICLES : BOOK ONE

for Susan —
who's looked after
me for most
of my life
Hugs & love

PEPPERBACK

KEANA DOYLE

Copyright © 2023 by Keana Doyle

All rights reserved.

No portion of this book may be reproduced in any form without written permission from the publisher, except as permitted by U.S. copyright law.

For Rachel – who redefined what bravery is to me.

Prologue

7^Th^ Century Northwestern Irish Coast

He walked into the village tavern's common room, wearing muted, worn clothes like everyone else.

No one paid him any attention, despite his being a stranger.

Of course they wouldn't. That was how he wanted it.

But I'd felt his presence before he'd even entered. No point in running since he only would've found me again... and probably would have been less happy about it.

I sat in a corner, continuing to drink.

The villagers no longer had any interest in me either, not with a knife stuck in the table, dripping blood from the last idiot who'd tried to press his intentions.

Not that I was particularly choosy these days, but that one had insulted my warrior status, regardless of my being dressed as such. He'd implied some less than flattering things that I hadn't been willing to let slide.

My gaze focused on the God-awful swill they called drink in this far-flung hamlet.

Thunder quietly simmered in the distance within the rolling grey clouds out the window.

The new arrival's power danced along my skin. I didn't know exactly who he was, but that he would be trouble was not in doubt.

He seemed to be in his third decade, standing in front me with his curly dark hair, brown eyes, and close-cropped facial hair. Glancing around, and then at the chair across from mine, he commented drily in Greek, "I would ask to join you, but I do not think that wise. In truth, I think we should step outside."

"I think I am fine where I am," I responded in the local Gaelic dialect. No sense in letting them know I, a strange surly female, was more educated than their druid.

A wry half smile filled his face.

I'd just outed myself by answering him, even if it was in Gaelic. My lips compressed into a grimace as I stared at my cup.

Aoife, he said into my mind, *that was not a request.*

No one had used that name in centuries. That identity had died a long time ago with my first lifespan. I dared a quick glance at him, and rapidly wished that I hadn't. My breath raced. While my body sat rigid, my heart galloped like a spooked horse.

He'd stopped hiding himself, from me at least, so now I knew. A member of one of the Higher Orders stood in front of me—in Human terms—an Angel. Aw, damn.

Thunder rumbled louder, closer.

The sky let loose a steady pitter-patter against the roof.

I yanked my knife out of the table, wiped it off on my pant leg, and sheathed it. Trying not to look nervous was a challenge.

With slightly trembling fingers, I slammed back my drink, bringing the cup back down harder than was necessary. I stood and gestured for him to lead the way outside.

Approval rumbled through those watching. A few snickered.

His glance silenced them.

Once outside in the rain, he didn't stop. He merely walked out of the village, not waiting to see if I followed.

I had no choice. Well, there was always a choice, but I wasn't feeling *that* stupid.

We walked through the soaking drizzle, though it seemed not to bother him at all. The cold wet slid down my back, so I expended a little furl of power to fix that. Soggy leather was damn uncomfortable.

The thunder rumbled again, closer this time.

He turned and speared me with an unfriendly glance.

I raised an eyebrow.

Shaking his head, he turned and kept going.

To the west of the druids' grove were cliffs overlooking the ocean. The grove was a peaceful place, a holy place. Lately, I'd felt less and less comfortable there.

He walked towards the open scrub grasses blowing in the winds along the cliff's edge, staring out over the sea.

I joined him.

"Where we stand is special. A spot out of space and time, though it does not seem it. Tell me, Aiofe, daughter of Bebinn, why should I not throw you off this cliff and let the sea do as it will?" he asked mildly.

Silence was my friend.

"You do realise that not saying anything could be considered an answer in and of itself."

Damn.

Lighting struck the sea.

"Will you please stop cursing, Aoife," he commanded.

If I didn't know better, I'd have said he sounded irritable and tired, which made no sense to me because he was one of the Higher Orders. That didn't happen to them. They were infinite, immortal, and able to shape Reality in ways I could only dream of doing.

"It does if we've chosen to take on a Mortal form."

I flinched. He was slipping into my mind without me realizing it. Rude.

"Necessary, Aoife. Since you refuse to talk to me," he groused.

"Fine. Please stay out of my mind. That's rude, and against the rules," I informed him.

"You are amusing. The 'rules,' as you say, have not been something that you have paid anything more than bare lip service to in quite some time. You forget yourself, Nephilim. Did you honestly think your actions were hidden from us?"

Uh oh.

"Or had you not noticed that holy spaces were no longer, as you say, 'comfortable' to you anymore?"

It was a hard fight to not roll my eyes. Though he did get a disgruntled side-eyed glance. What a holy—

"I would not finish that thought if I were you, Nephilim," he advised.

Thunder rolled closer as the rain gained strength.

I tilted my head with a raised eyebrow and glanced into the sky. "Why are you here? If it's simply to give me a hard time for misbehaving, then consider me chastised. I will mind my manners. There. Are we done?"

He swung around and grabbed me. Suddenly, we were both over the ocean in the open air. All in a blink.

If he let me go, I would most likely die.

He glared.

That angry gaze left his eye color shifting faster than I could blink. Angelic beings were too much to fit into such a finite package.

His now blue eyes pinned me.

Shite. I'd made him truly furious.

Thunder clapped and lightning struck the sea.

"Stop cursing!" he snarled at me.

My eyes went wide. "Y–Yes," I whispered as I slowly nodded my head. "My apologies, Holy One."

He stared at me in grey-eyed, thoughtful silence.

"Ma-may I be graced with who has come to visit me?" For all the rain, and being held over the sea, my mouth was drier than the great desert. This had just gotten very real. Very real and very scary.

I'd heard stories of what the dark place held for those of my kind who'd ended up there. I had no interest in being condemned to that. An involuntary shudder shivered through me that had nothing to do with the chilly rain.

"You may call me Gilchrist," he finally said.

"The Devadas?" I whispered in disbelief.

My body trembled.

Muscles screamed to fight and claw and get myself back on land and away from him.

THE Metatron, one of the most powerful Angels, was in the Human world! He'd taken Mortal form. Why? Why had he hunted me down?

I racked my brain. Yeah, I had been crossing the lines a bit, but nothing that would warrant a visit like this. Right? Right?!

My body twitched and squirmed as all my transgressions marched vividly behind my eyes. By the time they stopped, I realized we were back on land.

Knees giving way, I sank to the ground. Sodden grass tickled my dirty fingers as they massaged wet earth.

This was it.

Tears welled unbidden over how stupid I'd been. The lives I had needlessly cost; the ones I'd taken. All the lies and the arrogance. My mind flitted to all the places I had thought of traveling back to see. All the Humans I'd thought to meet along the way. Missed opportunities to do better, to do good, that would never happen. Máthraín would've been so disappointed in what I had done with the gifts I'd been given.

"What? No begging, no groveling, no requests for mercy?" Gilchrist inquired as he stood over me.

"No," I croaked. "I do not beg. I will never grovel, and mercy is for those who did not know what they had done. My transgressions are mine. I knew what actions I took and made those choices freely. They are mine to own."

Shudders wracked my body.

His frozen silence broke me.

"I am prepared for judgement, Holy One," I blurted.

My terrified brain wondered briefly if being smote would hurt, or would I simply cease to feel?

He sighed and crouched, putting his hands on my upper arms. "Aoife, little sister, we feel your regret for what you have done, and you are forgiven for your dark acts," he absolved me with tenderness in his voice.

My head swung up of its own accord. "Wha—?"

His warm blue eyes regarded me in amused exasperation.

"I—I don't understand..."

"There are many things in this eternal existence that you do not yet see. Others thought you would know some of them by now. Regardless, there is a task we would like you to take up, little sister. One that you are uniquely suited to do," Gilchrist explained.

"What would you have of me? What could I possibly be better suited for than one of you?" I asked.

"Unlike the Divine Caretaker, Holy Ones, even such as I, have limits. Concealing ourselves by taking on a Mortal form is actually more tiring than you would think. There are those who break the rules, whose dark acts cause Humans and this world much more trouble than would be a part of the natural order of things," he clarified, taking a hand to tuck a lock of soaked hair behind my ear. "But you? Due to the Human half of who you are, this world is yours. You are able to move freely through it, though you could stand some training in both your powers and how to fight those who are more than merely Human."

I blinked as my head snapped back. “Are you talking of other Nephilim? Or are we talking...?”

He nodded with saddened, green eyes. “The Fallen, yes.”

A beat of silence stretched between us.

My eyebrows rose and my eyes widened. “You’re serious?”

Gilchrist’s mouth lifted in a fleeting half smile as he stood. “Yes, I am.”

I let my gaze flit about as I considered his words. An earthly warrior for the Heavens. Now there was a job with a lot attached to it.

“It will not be easy, nor do I make this request lightly,” he said quietly and stared out over the sea. “There will come a time where it will cost you all that you will hold dear, but it could hold the key to an even greater happiness.”

That made me swallow hard.

“Come. What say you, Aoife, daughter of Bebinn, child of the Heavens, will you be our Devadas?”

I choked and held my hands up. “That’s your title, Holy One!” There had been stories for ages about ‘the Devadas’, the one who traveled the known world keeping others like us from running amok and Humanity safe from those darker forces.

He grinned like he knew something I didn’t...which was entirely possible, and then he shrugged. “It is a title, one that I may confer to whomever I wish. So?”

It felt as though I was going to regret this. Hoping I was wrong, I went up to one knee like any good warrior taking an oath to her chief. “I, Aoife, daughter of Bebinn, child of the Heavens, swear to be your Holy Warrior to the best of my abilities, protecting those who cannot protect themselves, and stopping all whose dark acts would cause Darkness and strife in this world. This I vow by the Light of the Heavens, salt of the Earth, and the will of my Soul.” I wiped the tear tracks from my face and created a ball of Light in that hand. My breath blew into it, causing it to flare.

Gilchrist inhaled as his eyes closed.

The light flew to him and he glowed, taking my smaller light into his own.

Bells tolled, but they were something as much felt as heard. My head whipped around trying to find the source of the sound.

He exhaled as the glow faded. "That is the sound of your Oath being accepted and Reality changing accordingly. Come, Aoife, we have much to do." He held out his hand to help me stand.

Hesitating slightly, I put my hand in his. It was warm, even somewhat human feeling, but my other senses could now feel him. We were connected in some way. I knew that much.

He grinned. "Indeed we are little sister, but not as intrusively as you think, nor will I keep 'listening' to you. Our bond is fresh, and Energy is running back and forth between us. It will settle."

I nodded. "Why me, though? There are plenty of us running around, so what made you choose me?"

This made him laugh. "Because little sister, you are," he began and paused, glancing up at the sky, "interesting. Yes, that is it. You are interesting."

Well, that would teach me to be "interesting". Ugh.

Now he belly laughed as we walked.

"You may use my name, you know," he said with a chuckle. "You barely even think the one that I gave you."

"Even I know names have power. I am cautious."

He stopped and turned, getting me to face him. "Say it. Please."

My gaze darted side to side. "Gilchrist."

"See? Was that so bad?"

"I suppose not, but Heavens help us all if I ever call your Name," I muttered.

His face grew solemn. "May that day never have to come, but should it, know that I will hear you."

Yeah...because that was a happy thought. We began walking again. What had I just signed up for?

1

2017 Northeastern United States

I browsed the comic book store in one of my more eclectic outfits: a rumpled butter and indigo striped short-sleeved shirt, black long-sleeved spandex underneath, teal cargo shorts, olive cargo jacket and tan work boots completed the outfit. Owl-sized bedazzled pink shades rode atop my messy, long coal black hair. Sometimes, the best way to hide was in plain sight.

No one said anything.

It was a rural shop in the middle of Nowheresville, western New York. I'd been coming here for years. They were used to my oddities. Amusingly, this wasn't the strangest outfit I'd ever worn. My messy bedroom floor tended to be an outrageous fashion assistant. Today's wicked hangover, fueled by hair of the dog, had gleefully helped.

Things had changed a lot over the years, and not for the better, so I made do.

Some woman with short, blonde hair watched me from over by a spinning rack in the corner while she supposedly read an indie comic. Temptation taunted me to walk over and whisper *Boo!* But I didn't.

A lean dude, some big guy, and a dark haired woman browsed the boxes.

The place seemed more crowded than usual, and instead of looking happy, Rhett (yeah, his mom—what was a guy to do?) didn't seem super thrilled. He swore my purchases were what kept his place open. Hey, even the semi-immortal had to have hobbies.

Still, it was too crowded for my taste, and I was too hungover to play nice. I threw on my shades as I got closer to the front windows and register, where the owner stood behind his counter.

"Later Mac," I called while exiting. He looked like Kurt Russel's character, MacReady, from *The Thing*, so I'd called him Mac from the first time I'd been in the store. He loved it. To my knowledge though, I was the only one allowed to call him that.

The June sunshine was already baking things as I walked out of the center of town, such as it was. It only took a half mile to get off the main drag and into someone's back fields. With a piercing whistle, I called my ride.

Snort ambled up from a stretch of woods and let me climb on his back.

Really wanting to get out of the late morning sun, I unfurled a little Energy. We ran faster than an east wind through the woods, avoiding cultivated fields.

Sadly, bears tire faster than horses, so when Snort stopped, throwing me (somewhat unintentionally) off his back, I flew butt over tea kettle and tumbled several yards in front of him. My jacket and shades had flown off into the tall grasses.

I got up gingerly. The hasty bun I'd thrown my hair into had come undone, complete with dirt and grass accessories. At least I hadn't hit a tree.

Walking over to where my poor ride lay sprawled, I sent him a rush of healing energy that left him wanting a nap. So, I walked away with him sleeping on a deer trail. That would be a curious conversation later as Bucky and his herd came through.

Did I mention I was in the middle of no—

Hold on.

What was this?

There was a jet, like an actual military jet, sitting at the other end of the open field.

How in all of Creation had those two clowns gotten a jet?!

I shared my stretch of nowhere with a pair of brothers who were simultaneously as brilliant as they were stupid… and crackpot conspiracy theorists from way back. Mostly, they left me alone. My little trailer sat on the far edge of the clearing among some trees, closest to the only dirt road that led into here. It guarded the rim of their property from civilization, and they'd happily rented it to me for cash under the table. Their place was somewhere off to my right in the woods.

Reggie, the younger one (which meant he was in his fifties), crouched on top of the jet. He was yelling something over some noisy mechanical sound coming from inside it.

Theo was in his sixties. He stood on the ground. "I don't know what's wrong with it, you fucking idiot," he yelled in German. He thought I didn't speak it. Heh.

Their whole setup took up most of the clearing. Boxes, tool chests, barrels, crates, and things I really didn't want to consider.

I walked under the plane trying to get to my trailer.

They were nuts to try and park this thing here. How they'd managed to steal or buy it was something I didn't want to contemplate, mostly because if I did, I'd feel obligated to do something. Just like those crates I pretended not to see.

"Throw the switch!" Theo bellowed.

Woosh!

Jet fuel slushed down on me.

"Ahhhhhh!" I hollered.

"No! No! The other—"

Theo's words were lost as he went up the ladder to where Reggie crouched, completely ignoring what they'd done to me.

It stank. The blasted stuff had soaked my hair, the back of my neck, and my arms. Ugh! Aaaannd of course it was starting to irritate my skin. Great.

I half-ran, half-stumbled to my trailer.

The freakin' fluid had seeped into my left eye.

Monkey monster pukey batter butts! That burned!

I went up a couple of steps and yanked open my door. Babbling in multiple languages, I staggered off to the right towards my bathroom. The dimness inside my trailer didn't bother me, but it had made things harder to see, or that could've been the garbage in my eye. Thankfully, a single-wide wasn't all that complicated.

Once in the bathroom, I yanked my clothes off as if they were on fire because it had begun feeling as though they were.

My thrift store armchair creaked.

I stopped moving.

It only did that when someone sat down or got up.

The top sheet from my bed was on the floor just outside the bathroom door where I'd left it earlier. Grabbing the sheet, I wrapped it around myself.

Cautiously, I stepped into the hallway, trying to remember if I still owned a gun. Adrenaline was not the cure-all for boozy hangovers that some people made it out to be. My head still throbbed.

A shadowy figure in dark clothes sat in my chair, one leg crossed over the other. Maybe a woman? Dark hair?

"Wow...and to think Harry wanted to find you," the shadowy woman claimed in throaty, accented tones as she waved a silenced Glock negligently just above her knee.

My head pounded now. "Who?"

"British? Last name starts with a B," she commented and paused while I suspected that she glanced around the place. Things were too blurry to tell. "You actually live here? On purpose?"

My wheels were slow to get rolling, but once they did—bullet train speeds.

"That's not possible," I told her flatly. "He's dead."

Shadowy woman's cell phone rang.

Seriously? Hi folks, while you're enjoying this break-in, please silence your cell phones.

"Yes. I'm here. She's cagey, or drunk. Could be both," the woman informed someone, "and misinformed apparently." She paused. "Then you try and do this!" Shadowy woman gave an aggravated sigh.

Thunk!

2

The ice cold institutional pillow felt surprisingly good on my head. However, the mattress and metal frame? Not so much. I was still wrapped in my sheet covered in jet fuel. How nice of them. Now I could add cold body aches, rousing headache, and messed up left eye to the list of crummy garbage that had happened today.

Someone had gotten the drop on me, and that was no mean feat.

I opted to lie still and regroup.

The lump on the back of my head throbbed. Ugh.

My choice to live in the middle of nowhere, US had been on purpose since I wasn't fully human. There were myths, stories, even biblical references as to what I was. Sadly, most of them didn't come close to understanding the truth of it. See, being a Nephilim wasn't easy. It was more like being extremely human with both light and dark sides—but on steroids.

My mother's explanation had been along the lines of: a very long time ago, Dad, though a fully divine Celestial, had committed what amounted to an infernal act; he'd seduced a woman after expressly being forbidden. That had produced me. It was also the reason for his Fall from Grace and being banished from both Earth and the Divine. So, I carry the Divine within me, but there's also the temptation to do things that would cause me to Fall as well, from both sides. Temptation rides me like a bitch. Like I said, Human potential for good and evil—on steroids.

And sometimes... when one has lived for a very long time, life could become complicated. And messy. Several decades ago, I'd worked as an international mercenary, though particular as to what jobs I took. However, I'd walked away from that world. The plan had been to stay off the grid. Apparently, that plan hadn't gone nearly as well as I'd hoped. Somewhere along the way I'd gotten sloppy.

Top question of the day was: who had taken me? Why? Sometimes the why could provide clues as to the who. As far as I knew, I hadn't left any loose ends. They had to have a partial Infernal on their payroll, whoever *they* were. How did I know this? A full Infernal, what Humans called a "demon", would've wrecked the place already. They didn't take orders well. Also, even though I'd been decidedly off my game at the time, it had to have been at least a partial Infernal or... ooh, or a Supernatural. Yeah, a lot of them actually existed too, just not in the numbers that fiction and Hollywood supposed. Oh, and none of them were sparkly. Entertaining thought, but nope.

Had it been one of my kind, I would've known. We can sense each other, for lack of a better way to put it.

I began to run through a list in my head of possible candidates: the British government, the Soviets, oh wait, scratch them, but possibly ex-KGB folks, there were a few third world dictators, a couple of mercenary groups who'd be delighted to bag me, a few Family organizations probably wouldn't mind hearing about my demise. Hmmm...

Pain distracted my train of thought. That, and the hum of some fluorescent tubes, which made piss-poor crown molding as they lit up my small cell.

The room was barely longer than the bunk where I lay. A small, wooden dresser with four drawers stood on the opposite wall. Hmmm...quarters then, not a cell. Had it been a proper cell, they would never have given me so much to work with to make my escape.

Begrudgingly, I pushed myself to a sitting position while holding the sheet against my body as best as I could. Being so old, it wasn't that I was against them seeing me naked—that ship had probably sailed when they'd brought me here—but it was darn cold. I hated being cold.

A man walked into the room. His facial structure mostly screamed Eastern European with a strong jaw and Roman nose (and let me tell you, I could spot one of those from a mile away). He had close-cropped facial hair and wavy, thick, ash blonde locks on top of his head. Steel blue eyes regarded me in surly thoughtfulness. Whoever he was, he wasn't happy to see me.

Then again, it could've been that I looked like week old garbage with my hair sticking out everywhere hosting grass and jet fuel, and my left eye mostly swollen shut, redder than a poppy. Or it could've been the incredibly disgruntled look I was giving him. Nah. I was always a model of decorum and tranquility.

"So, you are awake," he commented while shutting the door.

"And you must be the master of the obvious. Pleased to meet you," I replied. My enforced nap had not alleviated my hangover nor my grouchy state. Though I was a touch more sober.

"Lovely. Such a snarky young thing. You are even worse than we were told," Mr. Obvious said. He had a slight accent to go with those looks. My ear thought Polish, possibly Czech.

Though I nearly choked at his words, 'snarky young thing'. Wow. Did they have the wrong girl or what? I know I looked like a twenty-six year old, maybe twenty-seven but um...Heh.

"Where am I?" I asked, refocusing so as to not laugh in his face. See? Model prisoner.

"You don't get to ask the questions," he stated. "That's our job, and your information leaves a lot of questions to ask."

I'd just bet. Yeah, there was no way I was going to play twenty answers with this merc/paramilitary punk. He just had that kind of vibe to him. They had not chosen their interrogator well. "What's your name?" I asked as I stood, tucking the sheet securely around my chest.

"What is yours?"

"Well, I go by Nemo Dade these days," I informed him. Most people thought that first name meant at least one of my parents was a Jules Verne nut. That was fine. It meant 'no one'. The last name? Eh, I had been a complete sucker for Hackers. As cover names went, it worked for me.

He nodded as if that's what he'd expected me to say. His left hand went to his waist as his right hand went to his face, scrubbing the lower half in frustration.

Idiot.

I ran, jumped, planted a foot on his thigh, and kicked his chin with my other foot, knocking him back into the door.

He stumbled forward on the rebound.

With a grab and a twist of his wrist, I heard bad sounds.

He grunted.

Then I stepped into him and flipped Mr. Obvious to the floor. Part of him may or may not have hit the dresser on the way down. I wasn't watching that closely. My goal was to get out of here. Wherever here was.

I yanked the door open and closed it behind me. No sense in alerting the natives early.

Right or left?

Mmmmm...left it was.

There were cameras in this dull gray hallway. I felt that in my bones. No help for it though. If I used my extraordinary abilities, that partial Infernal would sense me. It would be like throwing blood into an ocean for a shark. Not that sharks were evil, but the analogy was sound in terms of noticing things long distance. That meant I had to play things the hard way. I ran.

Needed clothes, not only because running around in a dirty sheet was tricky when one was only five foot two, but because it tended to draw notice in public.

However, randomly opening doors was out because that would just risk his buddies realizing faster that I was out and about, so racing around on instinct it was then. Maybe I'd get lucky. All the hallways looked the same. I finally found a stairwell. It was tight. That was bad, not much room for fighting if it came to it. I ran up anyway and stumbled into the corner of a large lounge area.

Oops.

There were four women and two men in the room.

Every one of them stopped what they'd been doing.

One of the men slowly lowered his newspaper. Massive shoulders, covered in long, light brown hair were attached to a big bearded guy on a monster sectional. He was the heavily tanned, outdoorsy type, complete with a few small braids; this wasn't a pretty boy. His hooded green eyes watched me. That was a warrior sure as I was breathing.

A broad-shouldered, bald black man with a goatee stopped playing cards with a short haired Latina woman at a modest round table. They both stared. His face remained carefully blank, and I didn't think it had anything to do with the card game.

The Latin brunette tilted her head as she watched me. Ahhh yes, my shadowy visitor. She must've been wearing a wig earlier.

Another woman with terra cotta skin and long wavy dark hair stood. She swung her leg over the back of the chair she'd been sitting in at the table. Even without her boots, she had me by a good four inches. Inches she looked like she knew how to use.

Two young Asian women, possibly Korean, looked at me from the opposite sides of the room. The one near the warrior watched me in assessing stillness.

My eye met the other one's eyes. Bingo. There was Trouble. Note to self, don't let her get behind me again. Thankfully, she was the furthest one away from me sitting across an armchair beyond the table with a book and earbuds.

Everyone's attention was on me.

"Hi, wrong turn," I stammered. "Carry on."

"Where do you think you're going?" the beautiful lady with her long wavy, dark hair asked in a rich, British accent.

"Oh, um, nowhere special," I rambled, "just not here, no offense."

I turned to dash back down the stairs. Now that I knew where that blasted pain in the back of my head was, might as well use a little juice to get away—

Wham!

Hands snatched my wrists as I ran into a wall of solid chest.

I've had iron manacles, like very old school real ones on my wrists that held me less securely. This couldn't be Mr. Obvious.

A quick peek up stopped my heart.

He was like me! Sort of.

How had I not known he was there?!

His ocean blue eyes watched me impassively.

"Well, I see you've met everyone," a masculine voice stated.

I cocked my head and blinked hard. Then I did a slow horror movie head turn to see.

The owner of the voice had dark hair with a salt and pepper close-cropped beard and tanned skin. There was military bearing belying that relaxed stance. His thick-collared, steel-colored cable knit sweater made me think of a fisherman though. He watched me with a curious smile and flicked a couple of fingers in our direction.

Manacle man let me go.

Chairs scraped.

The others stood.

My right periphery caught that Trouble remained sprawled in her chair.

I walked right over to her while adjusting my sheet more securely. A hard stare into her eyes illuminated so much. It was true: the eyes were windows into one's Soul. "I can help you with that," I murmured to her.

She stared at me and blinked.

The difference was that I could see the other one within her, just under her skin, as if her outside were see through. It glared at me with sulfurous, glowing eyes and too many teeth. Something very nasty was trying to possess this young woman.

Big guy's newspaper fell.

He had a hold of the other Asian young woman.

Looking at her now, I could see the family resemblance. This was either her sister or cousin. I was betting on sister.

Fisherman still watched me. "Let's go to the conference room where we can talk." He walked back out the door. I could hear faint traces of an accent, but from where?

Mr. Card Player and Pretty Brit gestured for me to follow the fisherman.

Contrary to my wishes, the odds were definitely not in my favor... especially with *him* in here. So, I went with my only option; I followed the fisherman.

3

Most of us were seated in a good-sized room with an even-better-sized conference table.

The door we'd come through was far down to my left beyond the head of the table. There was another door, though, to my right about seven feet away, just past Newspaper guy, who sat at the opposite end of the table. I had taken the seat kitty corner to him. Always be as close to an exit as possible. If it came to it, I liked my odds against Newspaper guy. He was big, but I was willing to bet that I was faster.

"I suppose we ought to do some introductions," Fisherman declared from the head of the table. He gestured to his left. "This is Ivelisse Nazario, or 'Ivy' to us. Next is Josh Cooper." The man with the goatee sat on her other side.

My erstwhile interrogator stood behind the chair opposite from me next to Mr. Cooper.

Fisherman exhaled a little heavily before saying, "You've already met Aleksander Dobrek."

Dobrek glared at me as the bruises blossomed. Sheesh. Kick a guy in the jaw and put him on the floor; next thing you know, there's no talking to him.

"On the end is Braxton Edwards."

Edwards studied me.

I fought the incredibly strong urge to do something outrageously silly just to mess with him. Sadly, I was too tired and in too much pain to bother. He was lucky. Wasn't about to use my abilities to heal myself with Manacle Man or Trouble in the room.

"This is Chun Hei Kang and her cousin, Hyun Kang. Usually, they go by Clarice," he stated pointing at the slightly older one, "and Ellie." Hmmm...Trouble was in fact Korean, and went by Ellie. Having her names would help. Finding out the name of that thing, or even what it was that held onto her, was going to be harder though. If it had one.

"Nemo?"

They were all looking at me.

I'd stood up without realizing it. "I'm sorry, what?" Oops, way to look about as sharp as a bowlin' ball.

"This is Grace Fletcher," Fisherman said, presumably again.

She watched me with a curious tilt to her head.

"She doesn't need to know my name," Manacle Man muttered, his aristocratic British accent very apparent. He stood against the wall behind Grace's chair, his arms crossed and a sour look on his face.

Creepy-crawling chills danced over my proverbial grave. Something about him rang all my alarm bells. I flexed a little of my power. He really was as young as he looked. At least I thought so. "How old *are* you?" I asked less than diplomatically. There was no way he should've been that young, that new.

He scowled at me.

"Hey, you cheery bunch of banditos kidnapped me, remember? So, I'd say I am allowed a rude question or two," I commented with lots of snark.

"He's twenty-eight," Cooper informed me.

Manacle Man pushed off the wall.

Several glares went around the table.

"What?" Cooper demanded with a shrug. "What's she gonna do with that information? I'll tell you what—nothing. I mean c'mon. She ended up being a far easier grab than we were led to believe. If she were actually as badass as you'd said, then why hasn't she healed herself, done more damage, or simply poofed herself out of here?"

Oh yes, he was American through and through. I liked him. A small chuckle escaped.

"What's so funny?" Manacle Man asked. There was no mistaking the menace in his voice. He was angling for a fight.

"I won't fight you," the words slipped out quietly. Dagnabbit. I hated being sensible. "Whoever you are." Okay, a little bit of sass couldn't hurt.

He tried to tower over me.

It wasn't hard. The git was at least a full foot taller.

On the plus side, I was smart enough not to meet his eyes. Uh uh, nope.

His power grew within the confines of his body.

"Henry," the sharp one word command came from a voice that made my head snap up. "That's enough."

"No..." I whispered.

A quick turn and jump put me on the table. I strode down to the other end. The blasted thing was a behemoth because it never moved or shook. My brain idly wondered at that. Gibbering in shock was much closer to accurate.

The new arrival stood there in all his stern British glory of pressed slacks and a buttoned down collared shirt, all six-two of him. His dark wavy hair had streaks of gray in it. Lines fanned from his beautiful, warm brown eyes. Well, they weren't warm right now. It was more that implacable brown tree bark color. He was angry.

Yeah, me too.

"You're dead." I looked around to see if the others were seeing him, or if it were just Manacle Man and I.

The warrior was on his feet.

"He looks like he's breathing to me," Fisherman offered laconically.

"You're real? You're really here? You're alive?!" I babbled. My jaw worked, my head pounded, the room spun as my harsh breathing sped up to supersonic speeds.

"Noswearingnoswearingnoswearing," I rambled under my breath.

Sounds of movement catalyzed me from my stupor. I teleported.

Shouts and more sounds of chairs were dim, but could still be heard so I wasn't too far. A quick glance showed me that I was in someone's office. It had the standard nice comfy chair behind a desk, a couple of chairs in front, a bookcase behind the desk chair, a small bar cart to the left of the door behind me—that's where my inspection stopped.

I grabbed a bottle of very expensive Scottish single malt and poured myself three fingers. Downed it. Poured another three fingers.

Needed to hear what they were up to, as much as I didn't want to do it. My eyes closed as I extended my hearing.

"...ridiculous, sir," Manacle Man snapped.

"I believe the Commodore asked you a question," Fisherman said.

A rude noise. His power stretched out and found me. "She's in your office, Captain."

Great. Whose office was I in then?

I took another sip. My hand shook.

"Aw man," Fisherman groaned softly as he opened the door.

"Goldy gobblety horsefeathers," I mumbled.

His eyebrows climbed his forehead. "Well, the least you could do is drink something easier for me to replace. They don't export that."

"I'm not crazy, nor am I drunk," answering his unasked questions. "There are certain things that ought not to be said, or taken lightly. Language is a weapon. Words have power.

The power to heal and the power to kill...even the power to damn for all Eternity. Nonsense words are my workaround."

"Isn't the effect still the same if you're thinking it?"

"Not if I'm specifically focusing on the nonsense. It's distracting." I took another swig. "And yes, I know perfectly well that they don't export this one. I'll get you some more. I think I have some at home."

"What? That piece of shit trailer?"

I chuckled, but it was a sour, sardonic sound. "Language. And no, not there. That's not home." I finished what was in my glass and stared at the wall with my one good eye. At least the room wasn't spinning anymore. "What do you people want with me? Who the hell are you? Interpol? Can't be MI-6; they typically don't team up internationally like...well, unless this is a multi-agency task force in which case, I want none of it. Go peddle your cookies elsewhere."

Fisherman's face grew thoughtful.

"No, I wasn't skimming your thoughts," I groused. "That's beyond rude."

"But you can," he said, but almost like a question.

"Yes, but like I said, there are rules about that."

"No, you said it was rude," he countered.

"You're dodging my questions," I hedged and redirected. "I asked first."

He smiled faintly. "Fair enough. I'm Callister Mylonas, and yes, I run this little show...well, with the Commodore."

I jerkily poured more scotch and downed it. He'd been promoted huh?

"Greek-American," I said with a nod, "should've realized." The last I said in Greek and then added, "North Eastern United States though, that I got."

"Very good," he replied in the same. That alone told me he'd come from a bilingual home. His accent was good when he allowed it.

"He said you speak a great many languages," Fisherman observed. "You sound like a native. I never would've known the difference."

I stared down at the glass and fought not to break it. "Do yourself a favor. Don't bring him up," I said in rough tones.

Fisherman nodded. He didn't say a word.

I spun and threw the glass against the far wall. Broken shards flew all over a credenza and everything else.

"Feel better?"

"No," I whispered harshly, chest heaving in deep breaths.

"Why don't we take you to your room?" he suggested.

"You stick me in that tin box and I will be off this ship faster than you can blink," I warned. Not sure why I hadn't figured out that we were on a ship before now. Then again, it'd been a rough day all around, and I hadn't started it at my best in the first place. Current events weren't making it any better.

He laughed. The motley, flippity fart actually laughed at me.

"You're not exactly dressed for a swim in the ocean, and while I believe you are strong, I don't think you're good enough to send yourself that far," he quipped. "Besides, that wasn't your room. You have much nicer accommodations up here with us. There's a nice bed, blankets, a shower, your own booze." Fisherman seemed happy to set me drinking other stuff.

With a heavy exhale, I agreed. There was no fight left in me to argue. They hadn't tried to kill me yet. Fisherman hadn't let the troubled twosome come after me either, so I supposed they wanted me alive and in one piece. So be it. "Lead on, oh great Fisherman."

His eyebrows came down in a query.

However, I was no longer in a mood to answer questions.

He was smart enough to let it go.

We left and walked the hallways without seeing anyone. Heck, I couldn't even sense the other two, so someone must've told them to tone it down.

Fisherman unlocked a door and ushered me into a room.

As I walked in, my feet sank into a soft, plush carpet. Its deep ocean blue silence stretched across the room. Two windows told me it was at least early evening...well, depending on where in the world we were.

A lovely antique cherry armoire stood off to the left with a door to the bathroom beyond it. The bed had to be king-sized with an abstract watercolor comforter of blues, greens, and purples with scads of pillows to match. It had no legs, just a full base to the floor.

But it was the painting over the quilted pale blue headboard that got my attention. "Is that 'Water Lilies and Japanese Bridge'?" I breathed.

"Yes," he said quietly.

"How did you...?"

"It's on loan."

Turning my head to say words that flew away as my eye caught the other painting above the couch in an alcove off to our right. "San Giorgio Maggiore...that can't be real."

He made an indecipherable noise.

I tore my eyes away from the invitingly plump ivory couch with its thick throw blanket and bookcase resting in the inset to a bar cart nearby on a pushed out section of wall. Another bookcase stood next to it with a cherry desk and chair against the hallway wall. I spun around the room slowly, staring at everything and noticed a small dresser stood behind the door against the other hallway wall.

This room couldn't have been planned better than if I'd set it up myself. Creepy! I walked over to the armoire and opened it.

The thing was filled with clothes—nice, understated, and mostly garments I'd have chosen back in my professional days before being a mercenary, when I'd worked for MI-6. My hands hung on the handles as I stared sightlessly.

Fisherman coughed. “Before you ask, yes, *someone* designed this room for you with your tastes in mind and gave us approximate sizing for the clothes that were chosen.”

It was too much. He knew how much I loved Monet’s work, especially the sunset monastery piece. Tears prickled. Right then I would’ve sworn on my life that it was because of the jet fuel in my face. “I need a shower,” I murmured without turning around, not moving at all.

“Sure. Why don’t you get cleaned up, heal yourself if you need to, and get some sleep,” he advised. “I’ll make sure no one disturbs you.”

He set the key down gently on the desk and left.

Soon as he was gone, I rushed over and locked the door.

The bathroom was just as nice as the bedroom, complete with a full tub and lavender scented shower soap. Never mind that my shower lasted far too long, or that I sat curled up on the floor for much of it. The water was hot and wet on my body as its steam obfuscated details from my mind for a time, so if the water ended up a bit saltier than it ought to have been? So what.

4

Fisherman had been as good as his word. After my very long, very healing shower, I dressed in soft pajamas and passed out cold. Their beautiful big bed was as wonderful as it looked, so I slept heavily and long. At least I think it was a long time.

After another, much shorter, shower, I put on real clothes, like undergarments, jeans, a long-sleeved shirt and sweater. For some reason, I was freezing, and I didn't feel like looking too closely at the why. There were even thick fuzzy socks for my feet! Yes!

I was going to have to kill him. Properly this time. This was entirely too creepy for my liking. Though a little voice in my head had commented that it was rather lovely to have new things, nice things even. It'd been a while since I'd bothered purchasing real clothes or gear. I'd spent too long off the grid in my weird grungy thrift shop clothes, lubricated on bad booze and comic books. Although, the comic books were the highlight of that stretch of my life. If those knuckleheads destroyed my collection....

I sighed. I wouldn't do a thing. Most likely because these were a bunch of trained professionals and it would be too much of a pain in the patoot to get revenge for my books.

Speaking of books, I perused the titles on my two, new handy dandy cases. There was a range from history tomes to recent releases in science fiction, even a couple of literary pieces. Thankfully no 'classics' though. Drat that man! He knew me too well. I'd lived through most of those periods and read the books along the way.

My meandering thoughts were interrupted by a knock at the door.

The lock turned and the door opened as a room service cart came rolling in with the most wonderful smells.

Keys jangled as they were handed off to someone I couldn't see by Pretty Brit. Er, Grace. I was trying not to learn their names because I had no intentions of sticking around this place.

"Hi," she greeted in cautious tones. "I brought some brunch, though it is past lunchtime."

Dangit. Cameras. There had to be. I discreetly let my eyes roam around the room. I'd need to find those as soon as she was gone.

She rolled the cart close to the cherry coffee table that sat in front of the cream couch and pulled up a couple of the lids. "There's scrambled eggs, sausages, mash, some American waffles, toast, tea, coffee. I think they weren't sure if you'd want an American, British, or Irish style of breakfast.

My mouth watered. "All of it," I whispered. It was a hard fight not to go all Cookie Monster on the delicious foods in front of her, but I managed.

Without a word, I removed the covers and lined the plates on my arms like the most experienced diner waitress and brought them over to the coffee table. Then I grabbed the tea, the coffee, and oh! Orange juice! I sniffed. Yes! The real stuff, not some concentrate. I couldn't help it. I guzzled half the glass.

Pretty Brit sat in the far corner of the couch sideways with her legs tucked underneath and observed in silence.

I ignored her in favor of my breakfast. Never was much for morning chatter. That was something Wi—

My mind stopped there.

Mother Fletcher's Castoria sonofabastidge. My eyes closed as I paused eating.

"Are you all right?" she asked quietly.

"Yeah, just peachy," I quipped. She was not my BFF. She had not earned the right to my truth. Hairy Bumbles bounce. Fisherman had gotten more out of me than I'd liked, but I wasn't sleep-deprived and injured anymore. "You don't have to stay, you know. There's not far for me to go, and I'm currently well-occupied as you can see." I lifted my fork. Well, not far until I find a way off this love boat from heck, I thought at my food.

She stared, but belied that by propping her arm on the back of the couch and resting her head in her hand. "You don't seem nearly as scary as—"

"Stop right there," I interrupted her. "Do not mention him. Not if you want to stay here. You've been very polite so far, so I will give you fair warning.

"And while yes, you're quite pretty, and I'm sure more than one idiot male has fallen for those big gray eyes, gorgeous hair and body, I'm not that stupid. They sent you in here because I'm a girl, you're a girl, we're both kind of girly, but can kick butt, yet capable of being diplomatic. They're hoping you'll get me to open up—best case scenario, or to at least join your merry little band of whatever—worst case.

"Well sister, let me tell you, I have been here, done this, had the t-shirt, sold the cookies, have zero intention of ever going back to the Game. It's like I told Fisherman, ain't happenin', as the Americans like to say," I lectured her and took a long pull on my coffee.

Ahhhhh...caffeine, one of Humanity's better inventions.

She didn't say anything.

"How'm I doing? Close?" I asked. "Trust me. I don't underestimate you in the slightest. If anything, I'd rank you right behind warrior braids, and him only first because he's got reach on you."

Now she smiled slightly.

"But I think you're probably smarter than he is," I whispered, leaning closer to her. Then I showed her eyes full of power.

Pretty Brit didn't flinch. Huh. Bonus points for her. Then again. Manacle man was on the team. "Not your first time seeing something like this, is it?"

"Nope," she replied.

I nodded and went back to eating like a hospital orderly on a coffee break.

When I was mostly finished, I economically stacked my plates and put them back on the cart. "Please thank the kitchen folks. That was wonderful. I suppose if it had to be a last meal, it was a doozy."

Her mouth twitched.

"What?"

"Hm? Oh, nothing. You're very funny," she quipped back at me. "I'll be sure to thank—"

She paused.

"My uncle."

I choked and did a spit take with my tea.

Now she laughed.

"Your what?" I coughed.

"Uncle Harry," she announced. "He made your meal himself. Much to Henry's disgust and my curiosity. See, my father was MI-6 before he died. Afterwards, Harry scooped up Mother and me and brought us to England. He's helped raise me since I was four."

After wiping my face, I stared into space while she talked. "Let me guess, MI-6 as well, aren't you?"

"Yes."

"Grace Raeni Fletcher, do be so kind as to leave my room. You seem a lovely lady, I'd hate to have to kill you," I informed her in perfectly accented aristocratic British.

Her face expressed nonchalance, but her eyes lied and showed me her surprise.

It probably had to do with her being unaccustomed to dealing with a compulsion and my ability to use the Queen's own English as well as any of them.

Quite frankly, I didn't care. I just wanted her out of my room.

She got up and walked away.

The door closed softly behind her.

I decided it was high time for me to meditate. Meditation would allow my spirit self to move about the ship for a little reconnaissance, but I'd have to be careful about the tweedles. If they noticed me, the jig would be up. It seemed viable to avoid them, and this allowed me to not worry about looking for all the cameras in my room.

After cleaning up the remainder of my breakfast, I pushed the cart into the hall and decided a 'nap' was in order. All they'd see was me back on the bed sleeping.

I laid down and did my best to slow my breathing. The hard part was doing this without expending too much energy and alerting them that I was doing anything I ought not to be.

As my breathing slowed and I took stock of my body; something felt wrong...

"Aw, c'mon. You gotta be fudge...bucketburlybeefeaters. Sonofagoat..." I mumbled. They'd drugged my food!

Man, I had to be more careful than this, I groused at myself.

My eyelids slid to half-mast. A lethargy stole through my limbs. I couldn't move. Sickness seized my midsection, yet I couldn't puke.

The door unlocked and opened.

What was the piss poor point of a lock if everyone had a freakin' flip flop key?!

Fisherman walked in and stood by the side of my bed. He shoved his hands into his pants pockets. "Huh. Looks like he was right after all," he said. "Well, the drugs should wear off around suppertime. We tend to eat dinner later, so you should have plenty of time to contemplate your options."

I tried to glare at him, but he kept sliding in and out of focus. Now there were three of him. My mind slipped and slid like so many broken eggs on a floor.

He'd still been talking but I had no idea what was said.

Trouble swam into view. She stared into me. "He said, join us, or end up down a dark hole," she said, pushing the words into my mind so I'd understand. "Though I personally think we could pull off putting you six feet under." Trouble smiled full of teeth.

When that dark power touched mine, we both gasped.

She jumped back.

I actually managed to flop away as my back arched up in pain. It stopped. I fell on my back panting.

There *he* stood at the foot of my bed.

That gave me incentive. My fingers flexed on the comforter.

Grayness ate my periphery.

I flexed my feet and tried to use my Energy to deal with the drugs.

The room spun.

A pinch hit my arm.

Fisherman stood back. Syringe in hand.

My eyes burned.

Now trying to pull my power together was like trying to gather marbles on ice.

I was on the clock.

Then I was not.

5

Before I was fully conscious, I raced for the bathroom and threw up, a lot. Puked up a lot of blackness with my laced brunch. Darkness made manifest as it left my body. I'd had a lot of very bad thoughts as I'd gone under.

The porcelain throne and I hung out for some long amount of time. I lost track. Probably because I kept passing back out on the lovely cool tile floor and soft fluffy throw rugs...

***

Wine glasses sparkled. Silverware clinked.

"...so no, she will not be joining us," Fisherman explained and took a sip of his wine.

Manacle man and Mr. Obvious shared dark fleeting smiles across the table.

Trouble's face flushed red.

Her cousin placed a comforting hand on her arm.

Warrior shrugged.

"He meant for dinner this evening," the Commodore clarified. He sat on Fisherman's right. A blonde woman, slightly younger than them, sat on the left. I hadn't been introduced to her.

"She's uncooperative and too dangerous to keep here," Pretty Brit observed from her seat in between the Commodore and Manacle man. "I think we ought to send her to the Keep."

"You're just mad 'cause she got the better of you," Cooper commented from the foot of the table.

"It's a sentiment I happen to agree with," Manacle man said, "and I wasn't even there."

"Yeah, but you never wanted her here in the first place," Cooper countered.

"I still say she could be an asset," the Latin woman said with quiet finality.

"Pippa, Harry?" Fisherman asked quietly before putting his fork in his mouth.

They shared a glance. A lot was said with no words. It spoke of years of acquaintance, maybe something else.

***

I snapped back into my body. Who was Pippa? Did I care?

Nawwww.

Well...okay, maybe a little.

I tried to push up from the floor, but it didn't go very well. My arms shook. My body trembled. I fell, bruising my shoulder. At least I hadn't hit my head.

Okay, a little rest, then it was time to get the hell out of here.

Had I cursed? Yes.

Did I care at this point? Not so much, no.

Was that bad? Definitely.

6

After another unplanned but necessary nap, I woke up with a shaky ability to stand. The clothes came off and landed in a dirty heap while I baby walked my way into the shower. At this point, showers ranked even higher than caffeine on my list of Human inventions. And I'd been around in a time before those amazing suckers had existed, so I knew from personal experience.

The shower had done its job turning me back into a functioning being. Hot diggity. I walked into my room and grabbed a pale jade, silk robe out of the armoire. Darkness outside the windows and my internal clock indicated that it was late into the night.

I didn't have to turn around to know that he'd entered my room.

The door handle click-clacked shut.

His nervous energy danced along my skin like the pins and needles one got after a limb fell asleep. Both a relief and an annoyance at the same time.

"What do you want, Bradford?" I asked and retied the robe tighter with my back to him.

It was too dang late to be doing this. Rather, I wasn't anywhere near ready to do this. Then again, was a person ever ready to hash out baggage with their thought-you-were-dead fiancé? One that went ahead and had a life without you? Never bothered to find you to say 'hi, I'm alive'. Armed with my anger again, I turned around to face him.

Sir William Harrison Bradford stood barely inside the doorway. He would always be "Harry" to the rest of the world, but for me, it was different. He would always be my William, my Liam.

His eyes were wide, like he'd seen a ghost. Catching me seeing him stare, he began to glance around the room. Anywhere but at me. "Your hair," he murmured with a cough. "It's back to normal."

I still couldn't get used to the graying hair, the lines in his face, but if I closed my eyes, his voice had remained mostly the same. Lovely, like velvet.

Wait! I was angry at him and crossed my arms over my chest. "Yes, I changed my hair back to 'normal', whatever that is," I muttered. A small part of me felt absurdly pleased that he was happy with my natural amber and reddish waves. It was a fight not to slap my forehead at my own stupidity.

"Well, that gothic black was most definitely not normal," he said, regaining his verbal footing, "at least not on you. It looked rather awful."

"Glad I pass inspection, Commodore," I retorted, making a screwy face and saluting. "Congratulations on the promotion, by the way."

"You haven't changed at all, have you?" he sighed irritably.

"Oh no, I've most certainly changed, sir. I've learned that I need to be *very* careful what words I use and how hard I mean them," my mouth motored on without my consent. Why was I cluing him in on what had happened?

"What do you mean?" he questioned with a frown and a direct stare.

I'd gotten his attention. Great. Time for the bull and the horns and all that hooey.

"When I thought I'd gotten you blown sky high, when I'd thought you were dead, I sat in the garbage of an alley—filthy, bleeding physically, metaphysically, emotionally, and I cursed with everything in me to the Heavens for taking you out of this world. For allowing me to screw up so badly that it got you killed!

"I informed them of what they already knew, which was that you belonged in this world. It was a far better place with you alive. I raged at them! Threw Wrath at them with everything I had. Offered myself in your place and everything.

"Guess the joke was on me because it seemed like they were listening. Who knew the word of a Fallen's child carried actual weight? So they apparently brought you back. Though no one thought it was important enough to let me know this little tidbit," I told him in flat tones heavy with sarcasm and pain. "So, I went on with my life. Became a freelance mercenary. I refused any team jobs after that. Oh, I'd work *for* people just not *with* them. Did some work for a bit, but then I quit and went off the grid. Vagabonded around Europe for a while. Thing was—I couldn't stand it. Everything in Europe kept reminding me of you. That's why I left and went to the States."

"In other words, my intel was correct. You've been hiding off the grid, a washed-up drunk for decades," he surmised tartly.

I shook my head once and sucked my lips into my mouth, clamping my teeth down on them. I would not tell him to go to Hell. "Figgity froggy forkin' full of Casablanca go la-la-la," I sputtered trying to protect us both. My cursing carried consequences, serious ones.

He raised an eyebrow.

"Don't give me that. I know you know what I'm fighting not to say," I snarled. Wetness pricked my eyes, but I refused to give in to it.

William walked toward me. "If I had to guess, you want to tell me to go um, fuck myself? Possibly tossing in that I ought to tour Hell in the process?" he asked. There was a tiny bit of a smile trying not to show, but I could hear it in his voice. "How am I doing?"

I walked over to the bar cart.

He wasn't funny. Not-even-close.

Trembling shook my hands. His words rang in my ears—*you've been hiding off the grid, a washed-up drunk, for decades*..."FUCK!" I yelled in old Gaelic as I threw the cart at the wall next to the door.

It smashed everything, taking out the desk and chair.

Lights buzzed and browned out for a second.

Nephilim are stronger than Humans.

Ragged breathing made my shoulders shake and heave.

The pitter-patter of many footsteps sounded in the hallway.

Uh oh. Now I'd done it. I stood there staring at the wreckage.

Bradford stepped into the hallway. His words were quiet, but authoritative. That was him. Never needed to raise his voice. As far as I knew, I'd been the only one to ever get him cheesed off enough to yell.

He came back inside and locked the door. "Do you feel better now?" he asked drily, still facing the door.

I shook my head back and forth as I bit my lower lip again. The coppery tang of blood seeped into my mouth. He was seriously cruisin' for it.

Then I stood still.

He was deliberately pushing for me to unleash my power at him.

"Why?" I demanded in a strangled voice.

Bradford turned to me and shoved his hands into his pants' pockets. "I needed to know. I need to know if you can be provoked badly enough to unleash your powers wildly or if you can maintain control under duress," he explained. "Something we'd never addressed before."

"Wait just a darn tootin' moment. You just conducted a gratin gofer freakin' experiment on me?!" My eyes blazed with power as I spun to face him. Energy sizzled through my body and suddenly, I was feeling a whole lot better than I had been in a while.

Somewhere in the ship I felt Manacle Man's power flare in response. Trouble perked up as well.

"I wouldn't do that, Eliora," he cautioned. "It's a good probability that you've alerted the others to your state."

A growl left my lips. "Shut it, *Commodore*. Oh yeah, they're both awake and aware of my *state*," I snapped. "Blast you, you bloody bastard."

His lips compressed.

Energy rumbled and teased my senses from outside the ship.

Winds increased.

He glanced out the windows.

Rain pinged and pelted as lightning sailed across the sky.

The lights flickered. Sizzling hissed through the bedroom walls. There went their surveillance.

I took a deep breath and closed my eyes...three, four, five. Let the breath out. Yoga breathing had its uses. "*Don't call me that*," I added. "'Cause you sure as shootin' lost that right when you didn't tell me that you were alive, and for that matter, as far as the British government is concerned, 'Eliora' is dead. I know because I checked and made sure of it."

"Actually—"

My index finger shot up and shushed him before he could contradict me. "Do not tell me you've 'fixed' it, or I swear..." I stopped speaking and swallowed hard. "You fix it, you change it, you call whoever the freakity flip you have to and you lay her to rest because *that* particular young woman is gone, killed in action. Apparently though, her fiancé survived." I coughed on my incredulity, "I mean—you survived. How'd that play out? And why didn't you find me? What the hairy heckin' hootin' rootin' tootin' gosh-dang-it-all were you thinking?"

He watched me silently for several moments. "I woke up in a morgue van full of bodies. The memories are fragmented, jumbled. They had me in a body bag, but I fought my way out...I don't know who was more traumatized," he said and paused. "While I was in hospital, they told me no one else from my team had made it out alive. They hadn't found a body for you, so I suspected you might've survived.

"Years I searched for you, but when you don't want to be found you are bloody impossible to find. I thought that if you had wanted to come back to me, you would have. I ah, I finally made myself give up on finding you and moved forward, like you'd told me to do before that mission went pear shaped. That was quite an exit." His face soured as his eyes rose to meet mine. Pained anger filled them.

"That was not any kind of 'exit strategy'," I choked out as the power left my eyes. The extra Energy, juiced by fury, drained and got sent into the ocean. Safest place for it. Especially with those two on board. Hopefully that meant the storm I'd accidentally created would slow down.

We had fought before that last mission. That'd been when I'd said I was leaving him. One last mission, then I was going to leave. The impasse that we'd reached had created a stalemate. One I'd decided to break. Had to break. For both our sakes. Before the decision got taken from my hands.

This idiot thought I'd bailed when the job had gone so sour raccoons wouldn't have touched it? I glared at him, appalled. "You seriously thought I'd done that to you?" I whispered.

"The possibility crossed my mind," he hedged. "I had hoped not though."

"You're a fucking idiot, you know that, right?" I muttered running a hand through my riot of waves.

Thunder rumbled.

He inclined his head. "Well, it's not the first time you've told me that, so I suppose I can take comfort in the small consistencies." Bradford went silent, staring at me.

"What?"

"You look the same, young enough to be my d—"

I walked over and put a finger on his lips to shush him. My power flowed through his body, dialing back the course of time until he was in his thirties. His hair grew darker as the gray disappeared. Wrinkles faded from the corners of his eyes. The expenditure of power made me dizzy with the strain. Probably not the smartest thing to do with the other two on board, but in that moment, I didn't care. We were both here, alive, fighting, but alive...and my anger was turning to something else as his words gained purchase.

"What?" he gasped, staring at himself in armoire door's mirror.

"Eh, your thirties, my twenties, that's doable wouldn't you say?"

"Is this permanent?" he asked.

My shoulders shrugged without me. I couldn't tell if he was happy or appalled. "Does it matter?"

"Yes, it bloody well matters, Eliora," he sternly railed at me.

The blonde from dinner rose in my mind's eye. "You have someone else now."

"What?" he sputtered. "No! No, there isn't anyone."

I turned and ran a hand through my hair again. He was such an insufferable pain in the ass, but then, so was I–just in different ways.

More rumbles sounded outside.

My eyes found his in the mirror.

His face was full of fear, anger, frustration...and hunger. He'd tried to find me, but I'd been too good at hiding, too many centuries of practice in covering my tracks. He was right. When I didn't want to be found...The jerk had also been right about being a pissed slacker. I'd gotten sloppy, which must be how they'd managed to find me.

Despite my years of experience and knowing better, I let my emotions rise to the surface. My face drawn, my eyes wounded. It wasn't a good look. He'd always managed to get past my best defenses.

William stepped up to me and spun me around to face him. "I should've done this years ago." His hands cupped my cheeks in loving hunger. He kissed me. Gently, testing the waters, presumably waiting for me to reject him.

Tears spilled down my face. "Liam," I whispered with an Irish accent I hadn't let myself use in too many decades.

"Eli," he murmured back and kissed me with more intent.

Our arms wrapped around one another as a kiss decades overdue smothered us in a blanket of passion. Neither one of us cared that we couldn't breathe.

His body abruptly went stiff, and not in the good way. "No." He stepped back. "I can't," he murmured without meeting my gaze. "Change me back."

"What?" My head snapped back. "Yer serious? Ah okay, alright. Let me catch ma breath. I'll make us both older—"

"No. Stay the way you are. It's too much of a drain on you," he said.

"What are ya sayin', Liam?" My voice was hoarse with a deep-seated need to scream in frustration. What was happening?

Thunder rumbled.

"I'm saying that we can't. We shouldn't. It's a bad idea. Too many years have passed. Our time has passed. That was too long ago. We've both made our peace with what we'd thought had happened. Now we need to deal with what's in front of us," he informed me. "Our team needs your help badly."

I turned away from him and clutched the robe more tightly closed. "Are you saying that's the only reason you came looking for me?" I whispered, my accent had swung back to generic American. Eliora's Irish lilt was not for this cold, manipulative bastard.

Lightning flashed again.

Rain pelted the windows.

I stared him down through the mirror.

He'd aged again while I'd been turned around, and I hadn't even realized that I'd done it.

That was a whole new level of bad.

William drew himself up and crossed his arms. "Your image was captured when you stopped that man from harming the young woman. A policeman's car cam caught you before you left the scene. That was enough for our researcher to find you," he explained. "I was quite serious when I said that you'd managed to completely disappear."

I turned around and walked right into his personal space. "I get that. But why? Why did you come for me?" I demanded. "If this," I pointed back and forth between us, "if this is over, then why? Why now? You knew I wanted out. I was done. Wasn't doing this anymore. I have buried too many friends and colleagues, William..." My voice broke.

He stared out the window, at the painting he'd put over the bed, anywhere over my head. I could see the wheels spinning. Things he wasn't saying. "Because you're needed."

"Needed? Needed?!" I barked incredulously. "What about what *I* need?"

He stood there silently.

"Or did that not figure in your plans, *Commodore*?"

"Debriefing will be at o' eight hundred tomorrow morning. Someone will come get you for breakfast thirty minutes prior." He stiffly turned and walked away from me.

I bit my lip to not say anything.

Before opening the door, he stopped. His head turned slightly to give me a quarter profile. "I am sorry, Eliora, truly...Someone will come to clean up and restock things while you're in the meeting. Do I—Would you—Do you want me to send someone with some scotch?"

No, that won't be necessary.

His shoulders hunched.

I'd used telepathy. It had allowed him a glimpse of my pain. I didn't let myself peek at his. I didn't want to know. As much as I wanted desperately to know why he had rejected me, in truth, I didn't want to know, not really. It would probably hurt too much.

This was why I'd gone decades, once even a couple of centuries, without deeply connecting to a Human like this. It wasn't worth the heartache and the pain. He was the first man to breach the walls around my heart in a very long time. Moments like this reminded me why I'd had such a policy.

William's movements were jerky as he opened the door.

Manacle man stood in the doorway. Lowered eyebrows and a snarling frown filled his face. He searched William from head to toe, making sure the older man was okay.

How had I not known that he was there?!

My hard stare revealed something else as William looked at the younger man. "I'm fine," he murmured.

I gasped.

Lightning struck the ocean too close to the ship and the lights flickered again.

"Eliora," William began with resigned impatience, but he stopped, seeing my expression.

Blind snow storms had more color than I had in that moment.

My power pinged the younger man's feather light. "Henry Galahad Bradford, son of William Harrison Bradford," I breathed. "He's your *son*."

"Yes," William confirmed. So many emotions crossed his face. More than even I could track.

"What have you done?" I choked.

Henry glared at me. No longer could I just think of him as "Manacle man".

"You were the one who told me no in the first place," William reminded me tentatively.

"Yes! I had good reason! I still do!" I chastised him in a shout. "It's against *the rules*! I'm not supposed to have any children. None of us are! I would have done anything else. I just couldn't give you—*that*..." I raised a hand, gesturing to the young man whose eyes grew even darker with emotions that were going to get him into trouble.

My gut twisted with the knowledge that the man who'd almost been my husband had found someone else to break the rules. We hunted down our own for breaking those kinds of rules. It'd been part of my job to safeguard the world and stop our own from going rogue. He had no idea what he'd done. What he'd invoked.

By bringing me here and making me aware of Henry, Bradford had just signed his son's death warrant.

7

I tried to sleep. I truly did. Honest.

After flipping and flopping like the freshest catch of the day, I gave up and put on my robe. The room was dark, but I didn't mind. It was cold though, so I put on another pair of fuzzy socks. At least the storm had died down to a drizzling rain.

I sat on the end of my bed and forced myself to think for a moment about what my subconscious was pushing me to do.

Our fight before that last mission had revolved around children and marriage. We'd been engaged by then. In all my centuries of life, I'd only been married once. At less than a century old, I hadn't learned to keep any kind of emotional distance; I barely managed to hide my Otherness from the Humans.

Cairbre had been a strong and valorous warrior; though in private, his smile was tender and loving. My occasional lapses in hiding what I was hadn't scared him. If anything, he'd presumed that I was an itinerant priestess. An easy explanation as any I'd thought then. His love and our marriage had granted me safety, sanctuary within his tribe's village.

One spring had been much leaner than normal. Word came of raiding parties hitting the eastern coast far worse. The Crithni, now known as Picts, had decimated a nearby village where my husband's kin lived. He went with a group of our warriors to look for survivors, and possibly exact revenge, but he never returned.

After a moon cycle, our elders had allowed a few warriors and I leave to go hunting. All we'd found was the youngest of the group. He'd died of his wounds before reaching us. Tokens from the others, blood soaked, rested in a bag. I'd used them to rewind time in my mind's eye and saw the ambush.

My husband had died in that battle. His wedding torc in my hands and his grim death had nearly broken me.

The thought of losing Liam like that had terrified me, but worse than that, he hadn't known what I was, not really. Others weren't supposed to know. I'd only told him that I couldn't have children. He kept talking about the miracles of science, and that we'd find a way.

I finally caved and had explained all of it. William hadn't been able to understand how such good beings, champions of justice who fought to protect others, weren't possibly allowed to bring more of that into the world.

I'd tried to explain that the Nephilim were kind of like prisoners who'd been allowed to work off their sentence fighting for the good guys, but that didn't mean that we weren't still prisoners.

I'd seen the look on Henry's face. He hated me. It worried me about how or where he'd come by such feelings, or that William hadn't squashed them yet. That kind of emotional darkness was like waving fresh steak in front of a tiger cage before he'd had dinner. Somebody was gonna get dead.

"Dangit," I muttered. Time to search for a computer. This place had to be lousy with them.

I ventured out my bedroom door.

No alarms sounded.

Hopefully, no one was watching the hallways, either in person or via cameras.

It wasn't too hard to retrace my steps back to the lounge.

Most of the lights were dark, except for one smallish lamp over by the sectional. The wooden card table now had a laptop on it with a coaster next to it.

Jackpot! I could do what I needed to and slip off to bed.

Aw greasy grimy gophers. To use said laptop involved putting my back to both the stairwell and the door Fisherman and I had used. Using my extraordinary senses to feel for anyone was a bad idea since it would tip people off that I was awake and moving around the ship. The other option was to rearrange where it sat, but the blasted thing's cord had already been stretched to its limit. Another problem was the swirling colored screensaver prevented me from knowing if it had enough power if I unplugged it and the fact that those swirling colors still crawled across the screen meant someone hadn't been gone long and might come back soon.

Dagnabbit.

Okay, okay, it was doable, I told myself, sitting down on the chair.

I moved my finger on the touchpad to get a password window and held my fingers over the keys. I rewound time a little bit and watched what the shadowy hands from before had typed. It was a dangerous use of power, but there wasn't a choice.

No sounds.

Just the ocean outside.

My heart raced as I waited a couple of moments to see if I'd drawn Henry or Trouble's attention.

Silence.

I retyped what I'd seen.

Whew! Okay. I created a new internet tab and went to the gardening forum of the One World, One Garden website. It was about growing everything under the sun and moon. Those of us in the various Celestial ranks here in the Mortal world used it for communication in a pinch. Someone always monitored its various conversations.

Despite Bradford's words to the contrary, I had managed to learn some things in my time off the grid, and computers, being like Nephilim in having both their good and bad traits, hadn't been nearly as difficult to learn as I'd expected. At least not in basic operation.

I pulled up the arbor thread. There hadn't been any actual action on this one in a long time. My stomach roiled slightly as my fingers danced over the keys quickly enough to make an experienced hacker sit up and drool. Though my abnormally good reflexes were my ace, the message wasn't all that long. Merely a reply to an admin talking about apple trees. This admin was a member of the Triad. They watched over us Nephilim...and passed judgment when one of us screwed up beyond a certain point.

"I can see I'm going to have to change my password," Cooper commented from behind me, holding a steaming cup of coffee. He was still dressed in the slacks and polo that I'd seen in my vision of dinner.

I flinched. Idiot me had been too far into my own head and had stopped paying attention. "That smells heavenly," I answered, trying for casual. "No pun intended."

"Ah hm."

I cleared my throat. "Yeah, sorry about that. I just wanted to get online for a few minutes. I couldn't sleep."

"So, you're into," he leaned forward and read over my shoulder, "gardening, huh? That's why you were in the middle of nowhere? And you just had to post about an apple falling from its tree at—four in the morning?" He added an unsurprising 'I call baloney' look.

"I'm guessing you're not going to take a simple yes?"

He scrunched up his mouth and shook his head no, then took a sip of his coffee. Waiting.

I exhaled heavily. "Diggity dratty dopey dishes," I muttered. "Why do you have to be so cool? I like you. I could make you forget that you saw me doing this..."

We stared each other down in silence.

He watched me, waiting to see what I would do.

Visions of sending Grace on her way danced in my head, but my stomach flopped immediately after that thought.

Compulsions were decidedly frowned upon because they blocked a Human's Free Will. They fell into a grey area. To save a Human from doing something horribly self-destructive, we could 'nudge' said Human into a better direction. That was where the ability had begun. However, it was also possible to force a Human into an action.

I'd done it before to protect myself, or to protect others, or to prevent a half-Infernal's minions from stabbing me in the back while I fought said half-Infernal. Making Grace leave my room had not been an appropriate use of that power.

"That's true, but then it'd eat at your gut. 'Cause I'm a nice guy," he spoke while pointing to his chest, "and like you said, you like me. Which is more than what I could say about some people."

I held up one hand as I returned my attention to the screen. "Don't go there, man."

"Wouldn't dream of it," he murmured. "So, what message are you sending to whom?"

"Ooh, a Navy SEAL with proper grammar. What's the world coming to?" I joked.

"How'd you—"

"Your shirt sleeve doesn't completely cover your ink," I told him, "and I've been in the States long enough to know what that trident probably means. By the way, what're you doing up so late?"

"I volunteered to keep an eye on you overnight."

"What? You drew the short straw?" I snorted.

"No. I explained to the Captain that I'd probably be the least likely to shoot first and ask questions after, regardless of your healing factor."

Huh. Yeah, he had a point, so I nodded. I turned to the side, still sitting in the chair.

He dragged another chair over and sat down, pulling the coaster over to put under his cup.

My eyebrow went up.

"What? A guy can have good manners."

I chuckled. It was the first good laugh I'd had in a while. "Fair enough."

His equitable mood encouraged me to dare a question. "You seem to be taking me surprisingly in stride. Why?"

Cooper held up his fingers. "One, I'm pretty decent at taking care of myself. Two, you're a half-angel, so you're supposed to be one of the good guys. And three, I've seen things. I don't doubt for a second what you are, or what you can possibly do, and we need that. Junior's great n' all, but he's not you. Hear tell, you are damn—"

I raised an eyebrow again.

"Dang," he corrected himself, "old, which probably means more powerful and with better control. That's important. Like I said, I suspect that you've got too much of a conscience to do anything truly harmful to me, or anyone else here. Which means I'm also guessing you're wrestling with whatever message you're thinking about sending."

"Snickerdoodles," I muttered. An actual snicker escaped. "Junior, huh?"

His eyes went wide. "Only a couple of us call him that, and certainly not in front of him or the Commodore."

I sighed and rolled my eyes. With a deep breath, I stared hard into those deep brown eyes, and it showed me what I'd already suspected. He had a genuinely good heart. There was old pain and scars, but they hadn't broken him. Darn him.

Then he had the nerve to grin at me!

"All right, fine. Snot. Ugh." I muttered some more. "There's a message that I ought to send to...some—"

"People?" he offered.

"Sure. That I answer to on a higher level. I'm bound by the rules that govern us to do it. Could get into a lot of trouble if I don't." I added.

Cooper gave me a thoughtful look as he sipped his coffee. "What happens if you send it?"

I thought about what it would do to William. How it might hurt this team. Would they let themselves be caught in the crossfire trying to defend him? Would the Triad take out both Bradfords? Yeah...they probably would and yeah, they also probably would. One for doing it; one for existing. And there'd be a lot of bodies on the floor.

"People are going to get hurt," I whispered.

"Die?"

I nodded, unable to put it in words. A lump lodged in my throat. Truth be told, I didn't think there were that many of us left, easily less than a hundred.

"So, lemme spitball this back at you. See if I got it right. You send that message, and some...people," he said after a pause as I echoed the word with him, "will come to take care of business. Others will get caught in the crossfire. They might even pick up a bonus prize that I'm guessing wasn't included in that message, bigger fish first and all that, and there'll be a lot of hurt feelings all around. How'd I do?"

I nodded numbly.

"What if you don't send it?"

"They may find out, or rather, sooner or later they *will* find out. They'll come. It'll all happen, and they'll take me out with everyone else for not telling them."

"What if—now stay with me here—what if you don't send it, and stand by him, calling him like- a trainee? You guarantee his good behavior for them and stuff," Cooper offered. "You've been in the military. We take noobs under our wings all the time. We train them. We watch over them. We answer for what they do. It's called being a commanding officer." He winked at me.

I screwed up my face at him and fought the urge to throw something. "You're an ash-bucket, you know that right?"

He laughed. After a moment, though, he sobered and leaned forward, arms on his knees. "Look, everyone on this team knows you and the Commodore have a history. Heck, a blind man could see it. But remember, at one point, you two did love each other, a lot, from what I overheard the Captain and Pip say.

"Battles are lost as much as they're won. You two lost, big from the sounds of it. He went back to work. You went to ground. Both of you got kicked in the teeth and dealt with it differently." He sat up and shrugged. "So, do you really think it's worth it to destroy him by turning in his kid?"

My eyes went wide.

A fleeting smile crossed his face. "Just like the big guy, a lot of people underestimate me, too. They think we don't see stuff, or know anything, but we do. It's an old saying about the 'apple falling near or far from the tree', so it didn't take much for me to guess that you were going to rat out Junior's existence. I'm guessing children are a no-no for you?"

I nodded. "I'm duty bound to tell them he's alive. Once they find out about him, they won't just take him out. They'll probably come after all three of us. William for doing it, Henry for existing...and me, for knowing and/or possibly being his mother. They knew about William and I." I stopped talking.

"They're the reason you left him," he whispered in sudden comprehension. "They were worried you'd cave and have a kid when you weren't supposed to. Better to break you two up so it wouldn't happen, or get one of you killed. And since both of you have survived, and you've been off the grid for so many years, who's to say that you didn't go back." He sat back and whistled quietly.

"Yeah," I whispered. He'd guessed the truth of why I'd left William. They'd threatened to 'remove' the temptation from me. Wasn't sure if my ex-fiancé had figured out that bit. He was smart, but he had also had far more faith in my superiors than me. "I know you don't owe me anything, but please don't mention it."

"I won't," he agreed, "not my place. Though I find it curious that you're willing to talk to me like this."

"My Spidey senses tell me that you're someone worthy of trust."

He shrugged with feigned nonchalance. "People have always seemed to tell me stuff that they wouldn't tell someone else," he said. A series of images flashed through my head as strong memories flitted through his mind. "Pops said I had my momma's ability to listen. She was a nurse." The man in front of me did one of those side head nods to negate all that pain I saw deep in his eyes. His momma had to have been someone special and I'd have bet my freedom that she wasn't among the living.

The puzzle that was Joshua Anthony Cooper tumbled about in my head. He was right. I didn't typically confide in people unknown to me this quickly, or about something so important. It made me wonder about his lineage. Or that deep abiding Goodness, beyond his Human this-is-a-good-guy, my power sensed.

A gentle smile snuck out to put him at ease as I commented, "I can believe that. So how'd you end up here then?"

"Thanks. Yeah, that's a story for another night, and lots of booze," he deflected and glanced at the computer's screen saver swirling colors across the blackness of it. Cooper logged back in. "So what's it gonna be?"

I stared at the screen.

"Maaaannnn, I am gonna hate myself in the morning," I muttered, deleting the message and closing the tab. "Speaking of hate, you do realize he hates my guts."

"Hate's such a strong word," Cooper cautioned. "Let's just say he has a substantial dislike for you."

My eyes rolled at the gross understatement. "I don't suppose you know why? It seems a bit much for the 'you broke my dad's heart' thing," I wondered.

"Sorry, no clue there, but how's about I show you where the kitchen is and we can help ourselves to some cinnamon rolls and more coffee. Then you probably should get some sleep," he offered instead.

My mouth watered. The only food I'd eaten, I'd thrown back up hours ago. "Yer on!"

We got up and headed out the door in search of rolls and coffee. Hopefully, I'd be able to get some sleep afterwards. The non-drug induced kind.

I glanced over my shoulder at the laptop sitting on the table. He hadn't shut down the screen. His Falcon and Cap desktop picture stared back at me. "Nice desktop pic, but ah, shouldn't you—?" I started to ask.

"Naw. We're the only ones up and besides, the locking screen saver will kick in within seconds anyway," Cooper reassured me.

"They left your collection by the way," he added, gaining my attention. "As long as no one breaks into your trailer, they should still be there."

"Yeah," I sighed, "they're probably gone."

"Well, hear tell it, you wouldn't have any problems replacing them," Cooper cautiously teased, "my Lady."

"Dude! I will beat you," I joked back as we walked down to the kitchen.

8

Cooper had collected me for breakfast. He'd asked me to play nice, for now, over warm cinnamon rolls last night, and man, was I a sucker for good breakfast pastries.

So here I was dressed in tan suede knee-high boots, jeans, and a forest green silk blouse. I'd even done my hair into soft side twists down into a single, thick braid that hung to the small of my back. Call me childish, but if William was going to dress me in what essentially amounted to 'my old clothes', then I figured I'd repay him by wearing my hair in his favorite hairstyle. It was petty, but I was feeling Human enough to not only indulge, but also take ownership of that. Did I mention that Temptation liked to ride me like a brat?

We entered the dining room near the head of the table. Said table sat a little to our left and a sideboard stood against the right wall. Fisherman had his back to us. Soft string quartet music played from discreet speakers.

As we came in, though, all conversation ceased and Fisherman turned slightly in his chair.

Everyone else was already seated and eating. Including the elusive "Pippa".

She swallowed visibly and dropped her gaze when I glanced at her. Hmmmmm...Getting a better look at her, she seemed vaguely familiar.

Bradford sat on Fisherman's right, then the Pretty Brit, Junior, the Latin woman, and an empty chair at the end.

Pippa, older cousin, Ellie, warrior, and Dobrek filled out the left side of the table. Another empty chair sat at the foot of the table. Seemed Cooper carried more weight than I'd originally thought.

I bee-lined for the left side and came around to take the chair at the end of the right side row. Two things: I wasn't going to steal Cooper's seat, and two, I had no interest in being able to see everyone at the table. Nope. Especially, not after catching William's flinch around the eyes as I made my way through his field of vision.

Temptations were sweet in their first blush, but seldom settled well.

Of course, Junior glared at me as I walked past.

A British military server appeared at Cooper's elbow as he sat down. "Master Sergeant, the usual, sir?"

"Yes, that's fine," my new friend answered quietly.

The server came over to me with all deference and asked in his crisp, British accent, "My Lady, what would you like? A poached egg, some fruit and toast? Or a croissant and au chocolat?"

Junior snorted.

My stomach turned. I wasn't sure if it was a knee jerk reaction to the options after yesterday, or the fact that *someone* had outed my title. Yeah, yeah, when you'd lived as long as I had, unfortunately, you ended up acquiring a title or two along the way. Why he insisted on giving me such dignity and gravitas, I'd never know.

I cleared my throat. "You don't, by any chance, have any American cereals and some milk? You know, kids' cereals, bright colors, lots of sugar. Oh, and a nice big ol' mug of black coffee. I know there are mugs down there. That'd be great. Thanks."

The server looked like I'd asked for troll's brains and the blood of infants. He glanced down the line.

I smiled sweetly at him.

Cooper rested his elbow on the arm of his chair and hid his mouth behind his hand.

Someone from the other end must've given him the okay because he gave me a beleaguered nod.

"She has spent several years recently in the States," Cooper murmured to the poor thing, taking mercy on him.

The server's face cleared at the explanation. "I'll see what I can do." Then he left out a door near our end of the table.

"Interesting breakfast choice," Ellie commented from across the table. "I should've asked for that." She shrugged.

I corrected my previous supposition, Korean-American, west coast. Picking out people's nationalities and lineages based on voices, appearances, and behaviors wasn't just a hobby, it had long since become survival. Being able to blend was paramount, lest the Humans realize that someone more than them was in their midst.

More than a millennium ago, I'd been told to blend and lay low after my activities had drawn unwanted attention. Yeah, that lasted a few centuries. Then I noticed another upsurge in dark activity. Idiot me felt compelled to do something about it. However, I'd retired from that life decades ago. No way was I going back.

"So you have a title?" the warrior asked.

"Yes," I sighed.

"No," Junior interjected.

"Doubt it," Pretty Brit snorted.

"Yes," William said.

Fisherman's eyebrows went up.

Warrior's eyes went wide as he looked away, then back at his food.

"Well," Fisherman spoke up, "I understand we're to have clear skies and smoother sailing today, though the ship's captain thought I ought to check on that. What do you think, Lady Dade?"

I nearly choked. Lady Dade?! Smooth sailing? What was he on—crack?

"I think we ought to sedate her again," Junior muttered.

"If the adults wanted your opinion, Junior, we would have asked you for it," I snapped in perfectly withering and aristocratic British, "but we didn't, so do be quiet."

Dobrek choked on his orange juice. That's when I noticed someone had healed the injuries I'd given him. How was Junior hiding his abilities from me?

"Maybe if we sedated him," I informed Fisherman in Greek, "things would go more smoothly since he cannot seem to behave."

Fisherman didn't immediately disagree.

"No," William said in sour tones. Ah sugar daddies, I'd forgotten he spoke Greek, at least some, and apparently enough to follow what I'd said.

The elusive Pippa avidly watched us. She cleared her throat, "Ah yes, I'd—I'd heard that you spoke many different languages. How many do you speak?"

There it was. She was their 'researcher'. Her intellectual curiosity oozed from that polite British face. Despite scaring the heck outta her, she had lots of questions, so many written in those avid eyes.

"Enough," I answered obliquely.

"All of them," William countered and took a sip of his tea.

"Horse-shit," Dobrek said in Polish.

"No, not horse-shit," I replied in just as good Polish. "I speak perfectly fluent Polish, thank you very much. Which reminds me, I ought to get back to Lublin's Old Town. The food there was excellent."

"She cannot speak our tongue," Older cousin said quietly to Ellie.

"Yes, she most certainly can," I replied.

The La—Ivy—ugh, I was starting to think of them as people I knew. "Dagnabbit," I muttered as Ivy opened her mouth.

"Yes, I speak perfectly acceptable Spanish," I told her in her own Puerto Rican dialect.

"Anyone else?" I added in American.

Two servers silently stepped in and provided Cooper with fried eggs, bacon, toast, hash browns, and a tea cup with saucer full of coffee. A small silver tray with creamer and sugar was then set above his plate. They brought me a fine bowl filled with colorful, fruity balls, a small glass pitcher of milk, and a large, white mug full of coffee. As they began to set down another silver tray, I held my hand up with a smile.

"Enjoy your breakfast," Junior said.

I stopped pouring milk on my cereal.

William sighed. His tea cup clattered into its saucer.

I exercised a tiny thread of power and checked the food. It was all safe.

Ivy glanced at me with a worried frown. "Everything okay?" she asked in Spanish.

"Yeah, thanks," I murmured back in the same.

I glanced at Cooper and dug into my cereal, ignoring everyone else.

An awkward silence descended.

This was why I was against too much conversation first thing in the morning. I continued to hoover my cereal, letting the silence stretch, and refused to meet anyone's glance.

"Well, seems to be a good time to adjourn to the conference room to debrief on this mission," Fisherman announced. "Cooper, Lady Dade, please join us as soon as you're done."

Everyone else stood to leave. William was the first one out the door.

"Lady my arse," Junior snorted with a soft sneer.

Ivy made a face and opened her mouth.

I put my hand on her forearm. He wasn't worth the fight.

"Captain Mylonas," I called.

Junior half turned with a surprised and dark glance.

Fisherman made his way toward me.

Ivy smirked at Junior as she passed him. "Cabrón," she murmured.

The fight was hard won not to laugh a spit take at the look on Junior's face.

Fisherman displayed no outward reaction, so he either didn't speak Spanish, which I had a hard time buying, or he felt that Ivy had handled it just fine. Once he got past them, he remarked, "Move along Bradford. I'll be there in a moment."

The other two left.

I picked up my bowl and drank down the milk. Thank heavens everyone was gone, because taking the time to use a spoon for that would've driven me nuts.

Cooper ate his food with militarily economic swiftness, though I could tell we had his attention.

I stood and faced my lead abductor, addressing him in my lately adopted northern nowhere US accent, "Captain, two things please. One, don't call me 'Lady Dade'; that's not my name. Dade, or Nemo—"

"You're right, Countess Midleton, or should I say Baroness Brodrick? Maybe Lady Eliora Guillebert?" he taunted.

My mouth closed as he rattled off very old titles I hadn't used in at least a century or so. Well, the first two at any rate. Lady Eliora had been of Irish nobility and had worked for MI-6 and as far as I was concerned, she'd died with the rest of her team. I took a deep breath and let it out. Killing their researcher for being very good at what she did wasn't going to get me anywhere. And I had places I wanted to go, like off this ship.

"No. Nemo Dade will suffice," I corrected and held up a finger, "and, if you use my former MI-6 rank as a form of address, I will take my chances with the ocean."

"Fair enough," he agreed all too readily.

"The second thing is that I will hear out your mission pitch, but if I think it is poorly planned, or that I'm unnecessary, I want out. I want off this boat. I don't care where you drop me. I'll find my way to somewhere. You let me go, no strings."

"Why should I do that?" he asked, his expression shuttered to a mostly unreadably neutral. How unsurprising. I'd made the mistake of starting to prove many of the things that William seemed to have told this man about me. The captain didn't want to lose his newest 'asset'.

I forged on regardless. "Because having Junior, Trouble, and I on this little love cruise any longer than needed is a recipe for disaster, or hadn't you noticed that he wants to gut me like a salmon? And Trouble's shoveling popcorn in its face waiting for one of us to kill each other or Ellie to fail in containing it," I explained impatiently. "And as I've explained more than once already, I am out of the Game. Retired. Kaput. Done. Finished. How many languages and/or synonyms do you want me to say it?"

Junior kept pushing my buttons, and seemed like he wasn't going to stop anytime soon. Now I understood why William had conducted his little experiment. He needed to know I wasn't going to kill his son no matter how provoking the punk was...what fools these mortals be. Puck so had a point.

Fisherman and I stared at each other silently.

"The others are waiting, Cal," Pippa called diplomatically, appearing in the doorway.

He glanced from me to Cooper and back.

I wasn't sure what face Cooper had made from behind me, but it must've helped.

"I'll consider it," the captain conceded. "But I want you to hear the mission all the way out first. Then we talk about your refusal."

"Deal."

9

It had seemed prudent to wait for Cooper to finish his breakfast before going into the conference room. Neither one of us said anything. There was honestly too much to say, and yet nothing worth saying, so we opted for silence. He really was awesome.

After the mess at breakfast, I wasn't sure how ready I was for round two.

I would've loved to shove all this emotional garbage overboard like any other reasonable, tightly-wound warrior who punched, cursed, and otherwise used fighting to avoid thinking about anything painful and/or problematic. Unfortunately, like the man said, "you can't always get what you want, but if you try sometimes, you just might get what you need."

What I needed was to be busy, preferably away from here. Hopefully, Fisherman was about to grant me my wish.

The whispers stopped as we entered the conference room I'd been in on my first day here. Just like with the dining room, we'd come in at the head of the table.

Fisherman stood on my left with William just beyond him, standing at the corner of the table. Ivy had the first seat on that side. Next to her was empty, but my mind filled it with Cooper's presence from the other day. Dobrek was next, then their researcher with her laptop in front of her. An open seat next to her held a soft-sided satchel and some folders.

The warrior sat on the end like before, with Clarice, Ellie, Grace, and Junior filling the chairs on this side. There was an empty one next to Junior.

Cooper and I shared a split second glance as Fisherman watched. My new friend was going to take a proverbial bullet for me as he moved to take that seat.

I touched his arm with a minute shake of my head. If Thor could play nice with Loki, I could do this. Pulling on a deep well of discipline, I nonchalantly went to the chair next to Junior while Cooper took his usual seat.

Fisherman cleared his throat and gestured behind himself as a screen dropped from the ceiling. "Okay, so we have intel that Tvrtko Vukovic will be arriving in Marseille, France in two days for the start of the Festival de Marseille," he explained.

An image of several men stepping down stairs as they exited a building. Six of them wore suits and shades, two of them had very expensive suits. Another few images of various venues there flashed across the screen.

Huh, hadn't been in Marseille for a few centuries. I tried to think of who might be hanging out around that area.

Fisherman continued, "Chatter has claimed that Koloman Brazda is supposed to meet Vukovic, a middle man who knows all sorts of folks. His business is to put people in touch with others. Brazda is our person of interest. He normally deals in arms, but he has developed a new side market recently—human trafficking." A new picture flashed on the screen. Croat by the look of him. "Which is why he has come out into the open to take advantage of Vukovic's contacts.

Some murmurs went around the table.

The screen filled with headshots. Dozens of women appeared—all different nationalities. Yet, they were all young, bright, and fresh faced. My blood ran cold as suspicions raised their noses like cautious bunnies.

I cleared my throat.

"Yes, Ms. Dade?" Fisherman asked.

"Okay, I'll bite. Human trafficking is terrible and everything, but I know lots of organizations that deal in apprehending these sorts of criminals. Why aren't they taking the lead? For that matter, just how 'official' is this little club? You seem a bit small and flexible for this kind of op. Not to mention it hasn't been made clear as to who exactly is running this cruise ship."

Fisherman stared at me, seeming to weigh his words. The mysterious Pippa took a breath, but closed her mouth at a glance from Fisherman.

William crossed his arms and finally looked at me directly. "We are a low profile intelligence group who specialize in high priority targets that other teams are not equipped to handle," he told me. "Yes, this is an international team, but everyone here has volunteered and been vetted due to their unique field experiences and skills. We are a mostly off the books group."

"The American and British governments are spearheading this initiative, and the Commodore is in charge as he's had the most experience with these sorts of things," Fisherman interjected. "Technically, we both run things, but I've been content to let him take point as his instincts are quite good."

"Usually," Junior muttered.

We all let that slide, though his father compressed his lips briefly.

My stomach sank because I had a very bad feeling about this team. I glanced around the room. "You've all had contact with the Supernatural and/or are in fact more than Human, aren't you? That's the 'in' for this little club, isn't it? You're the freakin' Men in Black but for things that go bump in the night." I really wanted to slap my forehead and directed a very sour stare at William. "The gorsh bush be-spammed Bureau of Paranormal Research and Defense. You gotta be forkin' flippin' kidding me."

"Hey, I think we have better odds than Hellboy's crew did," Cooper countered.

I looked from Cooper to William to Fisherman. "Nope, nope, nope, uh uh, no way, not happening," I came close to babbling. My Spidey senses were tingling off the scale. I stood.

Junior snorted, his gaze on the table, "I knew she wasn't going to do anything useful. She's a drunken coward too self-absorbed to be of any use to anyone. I think all that talk of her having been an operative was some sort of illusion she wove. She's no operative."

William took one of his crossed arms and pinched the bridge of his nose.

"No, what I am is no one's trained pet monkey doing tricks on command, like you," I spat. "I have more years of martial and formal military experience than you can possibly count."

"I don't know, I can count pretty damn high," Junior snarked with a brief glance up at me.

"Henry!" William barked.

"Language!" I snapped.

"Whoa," Cooper cautioned.

"Our interest in Brazda has to do with intel that would indicate he may have a partial– 'Infernal', I believe that's what you call them, in his inner circle," Fisherman said, trying to redirect things. "We've been asked to deal with it. You're right. A normal criminal arms dealer broadening his horizons to human trafficking is bad enough. One that has someone like Ellie, without her scruples, is a major issue, which is why we need you." He glanced over at William. "Word has it that you've dealt with these sorts of beings before."

My attention swung from Fisherman to William. How much had he told them?!

He had the good sense to look abashed but then straightened, taking ownership of what he'd done.

They were all looking at me. Some were hopeful, some skeptical, a couple were outright hostile. All of them wanted something from me. Sadly, I was starting to side with the two hostiles who wanted me gone. I wanted me gone too.

"If you'd sit, Ms. Dade, I'll explain the op," Fisherman requested into the well of uncomfortable silence.

Warrior's movement caught my attention as a swift spasm of pain flitted across his face.

Huh.

I sat down and motioned with a negligent hand for Fisherman to continue.

"We have arranged a meeting with Brazda. At this meeting, the Commodore will act as Demir Kutay's man of business, interested in adding to his employer's household. Kutay is a businessman and information broker in US custody and has agreed to let us use his name in exchange for us putting his wife and children into witness protection.

"Dobrek will be the driver. Cooper and Edwards will be the muscle. Bradford will act as the Commodore's attaché. Fletcher will be on scope, covering the buy. Nazario and I will be in mobile command. You and the Changs will be young ladies being offered in addition to financial remunerations because his employer is looking for something different. He'll, of course, provide medical paperwork of your fitness for Brazda's interests.

"This is a scouting mission. They're taking, buying, and making young women disappear left and right. We make sure you've got trackers, and then we'll follow you to the holding place. You give us the inside intel and get out of there."

Had they been dealing with normal Humans, this wouldn't have been half bad, aside from that exit strategy.

"There are a number of problems with your plan, Captain," I started.

"The Commodore's plan," he corrected.

"*You* should know better," I said with a professionally disappointed shake of my head.

Junior glowered at me.

"Especially with him and Trouble around as examples. If Brazda's pet Infernal shows up at the meet, you're done. It's going to be able to skim thoughts and know it's a trap."

"Not if you're there to block him," William countered.

"All the worse," I responded stridently. "He'll know I'm there if he's looking hard enough. And if, that's a big if, he doesn't detect me in the first thirty seconds," I pointed at Junior, "or him standing by your side, then I can't do boo without the target realizing it. So I can't block him. Oh and to clarify, I can teleport myself certain distances, but I have never taken anyone with me. Are you two trained operatives?" I asked Clarice and Ellie.

"I am," Clarice answered. "FBI—four years in the field. She's an agent in the cybercrimes division, or was. She's been on medical leave for a while now."

William got another hard stare from me.

"So it's like Henry said," Grace spoke up, "she's no use to us."

"No, Agent Fletcher," Fisherman corrected thoughtfully, "she has merely pointed out flaws in the plan, which is part of her job. She knows far more about these beings than anyone else at this table. That's why she's here."

"She's here because you didn't give her a choice," I reminded them. Couldn't help it. This whole op was foolish in the extreme. These people had no idea what they were doing.

"Then help us keep our team safe and alive. You've hunted these creatures for centuries. Help us make this a successful operation, Eliora," William snapped. Ding, I'd gotten his cool façade to crack. He'd been watching my face.

The booger butt had never had too much trouble figuring out what I was thinking, even without the benefit of telepathy. For everyone else, my face was mostly poker blank, but never for him. Pain in my gorse. "You need to have actual intel by someone who can sense what in swampland's slimy sloop you're dealing with here. Is it someone, albeit a bad guy, like

Ellie with Trouble, or are you talking a half-Infernal like my opposite, 'cause those are out there too, or a full-fledged Infernal in hiding?" I threw at them.

Some of them paled. Good! They should! This wasn't a game.

Ellie coughed as Trouble flexed and stared at me sullenly through her watering eyes. I was giving away 'state' secrets, and it wasn't happy.

"Also, you have no idea how many of the Humans could be in this creature's thrall, which sometimes allows them to act as an Infernal's eyes and ears. There are always those who are willing slaves to Darkness because Supernatural beings dress it up pretty to sell their shlock until it's too late and the poor unsuspecting Humans become soul popcorn for a host of Infernals!" I lectured in exasperation.

"Like what you did to my father?" Junior accused with quiet venom.

Everyone stopped.

"Excuse you?" I demanded softly.

"You heard me," he said and stood, letting power seep into his eyes.

My stomach flipped faster than a con's coin, and it was a fight not to throw up. I suddenly understood who his mother was.

He smirked at me.

The proverbial gloves went flying.

Standing, I unleashed my telekinesis.

Junior went flying from his chair. His back slammed against the wall three feet off the ground. I held him there. It'd been more finesse than brute strength though because he hadn't seen it coming. Unlike some, I was old enough, and strong enough, not to need a physical gesture. Things just happened.

Gasps and murmurs sounded behind me. I didn't care.

The brat glared at me, but I saw the fear lurking in his eyes. His body, though he couldn't move it himself, lowered to the ground.

He stumbled a little but remained on his feet.

I stepped in front of him. "Your mother is that gosh dang diddly squat Gwraig Annwn-Nephilim," I spat at him. Yanking on the simple, touristy looking necklace he always wore, I shook my head in disgust. It appeared to be a cross section of a snail's shell, done in abalone within silver wire, completely innocuous. However, now that I'd found and focused on it, I could see its protective weave of Fae Energy. "This was how she hid you! And I'm sure she told you to only ever use your Fae abilities and not the other ones. Didn't she? You have no idea what you can truly do, do you? Mother Fletching idiot."

She had to have trained him not to use his Nephilim abilities so we wouldn't notice him.

While his face sneered and snarled, Junior's eyes screamed fear. Cornered beings who felt they had nothing to lose were the most dangerous. I had to shut this down—now.

"Okay, listen up fish face, you have two choices. You can unleash all that pent up power and fight me, probably hurt some of your friends here, and draw all sorts of nasty unwanted attention to yourself, or—you can *sit the fuck down* and SHUT UP for once!"

The lights flickered.

"You are living on borrowed time, Junior, and my good graces you putrid punk, because the minute those in the Know find out about you, your butt is toast. In case that's too oblique for you, let me make it perfectly clear–*you* are a guppy. I am a shark. They? They are freakin' kraken of legendary size. And if that's not enough to guarantee your good behavior, then think about this–they will *kill* your father for having had you in the first place!" I yelled at him as if he were a petulant teenager and not a man at least as old as I appeared to be. Sad thing was that I knew some teenagers who were way more sensible than this idiot.

I let him go and retracted my power.

He sat down woodenly and stared at the table.

Grace glared at me with narrowed eyes, like she was contemplating something foolish.

"Oh shut it," I snapped at her. "I didn't make him do that. That's a scrap of his father's good sense finally kicking in."

With a disgusted glance around the room, I shook my head.

The others' faces were a range of shock to guarded concern.

William wouldn't look at me.

"No, nope, uh uh, this is not happening, I am out of here. You made your pitch. This plan is pure rubbish. I want none of it. Especially not with that hateful lackwit on the team. I do not care how well-trained you think he is. Even Trouble would wipe the floor with him because he has no understanding of non-Humans, let alone what *he* himself is capable of doing," I ranted.

I teleported to the upper deck and let the winds, whipped up by our anger, slap me around for a bit.

***

Dissention in the Ranks - Cooper

Cooper couldn't believe the Commodore had allowed his son to disrespect both himself and Nemo like that! Especially considering how badly they needed her expertise on this mission. Man, officers' kids coming up through the ranks were the worst.

It'd been hard not to openly laugh at how fast she'd put that little bitch in his place. Arrogant punk had totally had that coming.

A tense, stunned silence fell, but it only lasted maybe five seconds.

"Dammit Henry!" the Commodore thundered. "That was beyond rude. Inexcusable! I know you don't like her. It is also obvious that you question her capacity on this ship; however, after how easily she handled you, I'd say that she has more than demonstrated her capability. A capability we desperately need."

He'd never seen their commanding officer lose his cool like this.

"We don't need her," Grace muttered. "She got lucky."

"We most certainly do," Cooper countered, blown away by the magnitude of Grace's blind loyalty, which was only matched by her obstinate stupidity. "*They*," he added, pointing to Junior and his father, "particularly do. As does Edwards for this op, and Ellie to help with Trouble, as Nemo likes to call it."

"What have you heard?" Dobrek asked.

"Cooper knows that he was the one who talked her out of reporting Henry's existence to her superiors," Ellie supplied sullenly. "I overheard them talking before they went to the kitchen last night. Hadn't been able to sleep."

Cooper stared at her. How had she been out of bed and neither he nor Nemo had noticed? Had Trouble hidden her? *Could* Trouble hide her? Frightening thought.

Clarice frowned worriedly at Ellie and shared a brief glance with him. They'd been taking turns keeping an eye on Ellie.

"Master Sergeant, care to share?" Mylonas asked.

He exhaled heavily, considering his next words carefully. "Henry's existence is forbidden. Nephilim are not supposed to have children. Any that a Nephilim finds are supposed to be reported and/or destroyed. Nemo speculated that it's only a matter of time until the higher ups find out and deal with the situation."

Cooper subsided into silence because the rest of what she'd told him was between her and the Commodore. Though if Mylonas asked, he'd feel compelled to share, if only so his superior would have as many of the cards as he possibly could because this whole mess with the three of them had the possibility of sinking not just the mission, but this whole ship.

"Well someone probably ought to go talk to her," Pippa ventured. "See if something can be done?"

"I'll go," the Commodore insisted.

Junior opened his mouth.

"No," his father snapped. "*You* have already done enough." They watched as the older Bradford walked out of the room, back ramrod straight, but stiffly, injured-like.

Captain Mylonas' gaze met Cooper's with a loaded look.

He knew that expression. That was his 'in my ready room in five'. Cooper gave a miniscule nod that the others didn't seem to notice because Pippa chose that moment to gather her things and leave. Despite exiting out the back door, she'd met the Captain's eyes. They were going to talk. That would give him a few extra minutes.

It was funny that no matter the country, military was military. As soon as the officers were gone, all hell was likely to bust loose. This was no exception.

"Are you really that fucking stupid, or just mental?" Ivy demanded in a thick accent as she stood pointing her finger. He could always tell how pissed off she was because her accent got thicker the angrier she was.

"Are you fuckin' nuts?" Edwards tore into Junior at the same time, also standing, which made the room feel a lot smaller. "Are you seriously trying to blow this mission?"

The punk erupted from his chair. "Look! She is a crazy narcissist who doesn't care about anyone else but herself," he fumed. "She's a loose cannon at best, or at worst, she'll walk out mid-op and leave us swinging in the wind. We can handle this without her. She can't be counted on in a clinch. The only reason she got the better of me was because I didn't think she'd do something that crazy in here."

"Between Ellie and Henry, we more than have this covered," Grace tossed in, standing and putting her fingers on the table.

Dobrek snorted and rolled his eyes. He muttered something in Polish that Cooper didn't catch. Though apparently Junior had.

"You son of bitch," Junior swore with a lunge.

Edwards maneuvered around the table, getting in close. He gripped Junior by the shirt. "Knock it off you little shit!" He slammed the younger Bradford against the wall.

Junior turned his head slowly to look at Edwards with energy laden eyes. "Let. Go. Of. Me."

Edwards growled at him, uncowed. "If *anything* happens to her because you blew this for us, I will go to Rome and personally make sure to shout your existence to everyone in St. Peter's Square myself," the New Zealander promised. "I'm pretty sure that'll get their attention."

Cooper knew the former Special Air Serviceman was tough, but this was nuts.

Henry's eyes narrowed. The glow of blue-green swirling light was still very apparent.

Clarice and Cooper shared a worried glance. One that Ivy and Dobrek shared with them.

Ellie stared thoughtfully at the men.

The air felt thicker, laden with the smell of ocean and electricity.

"Let him go, Brax," Grace murmured. "Please."

Edwards threw his girl a dark look. With one last shove, he walked out of the conference room.

Junior's muscles went a bit looser.

Good, the punk was winding down—now or never. "You might want to consider apologizing," Cooper suggested quietly. Someone needed to diffuse this or things were going to go completely off the rails.

The idiot glared at him.

He held his hands up in a don't shoot the messenger move. "Hey, have your own negative opinion of a new team member, but at least give that opinion constructively. The higher ups would probably be more likely to listen. You know better than to cause this kind of ruckus." Hopefully, Junior would read between the lines and take the hint.

The younger Bradford's eyes bled back to normal as thoughts obviously chased themselves across his face. His gaze darted back and forth across the table. Good! He was starting to think. The guy had a decent head on his shoulders when he bothered to use it. Problem was he'd been given way too much leniency.

"The apology isn't for having those opinions. It's for how you offered them—that was out of line," Cooper added calmly. "If you're gonna tear her down, do it in private in your ol' man's office. Not out here with all of us."

Junior's eyes darted around the room. "Yeah," he muttered. "I should go find my father." He gave a brief nod to Grace and left.

Ellie's head swiveled as she glanced around the room. A sly, half smile spread on her face. "Well, this place got a lot more interesting."

Grace rolled her eyes on a huff and stormed off, probably before she said something else problematic. Though which 'she' was up for grabs.

"I need a drink," Dobrek grumbled.

"Yes," Ivy concurred as they left together, presumably for the lounge.

Cooper put his hands on his waist and let his gaze drop to the table. He had a bad feeling those two had finally realized what kind of 'people' they had on board, and they didn't seem particularly happy. This kind of mission required that they trust each other, and right now, he didn't see this group being able to work together, let alone trust one another in a life-and-death situation. Something that he ought to share with Mylonas when they talked.

"It's going to be okay," Clarice consoled.

He glanced up at her.

Her expression filled with determined hopefulness.

Man, he wanted to hug her. They shouldn't. They couldn't.

"I hope you're right. I really do," he answered instead.

10

I remained on the upper deck. The harsh winds had subsided some, but still blew hard enough that my careful twists and braid were coming undone. I didn't care.

At least the sun still shone as fluffy white clouds raced ocean waves like a derby was at stake. The battle raged within me not to lose my cool. I leaned on the railing as my stomach argued about the position of my cereal.

They thought they could go after an arms dealer who was using, read that as being used by, a possible all out Infernal? That was beyond crazy! They had no clear intel on what they were after, and they thought I could counter anything that came their way. I mean, I'm good, but not that good. A real deal Infernal was decidedly out of my weight class.

That didn't even take into account the possibility that if the bad guys drugged me, the girls and I were borked. Then what? Fisherman was frighteningly uninformed, and William sure as shootin' knew better. Their operation had so many holes in it a colander would've been jealous.

And how did William think this had any prayer of working when his son—

My breath hitched.

When that miserable, hateful spew was more likely to throw me at the enemy as collateral damage than he was to work with me! Their mission didn't stand any kind of chance.

At least now I sure as sugar understood where all his vitriol has come from—his mother's teat.

Having lived many centuries, I'd been reborn into different personas again and again, mostly appearing as variations on a theme physically, but at the core—still me. Sometimes, I'm able to access memories, or knowledge, from those past lives. Certain personas had an easier time of it than others.

However, his mother's hatred of me was something fixed in my mind. No matter how old I became, or who I became, I was aware of it. She'd hated me from my earliest existence. Even from before the time I had defeated and reported her to the Triad. That was why Maelona, or Manon, as she called herself now, hid in Wales. She couldn't leave. I had proverbially chained her there, and the Triad had put her in a cosmic time out for misbehaving. Next step was them 'taking her out' of the equation.

I pondered whether Henry knew about it. Probably not, otherwise he'd have been nicer to me, knowing that I could reach out and have his mom out on a limb. How that one and only nasty Fae-Nephilim managed to hide all her darker shenanigans was still a mystery.

William approached the rail and stood close to me on my left. Probably because I was right handed.

"Don't touch me," I said, my voice low. "Better yet, leave."

He stayed put and said nothing, probably waiting to see what I would do.

I wiped away tears. He no longer had any right to those, such a private piece of me. "Your plan is worse than swiss cheese. Your son is a hot mess. And—and—"

I turned to him, my eyes bright with angry power and salt water that had nothing to do with the ocean.

"And you slept with that slimy no good greasy grimy witch?!" The words spilled out in a harsh croak. I couldn't even safely use her name because true names carried on the winds of the world. "*How could you?*"

Chest tight.

Couldn't breathe.

Had to take a deep breath.

Had to think of silly things, Looney Tunes, stuffed animals, comic books—anything! But my mind wandered back to the thought that had I been a comic book character, Manon would've been my archnemesis.

My fists clenched. I did my best to slow down my breathing. It was all I could do not to give in to my pain. That was a road none of us wanted me to travel.

"Do you realize that she destroyed an entire village of people, every Human living in a whole valley, to spite me because some young hunter wanted to be my mate and not hers?" I croaked, my voice cracking as the words tumbled out. "I didn't even realize he was making a choice! I was young, barely a century old. I didn't know. I had no idea she was even interested in him! He died trying to save those people because I wasn't strong enough to save *him*. That's just one example of the kinds of things she has done!

"She has hated me for centuries. I'm the reason she has to stay in one place. If it weren't for the fact that she hides in Wales and plays good little soldier for the Triad, they'd have taken her off the board by now. However, she doesn't just step on the line while they're not looking, or dip a toe across the line, she freakin' tap dances and does the samba on it back and forth! That monster kills like she breathes!"

He stared at me. Dampness welled in his eyes, but my former love said nothing. William dropped his gaze to his shoes. A tear hit the deck. "I was wrong. At the time, I was so very angry," he confessed, raising his head to look out at the ocean. "You're right. She's not the person that she'd led me to believe she was.

"As we got to know each other, she told me stories about how over the years you had made many...'conquests', as she called them. Then you left them behind, always. I wasn't new or special. It hadn't surprised her in the slightest that not only had you said no to me about children, but that you'd left me in such a horrible way. She said you weren't capable of truly loving anyone but yourself. All that mattered to you was your work.

"We—we ended up having Henry. He has always been everything I have ever wanted in a son...Please," he whispered, bringing his attention back to me, pleading with his eyes as much as his words, "please don't kill him. He truly is good."

"Could've fooled me," I muttered ungraciously. William had believed such awful things about me... and hadn't been able to find me to ask.

We'd never discussed my past lives. Now I felt compelled to refute the misinformation. "I have only ever been married once before, in my first mortal lifespan. You were the closest I'd come to changing that. Have I had lovers? Yes, I have. Do I know how many? No, not really, but considering all my centuries of life, not all that many. There's probably only a dozen that I could bring to mind, which considering we're talking millennia," I shrugged. "However, I can tell you that I have never, ever used a relationship to hurt someone like she claims. Not ever."

William's mouth compressed as he stared back out over the ocean. His jaw clenched. Words fought to come out, but he obviously didn't want them in the open.

"His mother had him until he was six, and then he came to me," my former lover explained.

I had the distinct impression that hadn't been what he'd originally intended to say.

He settled himself and looked at me. "I have done my very best to be a good father to him, to teach him to be better. Grace's mother helped. I sent him to train with the SAS. He even went to Oxford. Henry's learned so much. He is constantly reading, anything and everything he can get his hands on. He picks things up so quickly," William laughed a little as he rambled, like a proud father. The loving, proud father that he was.

"I still care deeply for you," he continued, "but he, he is my life. Please, don't destroy that just to have revenge on me. I know I deserve your anger, but I'm begging you, his only crime is loving me and being full of inaccurate information about you. I would never let him hurt you, just as I'm pleading with you not to hurt him. Please don't destroy him on my account." Silent tears slid down his face.

My jaw dropped, appalled. "William! I would never," I choked on my words because not long ago that was almost exactly what I'd been considering. Not to spite him, but because it needed to be done. His son trafficked too much in his Fae abilities and not his Celestial ones. That monstrous bitch had not only allowed, but encouraged, Darkness to grow in an environment of hate and bitterness. The combination had made Henry unstable and dangerous. His only saving grace right now seemed to be his love for his father.

Sharp winds quickened on my thoughts.

The man in front of me had asked for the world. This would cost me my life, protecting his young Nephilim who had no real sense of what he was, who I'd bet held entirely too much power for his own good, despite being the child of a Fae-Nephilim and a Human. Whose mother had set the youngling on a course his father could barely deflect. Who'd undoubtedly been taught from birth to hate me—

Yet there William stood, finally open in his pain and fear. He'd left himself open for me to see what was in his heart. What he hadn't articulated. His goodness and integrity, his guilt and remorse, his love and pain, some things which were shielded from me. Undoubtedly *her* doing. Even with that, I had never seen him this vulnerable.

I had never known him to beg anyone. Not ever.

All the negatives stacked themselves in my head, and yet, I'd been willing to die for this man a little over thirty years ago...

He stared at me imploringly, broken.

My heart lurched.

Cooper's suggestion teased the back of my mind as a way out of this mess.

"Fine," I choked out and cleared my throat. "I, Aoife, daughter of Bebinn, child of the Heavens, swear to you William Harrison Bradford that I will do everything in my power to protect and guide Henry Galahad Bradford so long as I draw breath. I will not seek to kill him; nor will I engender a situation to get him killed. He shall be as mine own to keep safe and hold dear to my heart.

"So I vow by the Light of the Heavens, salt of the Earth, and the will of my Soul."

I made a small ball of sunshine bloom in my hand. Took the other and wiped fresh tears from my face. Then let my power wash through us both. Blood oaths were one thing, what I had done was far more reaching. I'd shaped Reality according to my Will by using a piece of my Divine essence.

We felt, as much as heard in our minds, the cosmic bells tolling on my words.

The winds increased.

What I had sworn had traveled out into the ether and come back accepted as a new piece of Reality. I had created an Oath. "It is done," I murmured. "There is no greater gift I can give you. If They come for him, they must go through me first. I will undoubtedly die, but my death may suffice to save him. He has my protection from everyone and everything."

William's mouth opened and his eyes widened at my words. They widened further at seeing *me* as my true form fought to manifest, a vessel of Light and Love. It shone visibly beneath my physical one.

That's when I sensed him.

William turned his head in the same moment.

Henry stood at the top of the stairs that led back down into the ship, his face inscrutable.

I stuffed myself back down into my physical form. It hurt. Though it was probably for the best. There was no telling what I might've done or said in that state.

Retreat to my room sounded about right, but my Energy needed a break, so walking it was. Swearing an Oath of such magnitude took a lot out of a gal. I headed to the stairs, unwilling to let myself look at William.

As I drew close to Henry, there was bewilderment in his eyes as he watched me.

"That. That is what is within you," I told him quietly. "Don't make me regret my choice."

11

I slept.

Even Nephilim needed sleep, especially when we'd expended a lot of power. That was part of the gig. The Genie had gotten it mostly right, phenomenal cosmic power, itty bitty living body. Human bodies weren't designed to house that much Divine energy. As a result, we ate a lot and slept a lot.

Having woken in the middle of the night again had me feeling grumpy. That was my story and I was sticking to it. Also, it was doing terrible things to my sleep schedule. Then again, I was expending more energy now than I had in decades, so maybe I was just out of practice.

Fortunately—or not, depending on one's perspective–William had let himself into my room while I'd slept and left a walkie-talkie with a note for me on my nightstand.

The note didn't address anything from earlier in the day. All it provided was reassurance that only he had come in and just long enough to leave this for me since "other communicative measures had short circuited". Okay, that made me smile. The radio connected directly to someone who could provide me with sustenance when I woke. He'd rightly guessed I'd be hungry when I did. He'd also said Mr. Cooper would be in the lounge overnight if I needed anything else.

Not feeling particularly chatty for Cooper's company, I turned the walkie on and requested whatever they had left over from dinner earlier. No sense in making the staff's job harder. It wasn't their fault that their boss' son was a misbegotten prat.

His postscript requested that I not go to the kitchen because it bothered the staff to have me down there.

I shook my head. That pain in my rear must have them all convinced that I was, in fact, someone important, despite my two favorite hostiles' opinions. Great. So much for middle of the night kitchen raids. My imagination filled in Grace's grating, snarky voice in my head, *well, why don't you just pop in there and pop out again?*

Because you nit, I don't waste power like that. If I'm perfectly capable of using my own two feet, then that's what I'm going to do. I fought not to stick my tongue out at the empty air of my room. Overusing one's powers was a good path to abusing one's powers. It became addictive. That was an issue I'd experienced before. Snort's image as he slept on the deer trail rose in my head. Yeah...I'd been a real schmuck during my time in the States.

My food arrived. I was deeply grateful that the cart held enough to easily feed the warrior. With silent gratitude to William for having had the forethought to warn the kitchen staff to send me enough for a big man, I wheeled the cart into my room. My mouth watered at the lovely smells. Despite looking like a petite woman, I could eat enough to give a linebacker competition.

Two things popped into my half-asleep mind: say a prayer of thanks and check the food for poisons. The first was something I only did when my instincts dictated, and I kept it private. The other was now simply common sense.

Thankfully, the food was not only safe but delicious. After my meal, I rolled the cart into the hallway, locked my door, and crawled back into bed. Sleep claimed me swiftly regardless of my red-eyed stare at the Monet over my couch.

The next morning dawned cloudy with stiff winds. Not wanting to deal with Junior, or anyone else for that matter, I used my nifty new toy and requested breakfast in my room. After a moment's thought, I asked them to relay a message to the Commodore that this morning's weather was all Mother Nature's doing.

That got me a halting affirmative. Eh, let them think it was some sort of spy speak.

After a nice big breakfast, checked for safety, my body itched for activity. Even considering my years of drunken stupor, I had still walked everywhere all the time. Well, okay, except for when Snort and I had gone for short runs. But still...I stretched out on my bed, prepared to do a little out of body sightseeing when someone knocked on my door.

Getting up and tying my robe tighter around my pajamas, I called out quietly, "Yes?" My abilities were still sore, so only using mortal senses was going to have to suffice. Necessary recon was one thing, just using them as a proverbial peephole fell back into that unnecessary category.

"It's Cooper."

Oh. I opened the door.

"Hey, I just wanted to check in on you since you weren't at dinner or at breakfast," he explained. Poor guy looked seriously tired. Seeing my stare, he did a sideways head nod. "I not only stayed up for you, but Ellie had a rough night. Apparently, you called down some serious mojo yesterday because Trouble went ballistic."

"Ohhhh," I exhaled, feeling horrible. Caught up in swearing my Oath, I'd completely forgotten that there was a demon shard, a splintered portion of a full Infernal, on this ship. I winced. "I am so sorry. In the moment, I'd completely forgotten what that might do."

"What did you do?"

I gave a long blink and sighed. "Not only did I call upon the Divine, I basically let some of my Celestial nature manifest in order to reshape Reality because I swore an Oath to protect Junior and look after him, no matter what. All that Holy energy so close to any kind of Infernal would hurt it, piss it off, and in general, make it very unhappy." My tired eyes apologized as I spoke.

He nodded slowly. "Good deal. I'm proud of you."

"Whoa, wait, wha—?"

"I honestly think that was the best thing you could've done," he replied. "Here's for hoping it helps. Hey, I need some shut eye. Can I trust you not to string him up and use your new rookie for fish bait?"

That made me grin. "Girl Scout's honor," I said, laughing as I held up three fingers.

"Fibber. You've never been a Girl Scout."

"True, but I should have. They're great," I commented, "and they make the best cookies!"

He laughed. It was good to see him laugh. I felt better about having unintentionally cost him a night of sleep.

"By the way, there's got to be some sort of gym in this place. Don't suppose you could tell me where?" I asked.

Cooper watched me thoughtfully. "I'll tell you, but you have to promise no—"

I cut him off. "I promise you, Joshua Anthony Cooper, that I will do nothing untoward to the punk or his little friend," I solemnly promised, minus using my power. Didn't want to cause any more problems for Ellie. I took his hand in both of mine. "Seriously man, I'm just going to get some exercise. As you've seen, I'm wound tighter than an over-tuned Stradivarius."

"Josh," he corrected in quiet tones, "my friends call me Josh, or Coop." He gave me a wan smile. "I'm going to try something."

My mind got slapped with a very loud and bright tour of how to get to the gym. It was like someone slamming a VR experience on my noggin with no warning. I blinked as my head snapped back. “Wow! Okay. Got that loud and clear,” I laughed. “Let’s not do that again unless it’s an emergency okay? It was like getting in a car, turning it on, only to find that the stereo volume was jacked all the way up. Deal?”

“Fair enough,” he chuckled. “Be good,” Coop called as he walked away.

“Like my Thin Mints depended on it.”

His laughter followed me back into my room while I got changed.

12

The gym wasn't too hard to find. They'd apparently converted one of the holds into what amounted to a nearly full-service, commercial gym with cardio equipment, weight machines, free weights, a couple of heavy bags, and even a roped off sparring ring slightly raised off the floor. Only thing they were missing was a pool. Junior's mother had Water Fae blood, so I was perfectly okay that there wasn't a pool.

It was surprisingly airy with its white walls, a handful of squat rectangular windows up high, and full wall mirrors on either end of the room. Colorful exercise and health charts decorated the hull and hallway walls. I'd entered near the bikes, treadmills, and other cardio machines, thinking to start there to warm up...and saw Junior and his little friend. She was on an elliptical. He was running on a treadmill.

Clank.

Off to the right, on the other end, a weight machine's stack hit home a little harder than it should've. Ivy sat on a bench in front of a four-way machine with her back to the hull wall. She'd turned her head, watching the three of us. Her hands still gripped the lat pull-down bar.

The warrior sat on a bench press facing our direction. His elbows rested on his knees while he dried his face and hands on a towel. As much as we had Ivy's undivided attention, Edwards' gaze never left the floor.

I had no doubt that he watched us just as closely, no matter what his eyes were doing.

We could all hear the ocean outside as it lapped the hull 'cause everyone seemed to be holding their breath.

The punk touched something on the treadmill's control board as he pulled little plastic ear pieces from his ears. "C'mon Grace," he murmured with the barest glance towards me.

She punched buttons with more force than was needed and stopped her machine. The towel snapped as she yanked it.

I moved in front of the speed bags to my right, putting me further from them.

Slosh. Her water bottle audibly objected as she snatched it up with her towel and walked out of the gym. I only got one dirty glare from her in the whole process.

Curiously enough, Junior wouldn't look at me after his initial glance.

The silence stretched on the heels of their exit.

I stared at the cardio equipment, looked at Ivy and Edwards, and let my eyebrows go up with wide eyes. "Sorry," I mumbled. Seeing a few jump ropes on a small supply table next to the sparring ring, I walked over and grabbed one.

There was some open space down here, past the sparring ring but before the weights area. A second set of doors stood near the edge of the weights area and just beyond the punching bags. The doors led into the hallway just like the set down by the cardio area where I'd entered. With my back to the wall and doors, I began jumping rope. For whatever reason, I'd always found it to be a fun activity. Had to have been the inner kid in me.

After a few moments, Ivy and Edwards went back to their workouts.

I breathed a sigh of relief that I would forever claim was merely due to my cardio exercise. We all did our own exercising. Ivy made a point of showing me how the weight machines all worked while Edwards took some time on a heavy bag.

A couple of decades ago while living in the States, I'd developed a curiosity about boxing. Most martial sports interested me. I'd managed to find a place willing to let a scrappy little thing like me learn and train. It hadn't been hard to make myself seem human-weak back then.

Walking over to the supply table, I grabbed some tape and wrapped my hands. The other heavy bag wasn't being used so I began taking some warm up hits.

Ivy came over and stood on the other side, mopping her face and drinking some water, watching me. "Nice hits," she commented. "You've trained."

"Yeah," I exhaled. "I'm a bit rusty. It's been a few years."

Edwards kept working his bag, but I could tell he was listening.

"An actual 'few years', or more?" Ivy chuckled. "Because you were not this coordinated when we collected you."

"Oh, is that what we're calling it now?" I snorted a laugh and weighed the options. "Eh, twenty or so years, give or take." Wasn't sure what to do with the fact that Ivy seemed cool, like Cooper.

"He said you're old, like old-*old*," Edwards interjected between hits.

"Don't you know it's not polite to ask a lady her age?" I joked.

"By your own claim, you're not a 'lady'," he countered in that charming New Zealand accent of his.

I rolled my eyes and hit my bag hard enough to make the chains complain. Thoughts of William got ruthlessly shoved down into their box and back into my mental closet. The bag swung harder on my next hit.

"Tranquila," Ivy murmured in Spanish.

"Sorry," I muttered. "I survive by keeping a low profile. That means I'm not a fan of information about me getting spread around without my knowledge or consent. It tends to make me irritable."

Edwards snorted.

Ivy nodded. "Understandable."

"Think of it as a lifelong deep cover assignment in which the truth can cause problems. Significant, life threatening problems." I exhaled heavily and shook out my arms while bouncing on my feet in place.

Silence stretched.

They weren't going to let this go. For whatever reason, it was important to them. "Fine. You two guess people or events and I'll let you know if I'm older than that."

They shared a look.

"JFK," Ivy began.

"Older," I said while stretching.

"World War II," Edwards offered.

"Older."

"World War I" she guessed.

"Keep going."

"The French Revolution?" he asked thoughtfully.

I began hitting the bag again after giving him a side glance. "Older."

He stopped to stretch his head and neck side to side. "That was Pippa's speculation."

Ivy narrowed her eyes. "Did King Arthur exist?"

"Yes, and I'm older," I added.

Edwards stopped and stared. "The Roman Empire."

"Heh. We can call that close enough," I hedged.

Ivy's eyes went saucer wide.

"I was born before they got rolling by a couple hundred years, but ah...I don't try to think about it too much," I ended in a winded whisper. A hiccup-choke surprised me. I hit the bag harder than I'd meant.

Riiiiiiiiip.

The pitter-patter of sand spilling out from between the rag lining and leather seemed loud.

"Sugar daddies!" I muttered. "Tape!"

Edwards sprang into action grabbing some hand tape to help me seal the hole.

I flexed a little power as I put my hands over the taped hole. My overtaxed abilities groaned, drawing a hiss from me. However, the hand tape morphed and melded into a seamless replica of the bag's material. The bag appeared as if it'd never been ripped.

"Santa Ma—"

"Ivy," I barked without looking at her.

"Right, sorry," she apologized.

Edwards stood there silently, looking at what I'd done and the sand on the mat.

Ivy went over to a small mini fridge against the wall between my heavy bag and a speed bag further down. She grabbed a couple of waters and brought them over, handing one to me and one to Edwards.

His expression said he would've liked something stronger. Though he ripped it open and guzzled it down anyway.

I did the same, hoping it would help with my blossoming headache. "Bench," my mouth muttered without any real conscious thought as my feet found their way over to the free weights.

Edwards hadn't yet removed his plates from the bar. He had three hundred on it. I added another hundred and laid down on the bench. "You two spot me?"

They looked at me and then looked at each other.

"You're serious?" Ivy asked.

I shrugged. "Can do it myself I suppose."

Edwards rolled his eyes and guided Ivy to the far side with a glance that screamed 'get ready to save her'.

With a deep inhale and exhale, I positioned my hands and took the bar. Three reps and my eyes slid up to Edwards.

"Would you please let go of the end," I requested drily. "I swear I have this."

He stared with a blank face. "There is no way you should be able to do this."

We set the bar back.

I sat up and looked around for a towel.

Ivy threw one at me that I caught without looking.

Okay, okay, I was showing off for them, but to be fair, they had started to feel like new friends that I could trust with who I was. That was something I hadn't had in a very long time. While in the States, aside from some casual acquaintances, I'd kept myself mostly isolated. Who was I kidding? I'd hidden who I was and what I could do for a lot longer than that. After a while it became a very lonely existence.

"Talk to me," I cajoled. "Why do you two care so much about how old I am? How good I am?"

Edwards walked over to busy himself with putting dumbbells back on the racks.

Ivy went back to the fridge behind the bags and grabbed more waters. "I was born in Puerto Rico. Moved to Maryland when I was thirteen and began working for the CIA straight out of college. Who then loaned me to a joint team with the DEA, so I've seen things," Ivy told me in quiet tones. "We were told you are old, old and powerful. More importantly, he swore you were a good person. Sometimes, the higher ups, they tell their people things, things that they want to be true, or that they think could be true." She stopped and let her gaze slowly roam around the gym. "We really need it to be true. We need to know if you're actually that powerful, that good hearted."

Awwwwwww hossapples. What had he told them? After taking another pull from the water bottle she'd handed me, I wiped my mouth. "How much do you two understand about energy, matter, atomic structure? Physics, that sort of stuff?"

Edwards came back over and shrugged slightly. "I know some." He sat down on the bench next to mine.

"Okay, Celestial Energy is kind of like the source of all energy and can take any form—heat, electrical, mechanical, etc. We manipulate energy and matter, able to convert one to the other and back again. Being part Celestial, well, any of us can actually, I can create it too."

Ivy opened her mouth.

I held up my hands. "I know, I know, that defies the laws of Physics, but typically, in a cosmic sense, somewhere it gets destroyed—usually by an Infernal, or half-Infernal. They lost the power to create when they Fell to become what they are, but they sure as shootin' can destroy like nobody's business.

"Think of it like fusion versus fission. Fusion smashes atoms together and creates something new. It's very powerful, and there's very little waste byproducts. Whereas fission pulls atoms apart, destroying what was, resulting in bad things for Humanity, and then those byproducts come apart generating even more bad things. It's not as powerful but is very dangerous.

"Being what I am; I'm part Celestial Energy and part Human, so I can command energy, shape it, convert it into matter... basically shape parts of Reality." I paused. "However, it is a responsibility. Oftentimes, there are consequences, even when it is used correctly, because I am still half Human. My body pays the price when I've tried to channel too much Energy through it."

"You can do all that? You can shape the whole world?" Ivy wondered.

"Mmm...not on the level you're thinking. Like Humans, we all have different talents, ability levels, and affinities...Like, you will never ever get me into water with Junior." My face soured at the thought.

"Why not?" Edwards wanted to know. "I think you're more powerful than he is."

"I wouldn't bet your check on that just yet," I cautioned. "His mo—*she* is half Fae and half Celestial. *He* for some reason, is half Celestial, more than a quarter Fae, and a little Human. So, I'm not sure, but my instincts tell me that he is going to be much more powerful than he realizes." If he actually got a chance to grow into those powers, I mused unhappily. His psyche, powers, and emotional state were a hot mess.

"That doesn't seem right," Ivy mused aloud. "Genetics would dictate—"

"Yeah, 'cause the ones upstairs have never messed with genetics and statistics," I interrupted with a huff.

"But," she began, her eyes searching the floor, "how do you do it? If you're half Human, how do you stay sane living that long?"

I took a long pull of water and was slow to recap the bottle. "Reinventing myself after a fashion," I said to the bench. I'd meant what I'd said to William about Eliora being 'dead'. As far as I was concerned, she was gone. He'd said our time was past. So be it. Nemo was my identity now. My current persona. "Every so often, we are 'reborn' as it were. Not always as babies, but sometimes as children, or young adults; our physical features may change some. Old 'selves' have to die after a time to reset our minds, though I often keep mementos in my home." I smiled wistfully. Hadn't been there in too long.

"What? That ridiculous trailer?" Edwards snorted.

"Oh no, I have my very own Batcave," I replied with a mysterious smile.

He glanced at Ivy, clearly wondering if I was serious.

She scrunched up her mouth and nodded. "I can believe that," she replied thoughtfully and then her face lit up. "Ooh like Conner MacLeod kept a whole bunch of stuff."

I hated that movie. We didn't all run around trying to kill each other...well, most of the time. The Triad saw to that.

"Ah, I don't think she likes that movie, Iv," Edwards commented.

A quick body shake, rather like a horse's shudder, and I was right as rain. Sure I was.

Ivy opened her mouth to say something, probably apologize.

I held up my hand. "Like every ended relationship under the sun, there are certain things that remind us of that time, or that person," I confessed, why I wasn't sure. Maybe, *maybe* because I needed to say it out loud to someone. "Things went belly up at the end of January of '86. That movie came out two months later. Stupid me, I caught it in the theater out of curiosity." No more words came out because I had to swallow, hard, twice.

The silence stretched.

"So, you really gonna leave?" she asked quietly.

Her question rolled around in my head, one that I previously thought I'd had an answer for. "Not sure," I answered honestly. Having sworn my Oath, I was now kind of stuck, maybe. My head and my gut were still warring over where exactly I had to be to keep Junior safe.

"Please stay," Edwards asked the floor, and then he looked up at me. His face held a familiar expression.

"You have a personal stake in this mission," the words spilled in soft-toned surprise. I should've known.

He nodded.

"His older sister's daughter went missing," Ivy stepped in to explain. "Eden's only twenty years old. The short answer is that she was supposed to do a study abroad program. Edwards was already here with us when she went missing. Pippa's almost certain this crew took her, based on the information we've gathered so far."

My eyes closed as I shook my head. "You never do know what's around the bend, big adventure or a brand new friend..." I muttered. Dangity drippity doughy—

Edwards' bench creaked.

"Bless that man a thousand times over!" I swore and stood lightning quick. My water bottle flew across the room where it exploded on an elliptical machine, spilling water everywhere.

"Ahhhh, that did not sound like any blessing I ever heard," Edwards cautiously commented.

"That's because it wasn't," I snapped and then began mumbling a prayer of forgiveness in ancient Gaelic, apologizing for what I'd meant. My hands went to my hips as I stared at the bench. "He knew. That sonofawretchedblueberrybisonbillygoatgruff knew that once I became aware of what was going on around here—your niece, Trouble, Ellie, all of it! He knew I wouldn't be able to help myself. Especially after calling me out for my time in the States. A tendril of power showed me where a camera hid, discreetly secured in the upper corner.

Walking over towards it, I pointed upwards as if it were someone's face. "You! You and I are going to have words, sir! Sooooooooo many words," I snarled and spun. "Yes, we will get your niece back," I added to Edwards.

He stared at me with a guarded face.

"Yes, I am that strong," I barked at Ivy, who just blinked. My eyes found the wet elliptical. That didn't help. "I need a shower," I added in a growl.

"Team meeting at nineteen hundred hours. In the Conference Room. That plan is short bread. I want Pippa and all her notes, in my room, in two hours." I turned and stared up at the camera again. "You wanted me 'on board'?! Well buddy, be careful what you ask for, 'cause you got it."

Without looking at Ivy or Edwards, I walked out of the gym.

Whack!

Went the crash bars on the doors.

Wham!

Went the doors against the hallway walls.

I stomped all the way back to my room singing a children's show theme song in my head about a curious monkey because it had made me smile during my time of isolated misery, and right now I needed something to make me smile before I said things, even thought things, that were going to have very serious repercussions.

One thing that the military, medical world, and ministry shared–it wasn't possible to save them all. Sooner or later, the odds would go against you and you'd lose.

My heart had become too sore by the time I lost William. It was the straw that had broken the camel's back. Anger surged because I'd gotten out of the game and because William was right. I wasn't even close to being at my best, not anymore. A little over thirty years of wallowing and hiding had made me rusty. Rusty equaled risk. Risk liked to court death. I had little interest in seeing any of these good people court death.

My barely contained awareness felt Trouble wrestling with Ellie. *That* was going to have to be dealt with and soon.

13

Knock, knock.

The sound almost seemed hesitant. Surprising.

My eyes opened slowly. I'd showered, eaten lunch, and had been meditating. Seemed prudent. Something had to be done to lower my anger quotient.

The door swung open and gave me a good view of the mysterious "Pippa". Their scholar was taller than me by at least a handspan. Her thick blonde hair was cut just long enough to curl under and graze just below her shoulders. Bangs softened it. It surprised me to realize that her leanness wasn't just natural. There were muscles visible beyond her rolled up blouse sleeves and mid-calf skirt. She stared at me in consternation.

Apparently, she hadn't expected to find me sitting cross-legged and meditating. I stared back at her.

She shook her head and pursed her lips like any good British matron. "You are unbelievable," the scholar began in quiet, but terse tones as she stepped into the hallway to pull a small two-shelf cart into my room. It held her laptop, files, and books. "Absolutely beyond the pale with your behavior, frightening everyone, causing trouble with Ellie, picking fights with Henry, scaring Ivy, forcing Joshua into sleepless nights, and don't even get me started with how much you've hurt Harry." She shut the door, tugging her cart toward my couch and coffee table as her soft tirade continued. The scholar finally stopped to look at me with a huff. I think she'd thought to cow me with her motherly lecture being that she was nearly the same age as William, and I appeared young enough to be her daughter.

I sat there and raised one eyebrow as power crept into my eyes, taking them from a normal Human hazel green to an electric neon green.

She swallowed in the silence.

With power thrumming through me, I could feel her fear and racing heart. She was scared of me, and not just for generic reasons, like I was more than Human.

Annoyingly, Henry had extended his awareness.

Surprisingly, Trouble was ignoring me.

"Choose your next words carefully, scholar," I intoned into the well of silence.

"Ooh, you're just a rude bully," she spat. "Throwing your mighty power and weight around like that, and I am not so much a scholar as a doctor, actually. A medical doctor with years of research under my belt."

"What I am..." I began calmly as I unfolded myself.

She backed up into her cart.

"...is abducted, tricked, hoodwinked, hurt, crushed, abused, insulted, infuriated, oh–and let's not forget, drugged, trapped, threatened, and cornered." I finished standing in front of her. "Did I miss anything, Doctor Philippa Elizabeth Weatherford, scholar extraordinaire?"

She swallowed again. "No," Pippa croaked and cleared her throat, "No, I don't believe you did."

The punk's Energy reached out again.

It's nothing, just a discussion between Pippa *and myself. She's fine*, I thought back at him.

He withdrew.

"Also bear in mind," I added in crisp British accents to match her own as Eliora's arctic displeasure rose, "that all this happened because *you* found *me*." My eyes widened. "You were *ordered* to find me! After you tested my blood. You're the reason he had to come find me! Why all of this mess started in the first place. Wallace..." I trailed off not wanting to give away that I'd figured out something. Pippa's original, seemingly innocent research so many years ago, had given PM Wallace reason to rope William into all of this. Her panicking thoughts had been so loud that skimming them wasn't even necessary.

"True, but I had to, we needed you," she said in a tight whisper, trying to stand her ground. "He had finally confessed while we were looking for you that this was your job anyway, ridding the world of these beings, so someone needed to tell you about what was happening."

"*He* talks too much," I enunciated, still speaking like a native.

"*He*," she replied in more normal tones, imitating me, "barely talks at all."

I walked away and sat on the couch in my leggings, oversized sweater, and fuzzy socks. The couch was great for curling up on, so I drew up my knees.

She watched me with that silent stare all Brits learned in the cradle. It managed to convey disgruntlement, disappointment, irritation, and condemnation for extreme stupidity all while showing almost nothing outwardly. It was all in the eyes. William could give it in spades.

"Did you simply come in here to give me grief, or are we actually going to get some work done?" I asked, having switched back to Nemo's American accent and directness.

Her lips pursed again.

My hands went up in surrender. "Look, you win. He's yours. He wants nothing to do with me." The mediation had helped me see that all the emotional baggage with William and Henry had been turning my insides into a mess, still was. I barely had it under control. With Trouble on board, and Ellie at risk, that was a state I could not afford. Regardless, Gilchrist would've thrown me in a lake by now to cool off that Gaelic temper.

He'd been my mentor and guardian, and had made no bones about pulling me up short when I'd needed it.

I made a face as the thought crossed my mind that my memories were being nudged by a certain someone. Someone who wanted me to remember my inner balance. I let the power slip back down into the ocean.

The doctor's eyes widened as her hand flew up to the necklace pocket watch she wore. "What? Oh, Heavens, no," she sputtered. Her eyes closed for a moment and then she regarded me with a slight smile. "No, he and I are not 'a thing' I think the younger set calls it? As for the other, I can't speak to that because, like I said, he's not talking to anyone."

"Mmmm..." I responded and rubbed my face, letting my feet come down to the floor. "Not surprising at all. He's a veritable clam. Now, shall we get to work?" My voice had gone to polite observational tones.

"You two truly do love each other," she murmured, sounding surprised.

"Leave it alone, doctor," I told the table. She needed to stop pushing.

"I have a name you know," she quipped.

"And when you stop treating me like some sort of science experiment, or living artifact, I might consider using it," I replied.

"But you *are*! You are a living piece of history! You have anatomy of the rarest sort! If what he said is true, you are Heaven's Warrior on earth, their watchdog against the Dark. You are a being who is incredibly old, incredibly powerful, and yet this, this one Human relationship has you losing your temper and being as emotional as the young woman you appear to be. One would think that for all the centuries you've lived, that you would be so far beyond such things," she gushed.

I stood and got in front of her. Had to crane my neck as I got close.

Didn't matter.

She fought not to back up from me.

"Look, I will tell you this one last time, *Pippa*," I warned her. "My relationship with William, whatever that is, or is not, is off limits to all of you, and that includes Henry. That discussion is closed, done, verboten, over, not to be touched, etcetera, et al. Am I clear?" There was no power in my eyes. No cosmic awe. Just me. And I was pissed off and done.

Why William had rejected me and held me at arm's length despite coming to find me was a mystery. Why this one man's refusal wounded my heart so much and had sent me into such a tail spin was also a mystery. However, she had not earned the right to my personal pain, particularly when not even I understood it. So it was time to shut things down.

She nodded silently, having the good grace to look slightly abashed.

"Good. You're the resident smarty pants, so I need information from you, a lot of it," I informed her, going back to sitting on the couch with my arms on my knees, staring at the coffee table in front of me. "You people wanted the Watchdog. Fine. Sit down, and please start giving me the intel you've accumulated on our targets. Then we'll move on to our team assets."

Pippa stood still for a moment in thoughtful silence, but after a brief lip compression, she began pulling things off her cart so we could get down to business.

"Kolomon Brazda has been running his operations since roughly nineteen ninety five, when the Dayton Accords happened and shut down the wars in an official capacity. He started in Varazdin, in the northeast of Croatia and developed a second locale in Split, on the coast," Pippa explained, settling down to business and showing me her notes.

"So he's had plenty of time to dig in," I murmured.

"Yes. He was also Croat military during the wars, which gave him access to plenty of hardware. Currently, he has five lieutenants under his command who help him run things. The newest of which, Vinko Harvat, has taken over the trafficking portion of the empire. However, in order to expand things to farther markets, they need Tvrtko Vkovic's help."

"Why Marseille though?" I asked.

"Because Tvrtko's daughter grew up performing in Rijeka and landed a spot in a dance company in Marseille as part of the Festival, so that being relatively neutral territory, with thousands of people from around Europe being there..." she trailed off with a shrug.

I nodded. "Okay, yeah, that makes more sense then, but Fisherman said a meet's already been arranged?"

"Aleksander Dobrek has contacts in that part of the world. He came up with a list of names. Callister cross referenced those and discovered that one of them, Demir Kutay, had recently become a 'guest' of the US government. In exchange for the use of his name and reputation, Kutay's wife and children will be hidden.

"Ellie took the pertinent information and created Harry's cover. She seeded the trail and arranged the meet, with Dobrek's help."

"If Dobrek's got the contacts, then he should be William's assistant," I mused. "Okay, I need to see our team's files." My wheels were spinning faster.

"I'm not sure..." she hemmed and hawed.

"Pippa, either I am doing this or I'm not."

She frowned.

"You people uncovered my existence and dragged me back into this world kicking and screaming. You've put me in a position where I couldn't in good conscience say 'no'. Therefore, you are darn diggity dang going to provide me with the information I need to keep these people alive, which means, I want to see their files and what they can do." I stared at her expectantly.

She got up and reached down to the lower shelf where a bunch of files had been stashed. Her lips pursed as she handed them to me. "Needless to say those files are classified—"

"Yeah, yeah, yakkity smackity, I know, Pippa," I said with an eye roll. "I specialize in not existing. I think I can handle some classified profiles. Unlike some people, I have zero intentions of using this information against them." My glance slid sideways at her.

Dr. Weatherford had the good grace to drop her gaze and clear her throat.

I think that was about as much as I was going to get. So be it. We had work to do.

14

Knock.

I glanced up from where I stood in front of a map taped to the pushed out section of wall near the couch and coffee table, an area that was now littered with papers, maps, and files. Since I'd told them not to worry about replacing the bar cart, there was plenty of room. The eraser of a pencil tapped against my lips as my brain resumed its musings while sorting out all of the pencil marks on the map.

Knock, knock.

My head turned to stare stupidly at the door. Oh, yeah, someone had knocked.

The door opened inward as a dining cart slowly moved forward.

I exhaled and went back to my thoughts. "I didn't call down for anything. Sorry that you made the trip for nothing. I'll eat something later," I tossed out distractedly.

A male cleared his throat. "Actually Eliora, it's going on one in the morning," William reminded me diplomatically as he pushed the cart in and closed the door. "We rescheduled that meeting to tomorrow morning. I also had a feeling you'd forgotten to...eat." He'd turned and was staring at me.

My hand self-consciously went to the messy piled bun with a different pencil shoved into it. I'd abandoned the sweater and wore only the tank I'd been wearing underneath said sweater, and my leggings from earlier. We both knew it was a familiar sight. Me when I was deep into planning. Memories surfaced for both of us as I fidgeted, hands moving ineffectually.

He stepped over to the wall near the armoire and set down a black duffle bag.

"What's that?" I asked, glad for the distraction.

"Oh, this? These are some of your things from your trailer," he explained.

I marched over, grabbed the bag, and put it on the bed. He came over and stood to my left, watching. Dog-eared paperbacks, some comics—ugh, none of my favorites, a stuffed, pastel patchwork elephant that had seen better days, a wooden puzzle frame, a small, old hardcover book, and other assorted clutter that they'd thought I'd want.

"Who packed this?" I asked quietly.

"Ivy, Braxton, Clarice, and Ellie," William murmured after a moment. He wasn't paying attention, or rather, he was noticing something that made me nervous.

He picked up the small hardcover. Its embossed title had long since worn down to something illegible. "*You* have it."

"Yeah," I admitted guiltily. It was a cheap collection of Shakespearean sonnets he'd picked up at a yard sale before we'd met. We used to read it to each other for giggles on picnics.

"I thought I'd lost this," he murmured.

Then William noticed the frame and picked it up. An ugly thing, that housed two secrets.

I kept my movements very casual. The last thing I wanted was for him to figure out what that thing hid. I also would've bet all my substantial holdings that Trouble had fed Ellie the impulse to grab that and the book. Turning away, I took a couple of steps to return my attention to the map.

"Let me not to the marriage of true minds," he began.

His words pierced my chest. He was reading the page I'd ripped from the book and put into the frame. Sonnet one hundred sixteen. Once Liam had known who and what I was, he had loved quoting that one to me.

He stopped speaking.

"Dinner, huh?" I said too lightly as I walked over to the cart, deliberately ignoring him.

Two domed lids of equal size greeted me, with two wine glasses, two water glasses, a pitcher of water and a bottle of chardonnay breathing, just waiting for us.

Snick.

By the sound of it, he'd found the hidden compartment.

My eyes closed. My hand stilled on the handle of one dome.

"Your ring," he breathed.

The scraping of metal against wood and the tinkling noise of a chain unwinding. William had discovered where I'd hidden it.

A simple gold ring with its square cut emerald and two tear drop diamonds, one on either side. His Irish angel with her wings. The engagement ring he'd given me hung on a long, slender gold chain. A chain that was old enough to be worth more than this whole ship.

My hand dropped from the tray cover and I lifted my head to look at him.

He held up the chain and ring in one hand, the frame in the other. William stared at me.

For once, I had no idea what he was thinking. I cleared my throat. "That went with me to Rome. I had it consecrated, in your honor. Wore it for years to keep you close," the truth slipped out in a whisper.

William said nothing as he gathered up the chain and flipped the frame over, opening the back panel. The torn page came out easily and was moved to the front side of the frame. His finger gingerly touched the back panel. He pulled at the bottom fold of faux velvet. It came open under his questing fingernail. A photo slid out from its hidden folds. Us, roughly thirty five years ago. Him in a suit, wearing a rare smile, and me, looking much as I do now, but in a flowing garden dress forty years out of date. Both of us laughing gaily, not pretending like we were supposed to have been. An assignment that'd become far more than work.

He'd found both things that I expressly hadn't wanted him to–evidence of how badly his death had wounded me.

I stood there like the proverbial deer in headlights. Never had understood that one until now. A horde of ravening Infernals could've jumped through the windows and I probably wouldn't have been able to move.

William's gaze rose to meet mine. He gently set the frame and its contents down on the bed. He walked over to stand in front of me. Undoing the clasp, he put the necklace around my neck.

My chest ached. Whether that was from the ring's Holiness or my broken heart was up for grabs. Neither reason helped.

"This is yours. It shouldn't be hidden away like that," he whispered and kissed my forehead. "Things have to be different now. I can't change that...I am sorrier than I think you will ever possibly understand because I cannot explain why, and I cannot allow you into my head to see for yourself." My love stopped talking as a sour look spasmed across his face. A sudden flash of illness and pain.

My trembling fingers reached up to touch his cheek. It was on my lips to ask what that had been.

His eyes closed briefly and turned his head to kiss my palm, shaking his head in the negative. He didn't want to talk about it.

Then he put space between us. "I'd thought to take dinner with you and ask you how the planning was coming. See if you had any questions," he told me, "but I ah, I think I should probably go."

He got across the room and put his hand on the door handle.

"Please."

He stopped.

"Please don't go," I requested in a hoarse whisper. "Dinner sounds lovely. You were always so good at looking after me like that."

His mouth lifted in a fleeting half smile.

I pulled the cart over to the bed and pushed things out of the way so we could sit side by side and face the cart.

William's eyebrow rose.

Wryly grinning, I gestured to the overladen couch and coffee table.

That drew a chuckle from him as he came over and poured the wine.

I lifted the lids. "This smells wonderful!" My mouth promptly turned into Niagara Falls.

"Eighteenth century drunken English Somerset cider chicken with honey, fresh asparagus, some potatoes au gratin, freshly baked rolls, and warm apple slices with crumb topping," he informed me. William had always liked to cook and apparently had gotten much better at it.

It was a toss-up as to which was wider, my grin or my eyes. "Liam, you are brilliant."

He chuckled. "I try."

Napkins were draped, glasses clinked, and we tucked into our feast.

"So, from the looks of things, you have thoughts about this mission?" he asked drily after wiping his mouth and glancing around the room.

A soft snort escaped me. "You, sir, have *no* idea," I replied to my food.

"Then tell me," he said, forcing me to meet his eyes. "I'm serious, Eliora, we need to know where we went wrong."

My mouth scrunched up, and I exhaled. "Okay, but this is going to take a while."

"I've heard of worse reasons to lose a night of sleep," he joked, "and it's not like it'll be my first."

"Crazy Brit," I laughingly muttered, using an old joke.

"Saucy Celt."

That made me laugh harder and choke on my wine.

"Really Eliora?" he chuckled as he patted my back.

***

We worked through most of the night.

I surfaced in a sleepy state, having been put into bed. My room was predawn dark. Though I thought I heard his voice whispering, "I never writ, nor no man ever lov'd."

Sleep dragged me under again until a sharp knocking woke me, telling me I was late for my morning meeting!

15

My entrance was supposed to have been something cool like one of those kick butt slow motion walks to impressive music; however, it ended up being much more calamitous and crazy, like Kramer skidding into the room all akimbo, juggling folders, papers, and the laptop I'd been loaned.

I crashed into the open doorframe near the head of the table in an oversized, pale blue sweater with neckline askew to show a deep green bra strap and black tank. Dark rose yoga pants and bright purple fuzzy socks, sans shoes, completed the ensemble. A messy bun with a pencil holding it up really brought out my professional side.

Ivy's eyes were wide.

Coop covered his mouth.

Dobrek's eyebrows climbed.

Pippa's mouth twitched ever so slightly.

Clarice blinked several times while Ellie smirked. I suspected Trouble's hand in her less than pleasant demeanor.

Grace, of course, rolled her eyes as her cohort let his eyes drift shut momentarily, groaning while he did so.

Edwards' eyebrows lowered in consternation.

"Well, it seems we're all here," Fisherman declared, apparently choosing to ignore my brash entrance and colorful wardrobe.

"Finally," Junior muttered.

"Ms. Dade, I believe you had a presentation on the mission you wished to share. The floor is yours," he offered and moved to take the seat next to the punk, presumably to keep Junior in line.

I stepped up to the head of the table, laying out the folders, papers, and laptop. My hands shuffled things but my eyes couldn't find what I was looking for. A split-second glance over my left shoulder at William.

Please, you do this. I suck at this.

You'll be fine.

They listen to you.

They will listen to you.

I hated leading. My preference had always been to be behind the curtain.

Everyone waited for me to begin. Their stares were palpable.

A new team. They were becoming people I knew, people I would care about, would lead into battle. Ghosts from my past lined the walls, taunting me in my head. Some leader.

I'd worked alone for centuries. Somewhere in the mid-nineteenth century, people had insisted on helping me. Various groups had formed around my work, which was how my path crossed William's. So many had died over the years. Too many. I hadn't been joking when I'd told William that I was done. Humans were too fragile for this kind of work, and Infernals didn't care how many bodies they dropped.

I felt myself breathing get faster.

My hands trembled. Still couldn't find my flibertyjibbit notes.

A chair rolled backwards.

Ivy's hand grabbed my arm as she pulled me into the hallway. My new friend shut the door behind us. "¡Dios mío, cálmate!" She commanded me to get a grip while grabbing my upper arms.

"Language, Ivelisse," I replied automatically.

She bent over so our faces were only a few inches apart. "Seriously, Nemo, you have been around since before Arthur. You can handle them. Now get in there and do this!" Ivy gave me a lightning fast hug and went back inside.

I took a deep breath and went back into the room.

Quiet murmurs stopped as I entered.

My eyes homed in on a folder resting on top of the stack. Inside it was the page I'd been looking for. A fleeting smile crossed my face. *Thank you.*

He didn't respond.

Grabbing the paper, I walked back to the dry erase board and wrote down their plan with names and jobs on the left. "Okay, this is what you had," I began while writing. It was much easier to talk to them without looking their way. "This is how I think things ought to be changed." I wrote my list on the right.

Whispers blossomed.

"What about Ellie?" Clarice asked.

"I'll get to that," I hedged.

Rereading what I'd written reminded me of the *why*, which helped me walk back to the head of the table with more confidence. "Now. Koloman Brazda will most likely not be there. Though this expansion is important, he'll probably send one of his lieutenants, some muscle, and a money man. There's a decent chance that the Infernal will be somewhere in that mix.

"Ju–er, Henry, will act as the Commodore's driver. That puts him close enough to the action to be helpful should we need backup, but it also puts him farther away and hopefully, under the Infernal's radar. Edwards will continue in his position as bodyguard, because despite that sharp mind, that's what they're most likely to assume he is. Dobrek will act as the Commodore's assistant since he blends well, is poly-linguistic, and can shift gears quickly. Plus he has contacts in this part of the world. That adds legitimacy to the presentation.

"Mylonas can be in the van coordinating. Ivy will be on overwatch. Her shooting record is nearly as good as Grace's, and frankly, she can disappear into a crowd on her own. We need that ability in case she needs to move locations for any reason.

"Clarice and Grace will be bait since they fit the physical profile of the other victims: beautiful and exotic. Also, Grace is a seasoned agent and can help Clarice if she needs it. Cooper and I will work as bait guards. It would make sense to have a female merc on that detail. Also, that should keep me a little farther out of the Infernal's range. In addition to that, I won't be able to use my abilities without pulling attention, so having me armed for bear is a better choice," I informed them. "Questions?"

"Yeah," Dobrek spoke up, "I heard they were expecting three girls for delivery." He leaned back in his chair. "That is going to cause problems if we are not delivering what we said we would." He'd been a mercenary for years. Sadly, he had a point.

"We lost one in the crossing," I replied in matter-of-fact tones, thinking on my feet.

He made a face but nodded.

"So then we put Ellie back into the plan," Clarice interjected.

"No," I said. "Ellie is sweet and bright and I don't want to see anything happen to her. Trouble is none of those things. Under stress, let alone under life threatening duress? That's inviting that blasted thing to throw everything at breaking her." I leaned forward, my hands on the table and glanced around at them all. "If it breaks her mid-op, nine will give you ten that it'll try to ally with the other Infernal, or simply throw us under the bus to escape in the confusion."

"You're just worried that he'll out you to the other Infernal, oh great Watchdog of Heaven, killer of the careless and cold alike, destroyer of the Dark Ones, a being with a higher body count than most other non-Humans, even major demons," Junior muttered. "Aren't you, Devadas?" He said the last like it was an insult.

The others began to look at each other and then at me with curious faces. Pippa typed furiously.

My eyes narrowed. "Say that name again," I invited him and leaned further across the table. "I dare you." He was seriously testing the limits of my Oath.

Ellie squirmed and Trouble glared at me, snarling. Her breathing sped up dangerously.

I immediately backed off and stood straight.

She instantly settled down and visibly slowed her breathing.

My head shook in the negative as I looked away from them. "That. That right there."

"What?" the punk demanded with snark bordering on full out snarl.

"If you and I have to get into it with the Infernal, that bologna blasted borschwurtst will break her," I said, and turned to look at Clarice. "Do not pass Go, do not collect two hundred dollars, and go straight to bad. Your call."

"She could ride in the van with me," Fisherman countered.

"Possibly...it's still not a great idea."

"But if she were part of the bait, and the Infernal's not at the buy, she would know if he's at their holding site, just like you knew about her and Henry," he hypothesized.

"Yes, I would," Ellie piped up and added, "My senses are more passive than yours, and then we'd have all three girls as promised. Grace and Clarice are more than able to keep me safe." She glanced around, gaining confidence. "Besides, a lot of these operations work off computers. I'll know what to grab, or how to hack their security if we need it."

Fisherman grew thoughtful.

I gave him a minute shake of my head. Glass of bad idea straight up, don't bother with the rocks.

"I'll think things over and take everyone's recommendations into account," Fisherman declared to the room. "Sounds like a good time for everyone to get some air, exercise, get some work done. Dismissed people."

Some of them stood. Others murmured to each other.

The punk and his crony made a beeline for the door behind me.

In a blink, I was in close-quarters with him.

"Get out of my way," Junior growled. He went from staring straight ahead to head turned and looking down at me. Power rode in his eyes.

"I hear that name on your lips again—and trust me, my ears have a *really* long reach—you and I will have words, and it will become a coin toss whether I am able to keep my promise," I informed him quietly.

The room behind us had gone still.

He snorted. "Yeah, you're just full of broken promises."

My head did a side tilt shake as my mouth quirked in one of my best sardonic Tim Curry expressions

William stopped breathing.

"Well then...one more shouldn't make that big a difference then, now should it?" I quipped. "Rookie."

"You think you could take me?"

An unpleasant smile filled my face. I stood on tip toe and stage whispered in his ear, "Who do you think chained your mother to her home in Wales?"

With an outward veneer of confidence I didn't feel, I walked over to the table, giving him my back as if he was no threat to me at all. Managed to keep my hands from shaking as I picked up my papers, folders, and laptop. When I turned around to go out the door, he and Grace were gone.

My periphery told me that no one else in the room had moved.

Poor Ellie looked a bit green, but as I turned to study her more directly, she and her cousin left the room out the other door.

That was my cue.

I walked out and went straight to my room. Part of me wanted to go to the gym, part of me was afraid of running into Junior so soon. Another part was afraid I wouldn't be able to control my temper well enough regardless of who I saw.

So, I paced my room instead.

A quiet knock sounded at my door.

William poked his head in hesitantly. "Could we talk?"

"Now's probably not a good time, William," I answered and ran an agitated hand through my hair. My bun came undone. As the pencil began to fall. I caught it with faster than Human reflexes and threw it into the wall.

Thwack!

Its tip had buried itself in the wall where I'd hung the map. Reverberations echoed into the silence.

He arched an eyebrow, and I could see the exasperation in his eyes. William expected more from me...and he was right.

"It's just that the little punk always seems to know exactly what to say to cheese me off, William," I said as if we'd been talking aloud.

He stared at the carpet and shoved his hands in his pockets. "So, um, who or what is Devadas? You've never mentioned that before."

My throat closed. "Doesn't matter," I muttered. "That was a long time ago." This wasn't something I spoke about with anyone.

"I would beg to differ," William contradicted as he crossed his arms. "You were willing to break your Oath over it, so this very obviously still matters to you since you just threatened to kill my son for saying the name." His head came up so he could stare at me. He frowned.

"Your son just did his best to turn that name into an insult." I stopped, my traitorous voice choking up again. "He doesn't deserve to utter those sounds together, let alone throw it in my face."

"You loved this person very deeply," he said. He'd tried for matter-of-fact and it'd come out cold and stern. Holy hat! He was jealous.

"Are you seriously jealous?" the words tumbled out of my mouth.

"What? Me? No, of course not, that's ridiculous," he sputtered.

"You are!" I laughed.

His face got red. His eyes grew angry. "That is the most preposterous thing I have ever heard! You just threatened to kill Henry over—"

I walked over and kissed him.

He stopped stock still, blinking at me.

"He was my trainer in the seventh century, or rather, that was his title. He passed it down to me," I whispered against his mouth. "He was like an older brother to me whom I loved very much. It broke my heart when he left this world." William had gotten jealous. If he didn't care, then why? Why be jealous? My laughing smile held mischief. I kissed him again.

This time he kissed me back.

It was all too brief. He pulled away, taking several steps back. "Eliora..." he reprimanded. His breathing uneven.

Many mischievous thoughts filled my head.

William closed his eyes. "Please stop that."

"Stop what?"

"Stop deliberately sharing those thoughts. That's not fair," he requested. Pain had seeped into his tone.

I stopped. He was right. That wasn't fair—to either of us. With a sigh, I walked over to him, demurely taking one of his hands in mine.

He opened his eyes and looked at me. William struggled to regain his equilibrium. Anger and frustration leaked everywhere from him.

Guilt ripped through my heart. "I'm sorry."

"I can't explain," he whispered.

"I know," I answered solemnly.

"This impetuosity, this wild, aggressive, zaniness, it's all because of the new persona you've donned, isn't it?" he asked after a moment.

"Yes. Well, something like that," I said, sounding older, more like Eliora. "Every time I'm reborn, become a new persona, if you will, it's like going deep undercover. There's a legend, a backstory, a personality, and that's where I live. That's who I become. It's how I stay sane. So, Nemo?

"Yes, Nemo's an American: sarcastic, flippant, impulsive, aggressive at times, willing to throw down at a moment's notice, and loyal to a fault when she finds someone to be loyal to—like you, like Cooper, like Ivy....

"She is not someone Henry should be getting into pissing contests with because that is just going to end badly all around, William." My carriage was straighter, more like a dancer's, as I stood centered and calm.

We stared at each other.

I let him see centuries of existence and not the impetuous, short-sighted younger woman that he'd been seeing since I'd been dragged aboard this ship. "It was good of you to come and remind me that I am more than her. You've helped," I conceded and paused. "I am sorry for causing you pain. You are the last person I would ever willingly hurt." The last came out in a near whisper. Nemo was very outlandish in addition to being impetuous, thinking she could brow-beat or joke the world into submission.

"It's all right," he said softly. "You were provoked, and not under the best of circumstances in the first place. You handled the meeting well. I know how much you hate having to take point on such things."

"That would be because I work best in the background. You know that," I reminded him. "The fewer people who are aware of me, the better things go." I glanced around the room.

He stepped back towards the door.

"I'm going to go change and get some exercise. It'll help."

William nodded. "That sounds like a good idea. I should go."

"Okay."

He turned and left, closing the door quietly.

I backed up without looking and sank onto the foot of the bed, staring at the carpet. My awareness expanded, grew in scope and memory as it paraded the faces of loves from centuries past who'd mattered enough to stick in my head this long, not that there were all that many. They were pretty much gone, died along the journey because they'd been Human. I'd always done my best to stay away from the Fae, and Nephilim weren't supposed to have romantic, intimate relationships with each other. Too much temptation.

That was the hardest part of this existence. Having moments when I stepped outside of a temporary persona and regained my full faculties as Me. All of Earthly time and space spread out before my mind. It wasn't a frequent occurrence, not because I couldn't, but because I chose not to do so particularly often.

All it did was serve to remind me how isolated I was. Most Nephilim didn't want to be around the Devadas. They'd learned centuries ago that I took my job seriously. The same went for other Supernatural beings because I had to keep an eye on them too. That left Humans, who weren't allowed to know what I was for the most part.

My father had been a sentient being of Love, Light, Compassion, and all the other beautiful emotions. He fell in love with a Human and that had been forbidden to his kind. Mostly because as so many of them Fell, they'd taken Humans whether the women had been willing or not. So, he had broken the rules. He seduced her and loved her anyway, in so doing, he lost everything for all Eternity.

Some wouldn't call that love; they would say it's obsession. Hence, that contributing to his Fall. Some days I wondered though. We had such large hearts full of love and passion, able to feel on a scale I wasn't sure Humans could understand. Those enormous passions made us Nephilim, their children, dangerous, because even with all those good emotions, since we were also part Human, there were all the darker ones too... and acting on any of the darker ones: like anger, jealousy, lust, pride, wrath, etc. had a tendency to end badly. Sadly, Wrath and I were old acquaintances.

Those nearly bottomless wells of emotion were why I had frequently refused to become attached to Humans. There was too much risk involved, and I didn't have either my father's courage, or madness, to brave eternal punishment. Not when I wasn't sure that my own emotional needs weren't selfish.

My more than Human heart would give William whatever it was possible for me to give. However, my love had asked for the near impossible—to let him go. Those thirty-one years had weighed far more heavily on him than me. Considering his lifespan, that shouldn't have been surprising.

Such emotional thoughts crashed through my higher plane of thinking like a stormy ocean wave, and sucked me under just as quickly. I fell back into Nemo's sour frustration. Eliora's maudlin sadness.

He was right. Things were probably better this way. Of course they were; he was being sensible as always, reliable as stone. It would be easier all around, for everyone. Right. Sure.

Sniff.

I got up and began yanking gym clothes out of the armoire. There were bags that needed punching.

16

My muscles ached in protest, and I hadn't even started working out yet. I stopped outside the gym doors. Voices talked in the weight room area.

"You don't really think she'd go back on her word and kill him, do you?" Edwards inquired. He sounded concerned.

A set of weights clanked hard and stopped. Two others kept up a slow and steady rhythm.

"I don't think she would," Ivy answered. "Although that's not to say that the little—that *he* doesn't deserve some beat down."

I felt myself smile.

"What about you, Dobrek?" Edwards asked.

Another set of weights stopped. Someone took a drink of water. "If, and I am by no means saying I do not believe it, but *if* she is as old as you two have said, then I say nothing."

"You say...nothing?" I could hear Edwards' incredulity out here.

"Nope," Dobrek said.

Weights and pulleys started up again.

"Okay, I'll bite. Why not?" Ivy asked.

Indeed. Inquiring minds wanted to know.

There was a pause in the rhythmic sounds, but then they resumed. After a few moments of silence as we all listened to someone, presumably Dobrek, finish his set, and then he spoke up, "We learned as children, and it has been handed down for generations, never to speak of things whose attention you do not want centered on you," he explained. "*She* is most certainly one of those things."

Hmmmm...on the one hand, I wasn't thrilled at being in the same category as 'a thing', but on the other hand, he had a point. From the way he'd stated his thoughts, I got the feeling it was more than cultural background that had put so much certitude in his voice.

I opened the door and walked inside.

They all flinched.

Dobrek gave them what I'm sure they all figured was a mysterious to me 'I told you so' look and a nod. He stood and went to get himself another water while draining the rest of his current one.

"Hey Nemo," Coop greeted me. His voice was casual, but he went back to his leg presses, which meant turning his head from looking directly at me.

My tongue slipped out in thought to hit my upper lip and snaked back inside my mouth as a small smile bloomed in my head. I knew this game of old. "Hey Coop," I said just as casually and caught his eye in the mirror.

His discomfort at having been there for the conversation was obvious.

"So, Dobrek, what'd you run across back home that taught you never to utter names in the wind?" I asked just as casually as I'd greeted Cooper while letting the Pole have my back.

They all froze.

I held up my hands. "True confession—I walked up to the doors just as Edwards asked if anyone thought I'd actually kill the punk," I confessed. These were people I was going to need to work with, trust to do their part. If they thought I was some sort of unknowable boogieman, that was no use to us. My shoulders shrugged. "I'm more than Human enough to be foolishly curious and eavesdrop."

Cooper rolled his eyes with a quiet laugh.

Ivy shook her head in exasperation. "Rude," she teased.

Edwards watched me, his expression carefully blank.

I turned to glance at Dobrek. "Aleksander, forgiven?" I asked in Polish.

"Answer his question," he replied in English.

"Would I kill the punk?" I repeated as my eyebrows climbed.

He nodded.

A very heavy exhale left my body. I made a comedic show of looking around for more eavesdropping people, as I did so, I discreetly shielded against the camera up in the corner. Thankfully, shielding was mostly passive and didn't require much Energy.

Resuming my former stance, I crossed my arms and let my head loll backwards. Junior simply pulled that reaction from me. "This is between us for now," I started quietly, "because if he thinks there's some element of danger, he might possibly get in line, but no, I wouldn't." I brought my head back up.

Ivy nodded her head with a satisfied snap. "Knew it."

Cooper had moved over to the lat pulldown. "Figured," he said to me through the pulleys and weights. His eyes carried the truth of his relief.

My stomach twisted. Huh. His doubt bothered me. That was surprising.

Dobrek and Edwards watched me carefully, like they didn't really believe me.

"So how 'bout it Dobrek? I answered the question," I reminded him.

He regarded me steadily. "No."

I gave him my most charming, goofy innocent seeming smile. "Please? I can tell from experience that your advice to the others sounded like it came from more than just family tradition."

Dobrek laughed at me. "Oh you are good, but you are not that good, moja droga."

"Oh Aleksander, you sweet-talker you," I joked back. "You say the dearest things."

Edwards' eyes narrowed.

"Okay, no seriously, how 'bout we compromise? You think about the...being that you've met, and I'll listen," I explained. "I won't skim your thoughts or anything else. Think of it like broadcasting on a frequency only I can hear."

"Ah, but you are not the only one of your kind," he countered.

"True, but he's not here, and I can shield this room so neither he nor the other one would hear it."

"Will they not know something is up?" he asked as if this were all a bunch of hooey anyway. The beads of sweat forming on his forehead belied his nonchalance.

"Nope. It's a minor expenditure of power for me, and a relatively passive one," I reassured him because now I really wanted to know what had him so scared.

He glanced at the others behind me.

"That was how I showed her where the gym was since it was faster than trying to explain," Cooper offered.

Dobrek gave him a flat look that clearly thanked him for his help. "Go. Now. Do it," he snapped at me while looking at Cooper.

The gym fell away.

It was a warm summer's eve. Moonlight lit everything in silvers, blues, and greens.

A young man held our hand. We were young, small. "Shhhhh...don't be frightened," he said as we walked along a wide river to our right.

Parts of the water sparkled white in the moon's light.

Feminine laughter quietly trilled.

Our attention suddenly swiveled to the dirt road. The most beautiful young woman leaned against an old tree right next to the river. Big luminous eyes, long dark hair, pale sweet face...It was too dark to see much else for some reason. She stared at Uncle the way some girls did.

"Run," he whispered. "Go home."

She came forward with eyes only for him.

"Run!" Uncle pushed us away.

As the young woman got closer, Uncle's movements were slower. He spoke softly to her, tenderly.

She smiled.

In that smile, rows of small sharp teeth emerged. Her hands slid up the sides of his face and her thumbs covered his eyes.

Uncle screamed.

One word echoed in Dobrek's jabbering mind—rusalka!

We ran down the dirt path.

***

I came to bent over, hands on my knees. Ivy and Edwards next to me.

Cooper stood with Dobrek, helping him drink some water.

"You are right, Aleksander," I said, inclining my head in respect and acknowledgement. He didn't want my pity or my empathy, not right now. "Some things should not be spoken of out loud."

"I need a shower," he muttered in Polish.

Standing up straight, I stepped away from Ivy and Edward's hands. "Thank you," I said in English softly.

His hand waved me off in clear dismissal. Though he abruptly turned to me. "Never again," he informed me in English and pointed his finger.

I nodded slowly. "Fair enough."

He turned and headed for the doors down by the cardio area. Dobrek hit a heavy bag as he walked past. It swung hard with the impact.

Whack! The crash bar complained.

Dobrek was gone.

"What was it?" Ivy whispered.

A slow, negative head shake. "Not mine to tell," I whispered back to them, staring at where he'd left, "but if that's the price of admission to this little club..." Rusalka were nasty, not really Fae, not really Infernals, caught somewhere in between. He was right. They typically existed for a long time, mostly localized though. They could be destroyed, but it would take someone like Junior or myself to do it.

Maybe when this mess was all done, I'd bring little Aleksander home and we would take care of his nightmare once and for all. The thought of a little judicious dispatching cheered me immensely.

Cooper cleared his throat.

I released the shield on the camera and turned to survey my workout options, shaking my body loose a bit.

Josh still hadn't moved, obviously waiting for me to finish my sentence.

"Then all y'all need some serious therapy," I joked with an eye roll, hoping to break the tension.

They laughed or smiled, which was what I'd wanted them to do.

17

We were mostly done with our workouts, as talk turned to speculations on lunch and various diets. "I love the whole carb loading idea," I agreed with Edwards.

"I just love carbs," Ivy declared with a laugh. "Especially when the kitchen has those apple cinnamon tartlets!"

Everyone laughed.

"Wait, tartlets?" I asked.

"Oh yeah," Coop agreed. "To die for."

My mouth watered.

Clunk-crank.

It was Junior and his plus one.

The conversation stopped.

"Hey guys. What's up?" he greeted us.

I didn't trust that cheerful countenance for a second. He was up to something sure as sugar was sweet. His little minion was doing her best to seem all wide-eyed and innocent, all the while sneaking furtive glances at Edwards. Huh. I'd wondered about that. This just made me more curious.

"So how 'bout it, Nemo?" Junior asked me.

"How 'bout what?" I asked, hating that I hadn't been paying attention to him. Then again, it usually behooved my blood pressure to not pay him any mind. Still, careless on my part.

"You and me sparring," he replied and nodded in the direction of the ring.

Oh. Ah...That fell into a category of epically bad ideas. "Thanks for offering, but I've finished my workout already. Had a nice match with Edwards, but thanks," I said. See? I could play polite with the nit.

"Aw c'mon," he cajoled. "Braxton's good and all, but he's not one of us." Junior gave me a knowing smile. His eyes told me an entirely different story. He had a bee in his bonnet and very much wanted me in that ring.

"Like I said, I'm done for now, but ah, maybe tomorrow morning? After the morning debrief?" I offered. Time. Time was my friend. Stalling was good, getting Fisherman to tell him no was even better.

"Huh. Guess I'm going to have to wait to see that legendary strength," he pouted playfully.

Edwards crossed his arms.

Ivy gave me curious side-eyes.

I suspected she wanted me to just kick his butt and be done with it.

Cooper deliberately walked back to the machine to pick up his hand towel and water bottle, acting as though this conversation were nothing out of the ordinary.

My imagination speculated that Dobrek would've sided with Ivy via a dry snort.

The punk clapped his hands together. "So, I guess I'm going to have to find someone else. Braxton, since you sparred with Tinker Bell here, that leaves Cooper. How 'bout it? Or are you too tired too?" There was no mistaking the underlying taunt in his words, though on the surface they were delivered in the spirit of good natured ribbing.

SAS versus a Navy SEAL. Holy bragging battles Batman! This was ticket worthy, provided Junior didn't cheat.

Cooper glanced around casually. "Yeah," he said with a slight nod. "Yeah, okay. I can handle dishing out some hurt." He joked, but I heard his breathing. It had sped up, which meant he was concerned as well.

"Excellent!" the punk exclaimed and turned to go over to the supply table. Grace went with him and they began taping his hands.

The four of us slowly moved forward.

"Josh," I murmured, "you don't have to do this. He can wait until tomorrow."

"Josh huh?" Junior asked with a raised eyebrow. "Isn't that cozy. Don't worry *ma'am*. I won't break your new... friend."

He was goading me, and as far as taunts went, it wasn't half bad. And I really wanted to know where in heckadoodle he learned to make honorifics into insults.

Cooper ignored him as Ivy helped him tape his hands.

"Pendejo," Ivy mumbled.

I made sure my back was to the terrible twosome. My eyes closed as I shook my head, yet smiled slightly. When I opened my eyes, Edwards was smiling at Ivy and Coop.

Junior got into the ring and danced on his feet. "Gentlemen's rules?"

"Sure," Cooper answered, seeming to know what that meant. He climbed into the ring.

The two of them moved around a bit, taking practice swings at each other.

"What's 'gentlemen's rules'?" I whispered to Edwards, who stood next to me.

"Henry won't use his powers; otherwise, it's mostly military grade MMA fighting," he explained just as quietly.

We got a curt look from Grace. Oh yeah, she had it bad for him. "Are you and uh, Gr—"

He quickly cut me a look that clearly said not now.

Huh. Okay then.

Edwards' eyes flitted towards Grace to see if she'd heard me.

Yup. They were a thing. Thankfully, she seemed too engrossed in the fight.

Dragging my attention back to the match in progress, I could see they'd both gotten a couple of good hits on each other, but nothing too terrible.

They ended up together in a clutch.

Edwards called out, so they broke it.

Junior caught my eyes and smirked.

Cooper landed a solid uppercut.

The punk came back with a devastating blow to the side of Cooper's face. It wrenched Coop so hard, we heard something crack.

Cooper went down on one knee. He shook his head trying to clear it.

Junior swung at him from the other side, knocking Cooper backwards onto the mat.

"C'mon Cooper," the punk taunted. "That all you got?"

The SEAL rolled onto his side.

"That's enough," Ivy demanded.

"No, no. We aren't done until Cooper yields. That's how it goes," Junior informed her.

"He's on the mat, you idiot," she snapped.

Cooper pushed up onto hands and knees.

Junior kicked him in the side with enough force to send him rolling.

We definitely heard bones, emphasis on the plural, break that time.

The punk gave me a nasty grin.

That sonofa—I stopped myself and counted to five. This was on purpose to get me to fight him! "Fine!" I growled while stepping up to climb into the ring. "You wanna fight me? You got it, punk."

"No," Edwards said, with a hand gently on my arm, "you don't owe him anything."

"You're right, I don't, but I do owe it to Coop who stood in my place, and right now, I am more than ready to show this nimrod what it means to fight out of one's weight class."

"Oh, you think you're going to teach me a lesson?" he taunted. "That's rich."

I ignored him and went to Cooper. "Josh. Joshua? Joshua Anthony Cooper, hear me and sit up," I called on my powers as I called him, healing his wounds. "Be healed," I murmured the last in ancient Gaelic.

They all watched as his wounds closed and his eyes opened wide. His hand shot out and grabbed my upper arm. Coop's mouth opened and closed. He couldn't find the words.

Yeah. That happened. Healing on this scale tended to leave a Human without words. It made me dizzy for a moment too. "Ivy, help him get out," I requested in a tight voice.

I got up from my crouch. "Okay, punk, I'm here."

"No extraneous powers."

"Fine."

He danced around me like an MMA fighter looking for an in.

I merely circled him, walking.

Junior closed faster than I expected. His hit clipped the top of my shoulder, nearly knocking me over, but it had been intended as a shot to the side of my head, like what he'd done to Cooper.

The necklace slid out of my tank and sports bra's neckline.

He stared at it and didn't move.

Ivy immediately scooted around to see what had stopped us.

Grace's eyes went wide.

Ivy scurried back and whispered to the other two.

"What is that?" Junior asked me, slowly enunciating each word.

"None of your business," I informed him in matter-of-fact tones, "but if you must know, it's something of mine that was restored to me." Wearing the ring still made my chest ache, but that was a level of self-examination that I was not about to dabble in right now. A part of me wondered if he could see the holy glow or not.

Junior launched at me with no warning in a flurry of blows and kicks.

I managed to dodge most of them, and only grunted at his connected hits. It'd been a long time since I'd fought another Nephilim, or anyone who could be this fast and strong. Being out of practice was not my friend.

My swing had left me too open as I scrambled to pull back.

He took advantage and knocked me to the floor.

Edwards, Ivy, and Coop were cheering me on to get up.

As I rolled onto my side, I watched as he walked over to Grace.

She handed him a water bottle.

The side of his face showed me a dark smile.

My lungs stopped working. They were full of water.

I couldn't breathe!

Trying to push up didn't work. For some reason I was too dizzy.

"Nemo?" Coop's voice sounded far away.

My body trembled as I drowned while *on* a ship.

"Nemo!" Ivy called from a long ways off as I tried to hit the mat with my hand.

I fell onto my back.

Everything was becoming hazy and dark...

Our body drew itself upwards like a board pulled by a string. No clumsy staggering. Just suddenly on our feet.

"That–was deeply unwise, Henry Galahad Bradford," we informed the young Nephilim. He was foolish in the extreme.

It idly crossed our mind to warn Clarice.

Chun Hei Clarice, please get your cousin as far away from the gym as you can.

We tilted our head and considered what to do with the rulebreaker.

"Uh Nemo?" Ivelisse tentatively asked. She was standing in the ring.

We blinked.

She was back with the other two.

"Not—exactly," we answered her but went back to staring at the youngling. "I am taking care of this for now." We turned to them. "You might want to stand back."

As we turned back, we noticed that Grace had gotten into the ring.

Blink.

She was back where she'd been standing before next to the supply table. Her head whipped about in confusion.

That would have made the Nemo persona smile, but she was resting, healing, because of what *he had done*. We frowned and met him in the middle.

"Now Nemo, c'mon. It was a joke. It was nothing. Noobs get hazed all the—"

We hit him to the floor. "We are not your—moob."

He was slow to move.

"Get. Up." The soft hiss of our voice echoed around the room.

He still moved slowly.

"Nemo, or whoever you are, you made your point," Joshua Anthony Cooper delicately pointed out to us. He was a good man, a good warrior, honorable. Unlike this one.

We frowned harder.

It was easy to put the Nephilim on his feet with our power. He swayed.

The doors opened to admit Aleksander, William, and Callister moving quickly.

"Aleksander..." we murmured. "When all is said and done, we will deal with that which haunts you. This needs finishing first."

His eyes went wide as he glanced to the others, eyebrows high.

"Holy mo—her eyes!" Callister exclaimed softly. "Is that all white normal?"

"I have no idea," William whispered, eyes locked on us.

"Eliora," he said tentatively.

"Your son nearly killed the Nemo persona, had he succeeded, we would have allowed the Eliora one to come back," we told him. "We think you know what she would do about this."

"And you are?" he asked.

"We are—I am...Me."

"Is Nemo here?" he questioned and swallowed, watching his son sway. "May I speak to her?"

"Nemo sleeps. She must rest to heal." We turned our attention back to the young one and struck his sternum.

He flew backward into the ropes, bounced like a rag doll, and hit the mat.

A crack of thunder echoed.

The lights flickered.

We walked over to the body and gingerly picked him up by the shirt so he was on his knees. His glazed eyes swirled in blue and green.

"You, you broke the rules of engagement. You deliberately tried to kill someone dear to your kin. Were it not for this Oath, your life would be forfeit. As it stands, you will swear to Us that you will not willingly, nor accidentally, nor in any way cause another member of this—" we paused and looked to the ceiling for the word, "*team* to be harmed. Is that clear?" We healed him enough so that he could respond.

"Fine," his voice was a deep treble.

"Swear it!" Our voices echoed around the room like thunder.

"I, Henry Galahad Bradford, swear not to willingly nor accidentally nor in any way cause harm to a member of this team," he repeated grudgingly.

We healed him more until his eyes bled back to normal...

I swung and hit him with a vicious right cross to the mouth.

My own lip split as blood trickled down, but it was worth it. I was back driving the bus.

"I am a member of this team, am I not, Fisherman?"

"Ah, ah yeah," he answered. Oh the wheels were spinning.

"Okay, you putrid piece of pallid pond scum," I said as I grabbed him by the shirt and pulled him to his feet, "that means that I am off limits. You come at me again, you have a go at anyone else, and I promise you, you will not like what comes next. Am I clear, rookie?"

"Yeah, whatever," he mumbled.

I got in his face like any good military commander, and I'd dropped by a few American military bases to check things out over the years. "I CAN'T HEAR YOU, MAGGOT!" I shouted. "AM I CLEAR?"

"Yes," he said with a bit more oomph.

Leaning in with a hand to my ear, I yelled, "WHAT WAS THAT, PUNK?"

He glared at me.

No one else moved, though Coop and Edwards stood with a little more snap-to.

"DO I NEED TO GET YOUR ATTENTION AGAIN, JUNIOR?"

His gaze got intense. Power rose within him.

My Energy slapped his back down to a low simmer.

Junior's eyes widened.

I wiped the dribble of blood with the back of my left hand and smiled. "I can do this all day."

"Yes, ma'am," he responded, yet again making it sound like an insult.

"STAND UP STRAIGHT." I stepped on his instep and bit the inside of my cheek as my own ached. "CHIN UP. ATTT-TEEEEENNNTTTION!" I smacked the underside of his chin.

He actually snapped to proper attention.

"NOW, YOU PISS POOR EXCUSE FOR A MILITARY MOUSE, I ASKED YOU A QUESTION—DID I MAKE MYSELF CLEAR?"

"MA'AM YES MA'AM!" he shouted back in true military form.

What had me cracking up on the inside was that Cooper and Edwards, also at attention, shouted the answer with him.

Ivy stood with her arms crossed grinning like it was Christmas.

I couldn't even glance at anyone else. Ivy'd almost broken my composure.

"All right," I declared with a nod. "As far as you are concerned, I am your commanding officer. When I say jump, you say how high. Is that understood? In case you missed the memo, I am the only thing standing between you and annihilation, and after today's little demonstration, I don't know how inclined I'm feeling towards keeping your keister out of the crosshairs."

I got up close in front of him.

His gaze dropped in a swift, concerned glance.

"You tried to kill me," my voice dropped to a whisper. "I will not be forgetting that any time soon."

My hand went up to the side of his face.

He flinched.

I healed his jaw and mouth.

So too did mine.

"Permission to ask a question, ma'am." He actually sounded respectful.

I blinked in surprise. "Yes..."

"Why weren't you harmed when..."

"Ah, yes," I replied, weighing my options. "Well, we'll discuss that another time." I stepped around him and stopped before leaving the ring.

My senses went out into the ship. *Clarice?*

Y—yes? Nemo?

"Yes. Is she okay?"

Yes, I sedated them.

"Smart girl. Good. Things should be fine now," I replied.

"Who is she talking to?" Grace snapped.

"If I had to guess," William said tersely, "Clarice, to make sure that Ellie is okay." He glanced at me quickly in confirmation.

I nodded.

He redirected his attention to her and the punk. "I want both of you in your quarters and you will stay there until either Captain Mylonas or myself comes," he commanded them. "Do *I* make myself clear?" He was much quieter, but infinitely scarier. That much was clear on both of their faces.

They both nodded and left the room post haste.

I got out of the ring and back on the floor.

"Do I even want to know what started all of this?" Fisherman asked.

"Henry," Cooper, Ivy, and Edwards said in unison.

"Lovely," he muttered and rubbed his temples. "Nemo, are you okay? What was that, or rather *who* was that? Do we need to worry about a repeat appearance? Will she try to get revenge? Is this done? What—"

"Captain, whoa," I whistled and made a time out sign with my hands. "I'm going to be okay. Don't worry. I just need some sleep and food and we can talk later, probably, realistically, after dinner. Okay?"

Fisherman grimaced. He did not look like it was okay. "Fine. That'll give us some time to look at the footage and sort out those two."

I gave him a thumbs up and headed for the doors. Once in the hallway, my knees began to give way. I grabbed the wall and handrail.

The sounds of Fisherman, Cooper, William, Edwards, and Ivy all talking at once carried out to me. Drat.

"Dobrek," I whispered into the air.

I felt myself being hoisted as he slung my arm across his shoulders and had his other arm around my waist. "No kicking me this time," he joked quietly. "Why could I hear you like that?"

"Because you know how to listen," I slurred. "If I pass out before we make it to my room, please just leave me on my bed, I'll be fine. Used too much energy."

The hallway slid and tilted in my vision. I could tell I was passing out again, but I would've sworn he answered me with "Sure thing, princess."

Nawwww...

18

I had fully intended on eating dinner in my room, but Cooper showed up at my door. The snorty snaggle-toothed snotface.

"Wow, that's a mouthful," he commented from the doorway. "You kiss your momma with that mouth?"

My head went up as I blinked. Apparently, I'd been mumbling out loud as I'd looked for rubber soled loafers. They fit nicely over the warm socks, and with how much the ship was tilting from the waves, it was a good choice.

He got a look from me. "Whyyyyyyyy are you dragging me to dinner?" I whined and disappeared into the bathroom to run a brush through the mess.

"Why are you so averse to going?"

I shoved my head out and stared at him incredulously from behind the weeds of my hair. "I'm not even dignifying that with an answer. And this? This is a singularly lousy idea."

"It's going to be fiiiiiiine, really," he said with laughter in his voice.

"Ah huh. Sure."

"You worry too much," Coop informed me.

"Apparently, I'm on the payroll of 'worry too much'," I retorted and mumbled. "Someone needs to be."

"I heard that," he quipped.

"Good. You were supposed to," I replied coming into the bedroom, my hair in a simple braid. "There. Am I presentable?" I'd noticed that dinners tended to be dressy casual.

Though jeans, a pale green thick cowled sweater, and loafers seemed safe.

"You look fine, not trying too hard, nor as um, colorful as you were this morning," he answered, trying not to laugh again.

He got a mock glare and narrowed eyes.

I'd been asleep since Dobrek had dropped me off in my room before lunch.

Neither of us decided to mention earlier.

He seemed fine, and he'd showered and dressed in a collared shirt, sweater, and jeans himself. We headed to the dining room and the silence grew awkward. "Spit it out, Josh."

"Ah, how are you feeling?" he questioned tentatively. "Is there a plus one for dinner?"

I stopped walking. "I'm okay, Coop, and that? That was Me.

"She? Us?" I titled my head and stared upwards trying to explain. "Me exists far below the surface, like bottom-of-the-ocean dwelling, yet everywhere. As if you were staring at a map of who I am, Me would be in the deepest part where they label uncharted waters with 'here there be monsters', not that Me's monstrous or anything, more like she doesn't think like I do.

"Me isn't a persona like I am, like Eliora, or any of the others, those are transitory, nearly Human lives I live. They grow, they exist, they die, and a new one is born. Her? Me is my eternal core, who does not surface often, and honestly, that's best for all of us." I kicked at nonexistent dirt on the floor, my gaze on my feet. "He—he nearly killed me, Josh." The last part came out in a hoarse whisper.

The ship tilted again and forced me to grab the railing.

"Hey, you're okay," he reminded me. His hands went to my shoulders, forcing me to look up at him as he rode the hallway. "Remember?"

I half smiled.

"You are bigger, badder, and far scarier than he will ever be," he added.

"Yeah well, I don't know about that, but for a while, sure," I conceded. "He was drowning me in my own bodily fluids, plus a little he'd pulled from that water bottle." Thank all that was Holy that the punk really didn't seem to know or traffic in his Celestial abilities. His Fae ones were bad enough.

Coop frowned. "That's not good."

"No, it's not," I agreed and met his eyes. "We need to get going. We shouldn't be late."

He nodded, and we began walking again.

"They going to be there?" I asked in studied casualness that we both knew didn't fool him for a moment. Junior had scared me today, and I was in no shape to take him on again.

"Nope," he replied. "Commodore grounded both of them. Captain agreed. They're remanded to quarters until told otherwise."

My eyebrows went up as my eyes widened.

"We don't have a brig. Though I suspect if we had, he would've put them in it until we reached France."

I gaped at him. "Seriously?"

"Nemo," his tone got grittier, "you weren't the only one who noticed what he did today. There's a lot of people who aren't happy with him, or her, for that matter."

"Oh yeah, are she and our friend a thing?"

"The big guy? Yeah, but um...I wouldn't talk to him about that right now. Actually, team members aren't supposed to fraternize, but we've all looked the other way so far."

I held my hands up in surrender. He'd answered my question.

"I suspect he's rethinking some things," Coop speculated quietly.

There was no good response for that one. I didn't wish either her or Edwards ill, if fact, I thought it was a good match. Then again, what'd I know?

We didn't talk the rest of the way to the dining room. As we entered near the head of the table, I noticed that neither Fisherman or William were there. I paused. Grace and Junior's chairs were empty too, which made me wonder if they were still getting yelled at or something. I mean, Coop had said they wouldn't be here, but somehow, I'd worried that he was going to be wrong.

Pippa smiled at me. "Oh, Nemo, hello. Glad to see you up and about, dear. Why don't you sit here since it's an open seat; that way we can talk more easily." She pointed to Grace's chair...next to William.

My gaze drifted to his chair.

"Don't worry," she said with a wave of her hand. "They just stopped off on the bridge to consult with the captain."

I nodded silently.

Go ahead and sit, Coop thought at me a bit too loudly.

If he was going to keep doing that, I was going to have to teach him how so it didn't sound like he was talking to me with a bullhorn next to my ear.

Ellie studiously refused to look at me.

Pippa nodded encouragingly, her face eager. Great, she had questions.

Everyone else acted as though it weren't a big deal.

Feeling stupid, I sat down slowly.

"My lady," a server greeted me, instantly at my elbow. I flinched. "We have maple mustard tuna steaks, lamb chops with a balsamic reduction, and beef wellington this evening—"

"Yes."

"I'm sorry?" he asked, perplexed.

Ivy coughed into her water glass, trying not to laugh.

"Let's start with the seafood," I explained, "then I'd like the beef Wellington, and we can end with the lamb. Whatever sides the kitchen deems appropriate are fine with me. Thank you. Oh, and no wine this evening, please, just water."

He blinked a couple of times. His gaze sidled to the wall behind us and then he shrugged. "Very well my lady." Must've been new on the rotation.

With his departure, Pippa motioned to Clarice to pass me the roll basket. I gratefully took a couple and began to pry them in half for some butter.

The only sounds in the room were the quiet clinks and clanks of dinnerware and the soft classical music piped into the room. Yeah, 'cause that wasn't awkward.

Ivy cleared her throat. "So Clarice, I found that pattern finally."

"Oh really?" Clarice responded a little too brightly. "Great."

Cooper chuckled, but it quickly turned to a cough as Ellie gave him a look. He began talking to Edwards and Dobrek about European football.

"Pattern?" I asked.

"She knits," Ellie declared with a slight snicker, pointing at Ivy.

My eyebrow went up. "Really?"

Ivy's dusky skin flushed. She glared at Ellie. "Sí," she answered me though.

"Very cool. I'd love to see some of your stuff sometime," I replied after swallowing half a hunk of roll.

"You...like knitting?" Clarice wanted to know.

"Oh yeah, it's great." My mouth broke into a real smile.

"See, you can teach Nemo," Clarice announced as if it were settled.

"I'm sure El—Nemo has probably been knitting for some time," Pippa interjected.

I nodded, but declined to provide their scholar with just how long, nor to confirm beyond that fact that 'Eliora' had indeed been an incredibly talented knitter...as I was betting she remembered.

A server brought me my dinner.

Ivy grinned. "Ha, you're not off the hook," she said.

Clarice groaned.

"Hook would be crochet," I joked while cutting into my fish.

William and Fisherman entered. Identical grim expressions on their faces. William paused for a second, seeing me.

I began choking and grabbed my water.

Pippa started to rise, as did Cooper, but I waved them both to sit.

William gently thumped my back.

"I'm fine," I gasped.

He nodded and took the seat next to me.

The ship tilted more sharply.

Fisherman's eyes flicked to William's.

Pippa watched them with a worried frown.

Our eyes met.

She quickly wiped it from her face as she blotted her mouth with a napkin.

A couple of more bites of dinner got my wheels going as the two of them quietly gave the server their requests.

Once the server was gone, I took a drink and cleared my throat. "This wasn't my doing," I told them.

Two of the butter dishes and a relish tray slowly slid across the table.

"Seriously, not me."

"We understand," Fisherman said. He took a sip of something clear and carbonated. "She was in charge and it couldn't be helped, under the circumstances..."

The server came back and set down lamb in front of Fisherman and the beef in front of William. We waited until the server left.

"No," I corrected with a shake of my head. Now we had everyone's attention. "Me is powerful, but this storm isn't her doing, nor mine."

Fisherman gave me a thoughtful frown.

"It's all right, Eliora," William murmured.

"Ask Ellie," I said, pointing my knife in her direction. "She can tell the difference."

Ellie shrugged and gave a vague nod. She dropped her head, gaze on her lap. Her head swung a little side to side, then abruptly snapped up to stare outside the ship, glassy-eyed. Trouble's power made my skin crawl. "She speaks true," they whispered. "It is not her Energy."

Both of my eyebrows went up in a 'see?' motion.

The men exchanged looks.

"Then what is causing this storm?" William asked.

I shrugged. "Ahhhh...global warming?" Couldn't be the punk. He wasn't that stupid, was he?

"No," Fisherman disagreed. "Captain says this is too sudden, too strong, and it's getting worse. Not to mention that it's coming from the wrong direction to be natural."

Now it was my turn to frown worriedly. I looked back down at my half-eaten dinner.

Dagnabbit!

With the table manners of a starved castaway, or a pirate, I shoveled the rest of my dinner into my mouth. Crammed the roll in and swapped plates with William, stealing his beef. It was delicious and I was sad to have to shove it in my face like I was. My hand whipped out and took his water too.

Everyone stared at me silently.

Cooper wiped his mouth and began to rise.

"No way, Joshua," I directed with a mouthful of food. "I had to fix you once already today. This one's a little out of your league."

William's gaze darted around the table top, seeming to merely watch things slide. "No," he mumbled. "No, no," he said, each one gaining power as I stood.

"Sorry William," I said, wiping my mouth and hands with my napkin. I wasn't a complete Neanderthal. "You all need to stay here. It's safer that way."

"I don't want you two arguing again," he declared.

My expression was matter of fact as I shrugged. "We're not going to argue. He didn't do this either."

"Then who did?" Fisherman asked.

"*That* is what I need to go find out," I replied. "Coop, bridge?"

He gave me the path.

"Got it. Thanks."

"Now Eliora—" William started.

I left.

***

It really was cheating to be able to teleport out of a room when someone else was mid-sentence. I actually kind of felt bad about that one. Especially when the bridge crew flinched at my appearance.

The ship's tilting and listing from the waves and troughs was rougher up here.

"What the—Who are you? Get this woman off my bridge!" the man with a captain's insignia barked.

"I'm Nemo Dade, Captain," I said firmly, "and trust me—you want me up here. Now please show me the charts and anything else that will tell me what's going on with this storm."

He inhaled, scowling. "Fine," he answered on an exhale. The part where he did his best not to say, 'but I don't have to like it' hung in the air.

"I'm the EXO, ma'am," a younger man with short dark hair introduced himself. He was lean and weathered, a sailor through and through. "This is what you're looking for."

They brought me to a screen and showed me the parameters of the storm and where they'd tracked it as it had grown. Their perplexed tones were understandable because it came off the coast of the UK. Mother Nature didn't play like that. It shouldn't have been possible.

My heart leapt into my throat. No...She wouldn't.

The ship slid down into another trough. It was the world's worst roller coaster.

"...when death is on the line!" popped into my head. I couldn't tell if I wanted to laugh or cry, or both. Junior's mother was unhappy with me, and probably William too, so she was going to punish us all and bank on Junior surviving to make it home.

"Shite."

Thunder rumbled.

"Is there a way to communicate with the state rooms? Like Henry Bradford's?" I demanded.

The EXO blinked in confusion. "Ah yes, I—"

"Good! Patch me through—now!" I urged. There was no way that I was wasting power popping down there, arguing with him, and popping back up here.

He pointed to a com station.

An officer with headphones nodded to me.

"Hello?" Henry's voice came over the speaker.

"Henry, I need you on the bridge, right now," I said rapidly. "No time for arguing or questions. We've got a big, and I mean really big, problem."

The door burst open for William and Fisherman.

I was surprised it'd taken them this long to storm the castle.

"What? Look, if you're trying to get me in trouble by getting me to leave my room—"

"Henry Galahad Bradford!" I shouted. "I so do not have time for this! Someone we both know has sent a storm to sink this ship and I need your help to stop it. *Now get your butt up to command!* That is not an invitation to play. That's an order, rookie!"

There was a click.

"Now Eliora," William began.

I walked over, took his face in my hands, and kissed him. In front of everyone. "For luck," I whispered. We both knew that was a lie. That was me saying good-bye. With Henry's mother sending a storm that had reached this magnitude, and how whipped I still was, this had the possibility of being a very short Oath.

"I have to be out on deck, closer to the water, the wind. I have to be out there, in the elements," I tried to sum up for Fisherman. "Have everyone get to their safety stations, or whatever your protocols are, but be prepared for me to tell you to abandon ship if it comes to it."

Fisherman nodded. "That bad?"

"She's trying to sink us," I said. He deserved the awful truth. They all did. These people needed to understand what we were facing.

The door burst open again for Henry. He skidded to a stop. "Father, I—"

William didn't let him finish and embraced him. "Go. Help her."

I stepped up and grabbed the punk's hand. "Let's go."

Sadly, the fastest way down the deck where we needed to be was teleporting, or going out the bridge window, but I didn't want to break it, so teleporting it was.

We arrived a couple of feet above the deck and dropped down, falling. My joints protested. My everything protested because I'd never tried that before, and now I knew why. Adding someone else's Energy pattern to mine while I teleported turned out to be a very complicated thing. Now I could completely understand all those transporter 'accidents' as plot points on Star Trek.

Henry shook his head while on hands and knees. Water sloshed over us.

"You okay?" I yelled.

"I will be," he yelled back. "That sucked."

"Yeah, well at least you now know why I can't carry the girls out of that holding site," I replied, trying for some levity.

He ignored me.

The ship's shifting forced us to grab onto rails on either side of the door that had been at our backs.

"This isn't going to be easy," I shouted. "You're going to have to link up with me to get the storm under control. We need to disperse it!"

"I have to what?" He looked at me like I was crazy. "That will never work."

"If it doesn't, we're all dead. Including your dad and Grace. Now I know you could give a flying fart if I survive, which is what *she* is counting on here, but I gotta believe you love them. So if they mean anything to you, you need to work with me here," I shouted over the storm.

We rode up another wave. The slant threw us against the wall.

As the ship crested the wave, I yelled, "C'mon!" and grabbed his hand, pulling him forward so we were standing further away from the ship's bulk. Hand in hand, facing the bow, I fused our feet to the deck with power. Here was where we would live or die. "This is it!"

My Energy reached for the punk's.

His Energies slapped mine away.

After the afternoon's shenanigans, I wasn't surprised. "Work with me! C'mon!"

His eyes widened and went Fae, swirling blue-green.

That's how I knew that I'd gone straight David Banner with glowing green eyes under the strain of ramping up my own power. This was way too soon to be using this much energy, especially since my hastily inhaled dinner was threatening to exhale. I'd had the crazy hope that my body would've processed it faster than this.

"Rookie! We have to work together!" I shouted. Wind, waves, rain, and thunder overwhelmed us. It got harder to breathe. "You need to calm the waves! Disperse its energy! I'll work on the storm winds! But we have to be in sync or it'll become unbalanced, get even worse!"

Those otherworldly eyes stared at me as he rode the deck, storm and all. He was part Water Fae, this wasn't nearly as scary to him as it was to me. His face was all mask.

A lightning strike hit the ocean roughly a mile away.

He ducked into a crouch, hands over his head.

I pushed out with my arms and hands and power, shielding the ship in a sort of faraday cage bubble of Energy to redirect the electricity...and promptly threw up.

"Nemo?" Cooper's voice came over the intercom out to us.

With hands on my thighs, I wobbled a little, which hurt even more since I'd cemented our feet to the deck. I wiped my mouth on the sodden sleeve of my sweater and pushed my now seaweed-like hair out of my face. My arm went high with a thumbs up.

"THAT ALL YOU GOT? YOU MISERABLE MISANTHROPIC BITCH!" I screamed. "BRING IT ON!" Then I caved and called upon...Me. The punk wasn't helping, or maybe couldn't help, and I wasn't able to do it myself, not as weak as I already was.

As I let myself sink back to rest, an untethered feeling crept upon me. My body flinched like a sleeper sitting bolt upright. "This is temporary," I told Me.

She regarded me in watchful silence.

William had been right. A person couldn't go back. Things, once left, could never be like they once were. That lesson had been drummed into me again and again, yet I always needed reminding because I'd fall, not a big one, but a little one that would cause me to cling to the temporary, the finite, the Humans. It was why I clung so hard to my personas, because they made me feel like one of them.

Me didn't even come close to thinking like that, or so my Human personas believed, and that wasn't acceptable. I gripped my Human beliefs close, like the memories of a Human mother long dead. Thoughts that could still make me cry, millennia later. So Me didn't surface often. I had a bad feeling that this was going to be one time too many, too soon.

"Rest," we told Nemo. That persona kept courting near destruction entirely too often for our liking. It was not helpful that her progression from Eliora to Nemo had crashed and they were overlapping. It was breaking the new persona, affecting her ability to function.

"*You*," we breathed and grabbed the youngling's hand before he knew what was happening. Energy leapt between us.

He fought back.

Another wave crashed across the ship.

They will not survive this.

I will fight it my own way, he thought back.

Then fight.

His Fae energy flooded the ocean waters like a small Human trying to slap down a lake or a pool into doing his bidding.

The thunder and roaring ocean laughed at his efforts.

"You—AWAKE!" we called his inner One.

It felt badly beaten, submissive, forlorn, so dim.

Our fury swelled with the waters. We fed him Energy, reminded the One what he was.

His physical body bowed backwards as a scream tore his throat. A war raged. One eye was blue-green of the Fae, the other was all white.

"*You* know what to do, calm the waters as I calm the storm," we told them. His internal war was not our concern, but his ability to do as needed to save the ship was.

We sang, the One and us, we sang in a language that had been long since lost to the Humans. It did not roar, it did not fight, it did not force...it flowed. Music floated and flew. It filled the air from our bodies.

We could feel the anger-fed energies of the ocean subsiding. The great winds unraveled, slowing. They found other paths to travel.

Soon enough, the song subsided into a crooning lullaby as the World's natural order reasserted itself.

Our glance took in the One. The youngling's eyes were a swirling mix of pearl, blue, and green. Tears mottled his face. The curious thought rose to wonder if we had broken the Human part of him.

As the notes began to fade, so did our sense of Nature. Then we felt discord, a counter resonance stir before we had completely let go.

We grabbed the One and our energies raced over the waters to a coastline. There below us, a Fae male prepared to start again. One of her minions.

Damn yoooouuuuuu...you break the Treaty. You harm the World. No. More.

Thunder and lightning exploded in a blinding crack.

When we could see, the offender was gone.

We pulled the youngling back to the ship. The bodies were crumpled. Their feet still stuck to the deck.

The ship rode the ocean waves much more calmly, as it ought during this season.

We put the One back in and unfastened his body's feet. Our own body stood and turned as Humans came spilling out onto the deck.

Soft rains continued to fall.

Callister stood in front of us, distracting our gaze from watching the others swarm the youngling.

"The ocean should be safe for travel, Callister Isaac Mylonas. We will probably be watched over now. They will not allow that to happen again. The offending Fae has been dealt with by us, though there may be another. Regardless, we will be protected," we told him. "The youngling should be made warm, given rest, and plenty of food when he wakes."

The Nemo persona was awake. She poked and prodded.

We turned our head. "Enough!"

All the Humans flinched and paused.

We returned our attention to Callister. "She warns that he may not be himself when he wakes. Try to keep him calm. William Harrison Bradford ought to stay with his offspring to help with that."

"What do you mean, not be himself?" Callister asked cautiously.

"We have properly awoken his Celestial self. It does not sit well with the Fae within him. Their clashing may break the Human portion," we said with a shrug. "It is hard to say. Also, a great deal of Energy was expended to accomplish this."

"And what about you? And Nemo?"

A wrenching pain filled us.

My nose bled, both sides.

"Your eyes!" Fisherman exclaimed. "Get me some gauze!"

Trembling fingers touched my face, my fingers. My eyes were bleeding too.

I collapsed to the ground and threw up, part bile, part blood. Someone was crying. Might've been me. Didn't know. Was too tired to care.

"We gotcha," a familiar voice reassured.

My hands grabbed someone's clothes lifeline tight. "If she is the one who wakes next, throw me overboard," I ordered them. "Promise me!"

"We promise," Fisherman's gravelly voice responded.

I couldn't see anymore, my eyes were closed, and damaged. "Good. Doesn't trust me to drive the bus—wants to drive," I breathed. "Kyrie eleison." We needed mercy. I needed mercy. Unleashing her as I had may have caused irreparable consequences to Henry, to us all.

19

Beep. Beep. Beep.

Soft sounds of hospital equipment beeped and hummed.

Everything hurt.

Being awake brought pain, lots and lots of pain.

Even laughing in my head at my stupid, unintentional joke hurt. Although, I couldn't be dying, could I? If I could joke?

The beeping kept up its steady rhythm.

"...I'm sorry, Harry," Pippa's voice was even quieter than usual. "We just don't have the equipment here, or the doctors. He could wake tonight, tomorrow, or he might never come out of it."

Come out of what? My sluggish brain slumped over the mental card catalog, ripping out cards. Cornea, corona, combat... coma!

"What about Eliora?" he asked finally.

There was movement and then hands slapping legs, so she'd probably shrugged and let her hands drop.

"She's even worse," Pippa sighed, "however, her body's repairing itself slowly but surely. So, my guess would be that sooner or later, she will wake. Who will be in charge remains to be seen though."

There was no way either of my hands or arms would move. I could feel straps on my wrists and tons of tubes stuck in me.

My eyes wouldn't open. Trying to do it had me gasping.

"Hmmm...seems she's in pain," Pippa commented. There were some beeps. "There, that ought to help."

The pain eased, which allowed me the space to think. Though there were going to be consequences to my being able to think, right?

Junior. Junior was bad off. Coma? Coma. Yeah, coma. Not good. Could I break the strap? I could break the strap. Did I want to break the strap? Should I want to break the strap? I needed to break the strap if I was going to help Junior.

Riiiiipp!

BEEP BEEP BEEP!

Alarms sounded. Something was wet. Something was uncomfortable.

"Oh my God, no!" Pippa cried.

"Dammit, Eliora!" William swore.

"Thatsprobablygonna hurt," I slurred.

They tried to grab my arm.

We were playing keep away. Yippeeee!

"Juuuuuunnnnnioorr," I slurred.

"Well at least it isn't the other one," William muttered.

"He's sleeping," Pippa cajoled, "and so should you be."

"Liar!" I barked like Miracle Max's wife, "Liiiiiarrrrrrr! I'm not a witch...I'm a–I'm a–need Junior. Hold his hand. Gotta hold his hand."

"She's out of her mind," Pippa worried, still trying to catch my hand I think.

"Beatles," I snickered.

Then I heard more beeping. "There. That would put an elephant under."

"No, no, no," I murmured and grabbed sightlessly at the air.

A hand grabbed mine. William's. Well, it was certainly far too big and masculine to be Pippa's. "...iam, put our hands together, peas. Need to fix dis."

Leather slapped, a buckle clinked, and a limp, warm hand was placed in mine.

I pulled on my Energy. Something leaked from my eyes. Really hoped it was tears. My stomach roiled.

Aoife.

"Huh?"

My senses probed the punk's head. It was a mess. That was my oh-so-sober medical opinion. I had a medical opinion? Wait? Was I ever a doctor? The Doctor! No, wait, that wouldn't help. It might?

Aoife.

"Who's there?"

"Pippa, and myself," William replied. Except that hadn't been who'd used that name. Who'd called me. Neither of them knew to use that name. It had been my first name. My *true name*. True names were a very powerful thing. They could be used to help or to harm. I guarded mine as if it were an Infinity Stone. Had too many enemies to do otherwise.

"All right, William, that's enough," Pippa huffed. "They both need rest. We need to redo her IV, and oh look—she's bleeding from the eyes again. We'll have to examine her and redo that dressing. Seriously, this needs to be finished."

Was she always this cranky? Persnickety? Persnickety. Cool word.

Aoife, you are doing terrible things to yourself. You need to stop.

Gilchrist! How? What? Here? *He will not recover from what she has done if I don't help him heal*, I explained. Maybe Pippa was right, maybe I was stoned off my gourd. Gilchrist couldn't possibly be here, talking to me. We hadn't spoken in over a century.

Yet his voice filled my head. *You may do permanent damage to yourself...or risk her taking control again.*

A cold spike rode down my spine that I didn't think had anything to do with medicine or damage. Speaking of both, why could I suddenly think so clearly?

Because little sister, I am helping you.

Help! Yes, help. Yes, Please, please, please, Gilchrist, please help him. I have never called on you in all these centuries. Not once. This isn't for me even. Oh please let this not be a Nexus point. He is dear to them and this is my fault, I should've been more patient and I tried I really did but he is such a—

Punk, I believe is your favored term. His weighty silence filled my head.

Speaking of silence, why wasn't I hearing William or Pippa?

We speak inside the tick of a tock.

I stopped breathing. He'd frozen time for us. I really was dying. Oh that wasn't good. How was I supposed to protect the kid if I kicked the bucket?

He chuckled, a quiet, warm sound. Well, at least I'd amused him.

Little sister, this is by far your most...interesting persona yet. Why do you wish me to heal him? He very nearly killed this persona, nearly killed you, not long ago.

Why do you always have to ask me the hard questions?

I ask because you usually have a very insightful answer that you have not fully realized yet.

Had I been able to roll my eyes, I would have. At least he refrained from laughing out right at me this time. *Okay, I want you to save him because despite his being a petulant punk with a mean streak, there is honor in him, and kindness, and a potential that means he has not completely succumbed to being his mother's creature. Undoubtedly because he is also his father's son. I suspect, with her hold on him broken, he would be a very good force for the Light in this world. He has...potential.*

This all seems vaguely familiar.

There was a dry tone to his words. I was glad there were bandages covering my face so he couldn't see it flush. Though, we both knew that I knew that he knew anyway.

Very well. I will see what I can do—for you.

Thank you, Gilchrist! Thank you so much.

Tock.

"sankyousomcuh," I babbled. My hand fell from the punk's. The world spun. With a freed arm, I rolled to my side and puked over the edge of the bed. The Riders of Rohan trampled my skull, splitting it open.

"Eli, Eliora," William stammered.

"...out of the way, Harry," Pippa commanded.

Pinch.

"But will he be okay?" William asked.

"Yesblurthpblah..." what started as a yes, became more throwing up. Everything spun. I felt a presence circling from below.

My arm reached out and grabbed air.

A strong, bony female hand snatched it. Pippa!

Sedate me! All the way. Now! I told her, unable to speak aloud. My grip was slipping and for the first time in my life, I was concerned about what would happen if I lost control.

Pinch! Something cool whooshed through the other IV.

Sweet oblivion took me.

***

Place of Judgement - Henry

He raised his head. Tried to open his eyes, but they were tired, so very tired.

Light winds blew across his face.

His body wouldn't move! There were chains binding him. As he glanced down at himself, he saw that he was wearing a simple linen shirt and leather pants. It was like something from a ren faire or a medieval tv show. What the heck?

Blond bangs dropped across his eyes. He reflexively tossed his head to get them out of the way. This made no sense! He hadn't had his hair this long since he was at uni.

A stronger breeze blew from behind him as he struggled with the chains binding him. He craned his head to look behind. His body stood only a handful of feet from a cliff's edge, easily more than a hundred and fifty yards high. Gray clouds rolled and rumbled across the sky. He struggled to move further into the clearing, away from the edge but he couldn't.

"You have presented us with a difficult conundrum, young one," a male Irish voice commented.

His head whipped about, scanning the vicinity.

A tall, lean but strong-looking man with dark curly hair, close cropped beard, and modern clothes lounged on a rock outcropping that hadn't been there before. The man wore a forest green henley shirt, sleeves pushed partway up his forearms, worn jeans, and work boots. This stranger seemed utterly normal until he looked into the man's eyes. They changed color while he watched.

"Who are you?"

"You may call me Gilchrist," the man said. "I have been requested to help you."

"Good! Great! Wonderful! Please unchain me, or at the very least get me away from the edge here. Please!"

"Well, you see, that's not something *I* can do," Gilchrist said. "*He* has to decide to do it."

***

The world spun! He wanted to throw up! Henry fell to his hands and knees. His whole body hurt like he'd gone ten rounds with Edwards in a no holds barred match after a ten klick run.

"Mmmmm...yes, you haven't been very careful of yourself lately, have you?" Gilchrist asked conversationally from the rock outcropping. He jumped down and pulled Henry up by the back of his shirt, getting him to stand.

Henry glanced down at himself. He wore his usual jeans and a t-shirt with a pair of tennis shoes. As he looked up, he saw himself—the self with longer hair, younger seeming, paler, weaker, and chained with his arms pinned behind his back. Henry turned his attention to Gilchrist. Those kaleidoscope eyes reminded him of Nemo.

He growled silently. That stupid bitch. This had to be her fault. It was a fight not to snarl and roll his eyes in irritation. When he got back to the ship, he was damn sure going to make certain that crazy whore got sent packing.

Thunder rumbled. The winds picked up their pace.

One of Gilchrist's eyebrows went up.

"Henry, are you insane?!" his younger, bound self shouted at him.

"Will you be quiet," Henry told him.

"You just swore about a fellow Nephilim, to an *Archangel*, you nit!" he yelled.

Now Henry did tilt his head and roll his eyes at the bound one. "Right." He brought his head around to ask Gilchrist what this nonsense was all about anyway. The being in front of him was probably some greater Fae messing with his head.

Gilchrist had crossed his arms and had a thumb in front of his mouth. His gaze was on the ground behind Henry. As he watched though, Gilchrist raised his face.

Henry felt himself falling but not falling. The world suddenly became intensely huge. A vast place where he was so small, so alone. There was no one, and nothing and everything. He couldn't breathe!

"HENRY! HENRY, BLINK FOR HEAVENS' SAKE!"

He focused all his will on blinking.

Snap!

Henry was back in his body, standing in front of Gilchrist again. He turned to walk over to his other self when something caught his attention from the corner of his eye.

On the ground, several feet behind where he'd been standing, was Nemo lying broken and bleeding in dirty scrubs, her hair spread out from under her head almost like blood. Like the blood that seeped from under her closed eyelids.

She looked so small, so soft and fragile. A young woman pushed too far.

"She's dying," his other self murmured mournfully.

"What?"

"She's dying, Henry," his other self repeated. "Her Celestial avatar, for lack of a better explanation, accidentally shattered us. We're broken, fractured. Left like this, we will die. She used power that she no longer had to give trying to heal us. Her attempt caught *his* attention, which is why we're here. It is a place of judgement." He sounded awed, and scared.

Henry looked back at Gilchrist and frowned.

That is the Archangel Metatron, Henry, his other self whispered into his mind. *He was her mentor.*

"I still am, so I would choose your next thoughts and/or words about my Devadas very carefully, gentlemen," Gilchrist informed them blandly. "You, Henry, are here to be tested. Maxen swims in the waters below, your Fae self. There stands your Celestial essence given form, and you, Henry the Human, must choose your path.

"Your mother laid a trap should another Nephilim try to unbind your Celestial essence. It was supposed to kill them. In this case, my Devadas was strong enough to survive the trap, but its lingering effects have had consequences. One of those consequences has been that Maelona allowed the failed trap to break you. In her mind, if you weren't strong enough to stop her enemies, then you were too Human to survive.

"Maelona, or Manon I suppose," the Archangel paused thoughtfully, "has quite the low opinion of Humanity. Now,

Henry, you need to choose. Will you break the chains holding *him*, or will you allow him to perish in the waters below, becoming a purely Fae-Human hybrid? Or, will you save her? You have the ability to do it, so will you?"

"What are the consequences of my choices?" Henry questioned carefully. "And why does it seem like he has a name that I should know?" Frustration laced his second question, one that he felt had as far-reaching weight as the other.

"Henry! You know my name! We played knights and monsters for endless summer days for years," his other self reminded him earnestly. "You must name me!" His wide eyed stare urged him to remember.

Henry glanced back and forth between them, but some niggling unease made him glance back at Nemo on the ground. "Aoife," he whispered without thought as he stared.

Her hair turned darker, a deep chestnut color with more curls. Nemo's skin grew more tanned. A light dusting of freckles decorated the bridge of her nose.

Whoosh!

His head whipped back to see the other in the air off the ground.

"*Henry!*" his other self cried. "Name me!" Panic filled his face. "We have to work together to save the fair princess! You need me!"

*...save the fair princess...*It tickled at his memories.

"Galahad?" Henry wondered.

His other self was now over the ocean, chains tightening harshly. He yelled in pain. "Forgive him Holy One! He doesn't understand. No one taught him."

"We will keep your words in mind, young one. Your Essence will be missed," Gilchrist intoned formally.

His other self began to fall.

"Wait! NO! Galahad! Brothers together! Brother knights forever!" Henry screamed. "Save him!"

The Archangel raised his eyebrow at him.

"Galahad, I call you to me. I refuse to let you fall!" Henry shouted and pulled with all of his will.

A wet, bloodied Galahad flew up onto the ground of the cliff. He coughed on hands and knees. The chains were gone.

Henry rushed to him and yanked his childhood friend into a brotherly hug.

They both laughed in relief.

Galahad's face grew somber. "We still have to save the princess."

Henry frowned.

Galahad scrambled to his feet and ran for her, holding one of her hands. "Aoife!" His eyes glowed an electric blue. Not much changed with the dying Nephilim. "Henry, we have to save her together. I'm not strong enough on my own. C'mon! Knights save damsels in distress, and I'd say she was pretty far in distress."

His father's mistress from years ago was nothing to do with him now, other than to be a pain in his ass. Why was she such a big deal? Who the hell cared besides his father?

Henry turned his head away from watching Galahad to ask Gilchrist about all of it—

WHAM!

Gilchrist's fist connected with Henry's jaw.

The Human saw nothing but stars as he landed on the ground.

He picked Henry up by the front of his shirt and growled, "*I warned you!*"

Images of all the heroic and self-sacrificing things she'd done through the centuries overwhelmed his mind's eye. Then he experienced the fated, failed mission that had cost his father his life. Her in the alley raging at the Heavens. Unaware that she'd succeeded. The pain of losing all those lives who'd willingly followed her to battle the darkness, all the friends she'd buried again and again over time, her most current loss tearing at her, having driven her into the wilderness.

His own darker deeds over the course of his life. The people he'd hurt. Those that he'd harmed on his mother's say so. All the times he'd dug at his father, needled him about her, his worst trespass in trying to kill her on the ship.... Gilchrist showed him what that would've done to his father, the devastation it would've caused.

A hand touched his back tentatively and reminded him of the moments when he rose above, when he'd been kind and caring. The times he'd been generous and loving. When he'd protected others because it had been the right thing to do. The lives he'd saved.

Gilchrist let him go.

Henry fell to the ground.

Galahad stood behind him.

How had he been so wrong?! There was too much to absorb. His mind reeled.

"Give me one reason why I should not pronounce judgement on you here and now," the Archangel asked in those same kind of quiet tones his father saved for when he was truly furious.

His mind flashed back to another young Nephilim on her hands and knees in this place who'd chosen silence, to accept her fate, one that she had earned. He'd tried to snuff that light out in his arrogance. Among all his other transgressions, that one stood out front and center in his mind because he'd more than known better at the time.

Henry hung his head and awaited his punishment. "Please, sir, please just let Galahad pass on to...somewhere. Those transgressions aren't his, they're mine," he asked quietly. "He has always embodied what was my better nature."

The silence stretched.

His nerves couldn't take it anymore. He slowly raised his eyes.

Gilchrist wasn't looking at him. He was staring at Nemo. *Aoife*. Galahad, sitting on his ankles, held her upper body in his lap as her head lolled backwards, blood dripping down the sides of her face from her eyes. She was far too pale. Galahad cried silently.

No, no, no, no, no... he couldn't let that happen. Even if it was only for his father's sake.

Henry raced over, landed on his knees, and picked her up from Galahad. The Fae had a variety of ways of healing beings. In some cases, it meant reconstituting a body, restoring another's powers, or healing the spirit. Sometimes it required the magic of Creation. That was one of his mother's talents, using Creation magic. He had no idea if it would work, but there was nothing left to lose.

He kissed her and breathed his power into her pale shell. Henry's mind wandered to all those heroic, kind, and compassionate acts she'd done. Times she'd sacrificed herself for others. Healing him in the ring at the cost of herself. Nearly dying to save everyone on the ship. Killing herself now in trying to save him, all because she'd made an Oath. She'd reshaped Reality itself for his sake.

His kiss took on a new quality, a different one. There was respect. And something else. He sunk himself into passion, not wanting to see that something else. That was for Galahad to handle.

Her spark lit up and he felt her Energy pulse within her again.

Henry pulled his head back. Galahad was gone. Henry noticed he was wearing Galahad's clothes, though his hair was still his own modern style. A blending of them both. Huh. Yet he felt Maxen sulking in the back of his head. Annoyed that Henry had used his abilities. What a mess.

"Nemo. Aoife," he called gently. "Time to come back."

Nemo's eyelids fluttered. Blue eyes greeted him. Blue? Her eyes were hazel green. What?

She smiled vaguely at him. *Thank you so much, punch.* Then she disappeared.

"Punch?" Henry turned back to ask Gilchrist.

"I believe that was meant to be 'punk', but Pippa has drugged her heavily again so..." Gilchrist explained and stared at him thoughtfully.

Henry sat quietly and waited.

"We have much to discuss, you and I."

"Am I to be allowed to live?"

"Yes, for now." The look on his face told Henry that the Archangel still wasn't sure how good an idea that was as yet.

He swallowed hard. There was too much he still wanted to do in his life. Places to go, people to see, simple things to do, to live. He hoped that he could find a way to make up for some of what he'd done, to make things better.

"Oh yes, we will find a way for you to make good on that," Gilchrist said drily. "Stand Henry Galahad. Walk with me. We need to talk before I send you back."

"Yes sir." Henry stood up and followed the Archangel into the woods.

"This place is an ancient Druids' Grove," Gilchrist began. "Aoife once stood where you did, or rather, kneeled as you did, awaiting her judgement."

They talked. Well, Gilchrist talked. Henry Galahad listened.

And when he awoke, his head hurt worse than after a long weekend of leave. His father sat asleep in a chair, snoring away, watching over them both.

Henry's eyes welled up with tears. He couldn't quite remember why. All he knew was that the sight of his father there hurt his heart.

Turning his head, he saw her in a hospital bed next to him. Her hair was still its reddish blonde and her skin was so very pale. She seemed incredibly tiny with all those leads and tubes stuck to her body, blankets piled on top. A small portion of shackles remained visible against the bed rail. Racks of monitors and devices stood sentinel on the far side of her bed. The bandages were gone from her eyes, but they still were red, angry, and awful.

He watched her chest rise and fall to be sure.

She breathed normally.

Gilchrist had promised that she would be alive when he got back. Provided Henry made strides to clean up his own mess.

He had to find a way to pull himself together and fix the wrongs. His head was killing him. Much of what had happened was fuzzy. At least it seemed like he'd have time to sort it out though. So, he stared at the ceiling and tried his best to piece together what had happened.

20

Quiet snoring reached my ears, even over the pelting beeps of machines.

My eyelids rose slowly. Everything was a fuzzy blur. But at least the bandages were gone. That had to be good, right?

Clank, click.

Heavy metal manacles encircled my wrists. Some thoughtful person had at least covered them in a thick cloth, but there was no mistaking the message. Pippa had taken me seriously.

I let my body relax. Wait. Who was snoring? I turned my head.

Despite the fuzziness, it looked like Junior, asleep in the next bed, but the noise wasn't coming from him.

Gingerly, I lifted my head.

A blurry image that I thought was William sat in a chair at the foot of our beds. His head rested at an odd angle. On his hand? And one leg crossed. The shape of his body screamed contorted, which had to be why he snored. It was probably the most uncomfortable position I think I'd ever seen outside of a torture chamber.

He snored once more.

"He's been doing that for at least an hour," Junior commented quietly. "Good to see you awake."

I blinked. Had to still be sleeping. Or stoned. That's it. I was still drugged to the hilt and this was a hallucination. My right hand came up and rubbed down my face.

"Hey," he murmured an admonition.

I stared at my freed hand and the IV coming out of my forearm. That hadn't even hurt. That should've hurt. And I had never teleported only *part* of my body like that. What the higgity heck? "I have no idea, rookie," I mumbled, more to myself than anyone else.

Coolness whooshed through the other IV again.

Nothing.

***

A bright light shone in my eye.

"Ow!"

A bright light shone in the other eye.

"Hey! Stop it."

"What language was that?" a male voice asked.

"Ancient Greek, maybe," a familiar female British voice said.

I knew her, didn't I?

"Who—who are you?" my voice rasped, wasn't sure what language. Couldn't see much. Between the dancing light spots and the blurriness, eyesight was a wash.

"She asked who are you?" another British voice said, more familiar. I knew him. Maybe? He sounded tired, weary.

"Do you know who you are?" the male voice questioned. Faint echoes followed it.

I turned my head to the left trying to get away from the bright lights. The whole world spun. My hands gripped blankets.

Chains clanked. Chains?!

Beeping sped up and got louder. Beeping?

Where was I? Who were these people? Was this a bender? Had I been in an accident? Was this a hospital? Where were my clothes? Why did everything hurt? Why was I in scrubs?

What had happened? Wait! Why were we on a boat? Had I been kidnapped? Kidnapped! My trailer! My head!

I teleported off the bed.

And promptly fell to the floor.

"Where'd she go?" the male voice shouted.

"Oh no! Not again," the British female complained.

Sounds of people moving behind me.

I scrambled against the wall, looking for a way out of here.

Blood trickled down my arms. How'd they get hurt?

"Nemo, Nemo, it's me," the male Brit said.

Warm hands on my cheeks.

My hands grabbed where wrists ought to be. That hurt.

The hands and wrists rotated out of my grip.

Blue eyes.

His face was blurry. I felt like I ought to know that face, but my mind knew those eyes. His hands moved to my upper arms. "Hey, hey, it's okay." *It's Henry*, he thought at me.

The name rolled around in my head. Wait! He was a Nephilim! Henry! Junior! The Punk! My Rookie!

Most of those aren't terribly flattering, you know.

Images and memories crashed through my head in a high speed maelstrom. I curled in on myself, whimpering. Breathing came in uneven hitching noises.

He pulled me into his arms and held me on the floor. "Shhhhhhhh...Don't shoot her. Don't drug her," he informed someone. *Aoife, you're going to be okay*. "It's just hibernation sickness," he took the joke from my head.

Punch knew my Name? How? Why?

"Someone thought it was a good idea," Henry whispered.

Huh? Oh yeah, Gilchrist.

I risked opening my eyes and stared at blurry floor tiles. "He really healed you all the way, didn't he?" My voice rasped like sandpaper. Husky would've been an improvement.

"Yeah." He hugged me a bit more tightly, discreetly. Then his body tensed.

Our minds were linked. I felt his reluctance to have anyone notice, even us.

My mentor and I had saved his life, and he knew it. There was something else though, something different.

Henry gently nudged my staggering mind out of his. Now I really wanted to know what Gilchrist had said to him.

Hold the phone...Henry. Junior. Staggering pain in my rear. Was holding me?! I stopped breathing.

A door banged open from somewhere behind the punk.

My body flinched. I tried to scramble away.

He'd flinched too. "Whoa whoa whoa," he said while scrabbling to catch me.

It wasn't that hard.

His warm body wrapped around me again. He winced and grunted while doing so.

I heard others moving. Even over my harsh breathing.

"It's okay. I've got it," Henry told them. *Hey. I'm not going to hurt you. I've got your back, literally at the moment, so please stop.*

Why? This made no sense. My head throbbed trying to figure it out. Had Gilchrist ordered him to help me? I wondered if my mentor had kicked his butt.

That's when I realized no one was moving.

I risked raising my gaze. Someone stood near us with something, presumably a gun, pointed at me. "Fisherman?" *He doesn't look happy, does he?* I asked Henry.

Nope.

Great. "Please don't shoot me, Captain Mylonas," I requested dully. "I will haunt you by turning all your single malt to vinegar for the rest of your life if you do."

A snort.

"Pippa!" I called out and promptly began coughing. "Still chasing wabbits?" I asked when I could talk again.

"That's definitely her, though I would still question her clarity of mind," she declared.

"Dr. Weatherford, I would have you know that the clarity of my mind is clearly not in question nor concern, provided you can, will, and do follow my logic, logically speaking," I replied in aristocratically stuffy British right back at her. "Though everything's still a blasted blur," I murmured.

"He said your eyes would be the last to heal," Henry whispered into my hair.

Great. She's pissed, isn't she? Arms crossed? Fuming?

Check, check, and check.

"Wait. Fisherman and Pippa were in here," I muttered, "so who came in?"

"Not sure," he whispered back. I felt him strain to see. His whole body stiffened.

That instantly told me who was in the room. Without asking, I borrowed Henry's ability to see... and so wished I hadn't. He looked angry and worried and scared and an extra dollop of not happy. My head throbbed. Whether from the power expenditure or tension was debatable.

"I wouldn't do that again," Henry murmured sourly. "No power for at least a day once you are awake."

"Who told you that?" William asked.

"Help me get up," I mumbled.

Pippa stepped forward to help Henry. She tsked about my arms and went to get supplies.

I stood, but it was a shaky go.

Fisherman had mostly lowered his weapon, but I was betting the safety was still off, just in case.

"Callister, please put that away. Seriously. I'm about as threatening as a newborn kitten right now," I reiterated. "I can't even see properly."

"You can't?" Pippa asked as she walked over to me.

"No. I can see shapes and colors, but everything's blurry," I complained, "and my head is killing me, and my mouth feels fuzzy gross awful. Wait, what's for dinner? No jello, please!" I still sounded hoarse, but my tones were sounding more and more like me.

Fisherman barked a laugh. "Yeah, I'd say our girl is back." I heard a click and the sounds of a gun being holstered.

I turned my head in his direction. "Thank you."

"She can't see, but her hearing is spot on, sir," Henry explained.

"Ah, yes. Well then, you two should be back in bed for now. I'll wait for Dr. Weatherford's decision on visitors other than the three of us," Fisherman said.

"Yes, in bed. Both of you," Pippa directed us.

"No chains, no drugs," I said, standing my ground.

There was a silent pause.

Again, it seemed like no one was moving.

My head throbbed and I resisted the urge to rub my temples. Sweat beaded on my forehead. I knew I wasn't going to last in this standoff much longer. "William," I said, turning my head in the direction where I suspected he was still standing.

Audacious of me under the circumstances, but I wasn't about to let them chain me down and drug me that deeply again.

***

William

Eliora looked terrible. She wasn't going to cause trouble. If she'd thought there was a chance for a problem, she would've said so like before. Her blind gaze swung in my direction. "William," was all she had said, but it was the way she'd said it. She expected me to fix this, to help.

Henry had stopped breathing as he watched the other two. He refused to even glance my way.

My gaze took them in and traveled to the cupboards in the far corner. "Fine," I said on a tired exhale.

This was what I had wanted, right? It'd been my hope that once they stopped fighting, the two of them would find a way to each other. That was for the best, wasn't it? My mind said yes. However, my heart only saw Eliora, my former fiancée, being cared for by another man. A younger man. A younger man who would be able to live a long life like hers.

Mylonas walked over to her bed and began removing the restraints.

Eliora baby-stepped towards the bed.

Pippa immediately rushed over to help her.

With a lightning fast, peripheral glance towards me, Henry stepped back and made his way to his own bed.

As Pippa got her patient settled, she continued to mutter about all sorts of things. It faded into the background as I watched my very broken love being gently tucked into bed as if she were the young woman that she appeared to be. Pippa smiled. "I'll send some broth, bread, applesauce and some ginger ale. If you do well with that, then we can discuss more substantial foods. If you can manage to drink your water, I don't see a need for an IV for now. Think you can do that?"

Eliora saluted her with two fingers. "Got it covered." She undoubtedly would've promised the moon if it meant Pippa didn't have another chance to drug her again. As she curled up on her side with her eyes closed and facing this way, memories rewound time.

Pippa and Mylonas left the room with brief glances at me. I couldn't help myself; I walked over and clicked off her lamp. Then I remembered my question to Henry and stepped to the other side of his bed. "You never answered my question," I asked in a whisper, not wanting to wake her.

Henry lay on his back. His eyes flicked to me briefly before going back to the ceiling. "Just an instruction I woke up with, sir," he answered. "Guess someone wanted to make sure she would be okay once she was awake." He'd lied, at least partially. I believed that someone wanted to make sure she was okay. I even believed someone had provided that information to my son, but I also believed that my son knew who it was and wasn't saying.

"Get some rest," I replied.

"Yes, Father."

I walked to the door and turned the handle, "Oh, and Henry?"

"Sir?"

What could I say? What was there to say? I felt as though I ought to acknowledge what had happened, what I'd seen—something. Yet, a small, selfish part of me hoped that if I didn't, maybe we could simply arrive at a place where they weren't trying to kill each other.

"Good job, son. You've done well. It's good to see you back on your feet. You did well... helping her," I said, instead of all the other things I could have. Like how much what had happened had terrified me. How much I loved him. Possibly how relieved I was that he was safe and healthy. Or how proud I was of the man he'd become.

"Thank you sir." His voice sounded stiff. He was upset. Too many possibilities as to why, and I wasn't sure that it was a conversation either of us were ready to have.

I left the room because sometimes the best thing one could do in the face of so much conflict was retreat.

***

The door closed.

I opened my eyes. Things were still blurry but the shapes were getting clearer. Pretty sure Henry was on his back, staring at the ceiling. "Henry," I whispered. Lots of questions played dodgeball in my head, not the least of which was where the howdy doody howitzer his sudden gentle helpfulness had come from.

"Not now."

"But—"

"Go to sleep, Nemo," Henry muttered and rolled onto his side facing away from me.

"You're still a punk," I mumbled.

"Yeah, I don't like you either. What's your point?" he groused.

At least that sounded a lot more normal for him. I waited, listening to him breathe. It took a bit for him to sound like he slept, but I was also falling asleep, so I thought, *you aren't half bad when you actually try to be...*

Snore.

***

Placing Dark Bets - Fisherman

Callister Mylonas stood behind his desk and frowned at the cup of coffee there. His gaze flicked to the bar cart. The clock on his desk said another hour until noon. For the fifth time, he wished what was in his cup were something stronger. Fuck.

"...though this morning was something of a setback, but she rebounded rather well, and I think it's a positive sign that Henry was so willing to help her. It's concerning that her eyesight isn't healing as quickly as we'd hoped, however as he'd said, she should have that back by tomorrow morning. We could wake her around eight in the morning for breakfast and some preliminary tests to see if I'm right. Henry seems to already be in good shape, just in need of some rest," Pippa finished her recommendation.

"No," Harry snapped and grimaced. "As much as I hate to say it, we can't be so ready to trust that he'll continue to play well with Eliora. Considering how wounded she is right now, I think she should be allowed to sleep. You saw what a mess she was this morning. We don't want to push her too fast. There's no telling what will happen."

He could hear the worry under the Commodore's clipped, sharp tones. What did the Commodore know that he didn't? They needed Nemo up and running, just not stuck in the middle of such a fucking mess. He'd seen the look on Harry's face earlier when his kid had been holding Nemo.

"Harry, I wouldn't suggest it if I didn't think she could handle it. The girl is much stronger than you give her credit for being," Pippa argued. "We have no idea what she can and cannot do—what her healing factor is like. This is the first time we've seen it pushed, seemingly, beyond its limits. I had no way of knowing. I'm a doctor for God's sake. You talk like I would put her in harm's way for the sake of the mission."

"Wouldn't you?" his friend inquired with deceptive quiet. "You went and woke her after I had explicitly said no, and look what happened." The Commodore gave her a hard stare.

There was something more to that look.

Pip paled. Her eyes widened as her head snapped back. Pippa's hand flew to the watch necklace Callister had given her years ago, a sure sign that she was nervous and agitated.

He didn't know all the history Harry and Pip had, both having worked for MI-6 for years without him, but he hadn't thought that it'd been anything to be concerned about—until now. It seemed Harry's history was catching up with him left and right lately, and their team was getting caught in the middle. That shit was going to stop. Now.

Callister cleared his throat and stared unseeing at the papers on his desk. "Pip," he got her attention, "would you give us the room?"

"Yes, yes of course," she replied with a slight nod of her head. Her eyes shone too brightly.

He closed the fingers of his right hand into a fist and slowly uncurled them. She'd been working too much and not getting enough sleep. It worried him.

His office door closed softly behind her.

The admiral took his time sipping some barely lukewarm coffee. Otherwise, he was going to take a serious strip out of his co-commander and friend. Either that, or start drinking before noon. Neither option boded well for his day.

Callister didn't look at the other man. He set down his coffee and shuffled a couple of papers. "Mind telling me what *that* was all about, Harry?"

"It was nothing. Just lack of sleep," his friend muttered. "I'll apologize to her later."

He knew better. "The fuck that was nothing."

The Commodore blinked. His head tilted slightly as an eyebrow went up, "Excuse me?"

"You heard me, Harry," he growled softly. "I'm calling bullshit. It's time to deal me in. I want some answers."

"It would help if I knew what the bloody hell you were talking about, Callister."

He looked back up and locked gazes with the Brit.

"Don't fuck with me. And if that's too oblique and déclassé for you, then let me put it another way—do me the incredibly basic courtesy of explaining what in the fucking Hell is going on," he said and took a breath. "Your son's mother tried to kill us, at least once that I know of, your son attempted to kill the asset we've brought in from the cold, and if you were wound any tighter, you'd be shitting diamonds. So, I will ask you again, what kind of shitstorm have you brought down on us?"

The Commodore glared at the wall. He bristled and retreated into his cold, sternness. "I don't believe I have any answers that will satisfy you. My personal life is exactly that—personal. As in none of your business."

Callister's fist came down on his desk, sloshing his coffee. "Dammit Harry! The fuck it isn't! Your personal life is not only risking this team, but the crew—all of us! That would include your son and foster daughter. Look, either take her back or don't, but this messy 'personal' shit is done. This stopped being about you and your personal life about two near-death scrapes ago.

"We are still in the middle of the Goddamn ocean! What am I supposed to do? Call down an F-22 strike on some Fae? On the shores of fucking *Wales*?! How do I even begin to explain that one? I knew Infernals were bad news, but this is insane. Who exactly attacked us? Why? How? How do we safeguard against it happening again?" He jabbed his finger into his desk. "A better question—how the fuck do I keep that young buck from tearing this place to shreds while he tries to take her out of the equation? Because obviously taking orders seems to be off the table."

Harry's mouth worked silently.

"Dammit, man," he swore softly and began blotting up the spilled coffee.

"His mother is apparently as old and as powerful as our new asset," Harry answered finally, his voice tight. "I would imagine she took exception to something. Being half Fae and a Nephilim, she's rather strong. Though she has those who work for her, so it could have been one of them."

He had just thrown the napkins into his trash can. Callister went still. She was as powerful as Nemo, and there were more of them? His eyes pinned the Commodore's. "Harry..."

"I don't know how she knew," Harry replied as he dropped his gaze to the floor.

"If he betrayed us—"

"He didn't!" Harry asserted as his head snapped up.

Callister picked up the phone receiver off its cradle. "Yeah, we'll see about that," he muttered.

The Commodore reached across Callister's desk and pushed down the switch, stopping the dial tone. "Don't. Please. He's resting."

He stared the other man down. His eyes drifted down to Harry's finger on the phone.

Said finger withdrew.

"Henry didn't tell her anything, at least, I'm almost certain he didn't. Pippa tracks his calls for me. He hasn't called her. She made me swear some things years ago. Things I can't explain because that's part of the swearing...I ah, I broke my word. I think that tipped her off to something being up as it were."

Callister exhaled heavily. "And how are we supposed to protect ourselves from them?"

"Well, Eliora's..." Harry searched for the word, "Me-self said that we would be watched over from here on out and that they wouldn't be allowed to attack us like that again."

"This is something you think we can trust in then?" His head hurt. Fuck it. He walked over to the bar cart and poured them both a couple of fingers of his good stuff, twenty year old Kentucky bourbon.

Callister went back to his desk and handed a glass to Harry.

His friend took a deep sip. "Yes. Whenever Eliora had made assurances that couldn't be explained, it was something we could take to the bank."

He shook his head and scratched the side of it briefly. His ex-wife would've known that sign. It meant he was two seconds from utterly blowing a gasket. The intel he'd been provided had been woefully inadequate. His co-commander was keeping secrets that were going to get them all killed. Two *very* powerful beings were fighting on his ship and the only thing keeping them from sinking the whole thing was the older one's sense of ethics, provided she could stay in charge of herself.

"And what...assurances," he strangled the need to swear more. Had to tread lightly with this one. "What fail-safes are in place to keep him from trying to kill her again?"

Harry's mouth flattened before he took a deep pull of his drink. "He won't."

"Once upon a time, I would've trusted in that assessment, but now," he paused, "now I've had a fucking crystal clear batch of examples in the last twenty-four hours of just exactly why I can't."

"She has a mentor. I figure it has to be an Angel, or maybe another Nephilim, but I think that's who she got to save Henry's life," the Commodore said into his glass and took another sip, "and whoever that someone is, it seems he's talked to Henry, probably brought him up short, which would explain his change in behavior."

Oh great. Another one.

"In any event, that's why I don't think he'll go after her anymore. One of those 'bigger fish' she talked about most likely made Henry very aware that they are now *aware of him*, so he'll mind his manners."

"I really hope you're right, because there is a metric shitload riding on this," he warned.

It might be time to tackle things directly. Him and Nemo. Just them.

21

The next time I'd woken, all those fuzzy shapes had more color and definition.

I'd noticed Henry's empty bed.

A groan inadvertently had escaped as I'd tried to sit up enough to feel for my water.

Someone entered the room.

"Here you are ma'am," a British male had informed me as styrofoam found my hand.

"Where's Henry?" I'd asked after a long sip.

"Agent Bradford has been transferred back to his quarters," my helper had explained. "He passed all of Dr. Weatherford's tests yesterday evening."

Of course he had.

That had been the start of it. Pippa had watched me incessantly. For everything. Which meant I hadn't been about to ask her a thing. Especially not to see how Henry was recuperating.

As he'd foretold, my eyesight returned over the course of that morning, bearing out his speculation of it taking roughly a day for my eyesight to get better.

After that moment I'd woken, there'd been much arguing over whether or not to let the mission proceed. Once I could see again, the conversations got even more interesting because I had been able to actually direct my comments at people. My more than Human abilities were still mostly offline, which had been their biggest argument.

I'd disagreed.

Grace appeared practically glued to Henry's side after he'd gotten out of the infirmary. Or so Ivy and Coop had told me when they'd visited me later that day.

This morning had been more of the same: breakfast, very minor physical therapy, medical staff testing me, late morning tea, more tests from Pippa...but then something strange happened.

"Oh, by the way," Pippa began as she made notes on her tablet, "Henry will be here soon so I can do a fast checkup on him. Do play nice, please." She smiled at me absently like a busy doting parent, pleased to have her troubled child finally subdued.

"When can I leave the infirmary?" I asked, ignoring her statement. Though it was odd that she was going to do his checkup here. I was sure there were other rooms she could use.

As my mind pondered that one, her watch beeped at her. "Ah, I need to take this call. I'll be back soon and then we can talk."

The door opened before she could reach it.

Henry walked in with Grace hot on his heels. Her eyes found mine and narrowed.

"All right, Grace. Not now. You can talk with them later," Pippa shooed her from the room. "Henry dear, I'll be right back. Just a tick."

He took a few steps, his gaze darting everywhere but at me and all the monitors.

"How are you doing?" I asked him. He looked good, healthy, which was a relief since I hadn't seen him in two days and that last time had been a doozy. I think. Some things were a bit fuzzy still, but sure as shootin' wasn't going to tell them that.

"Who me? I'm fine," he said and shoved his fingers into his jeans pockets, wandering slowly around the room. "She still waking you every two hours?" he asked the wall.

"We're up to every four hours now," I replied blandly.

"Oh good. That's good."

"We really should—" I began.

"Look, I really don't—" he said at the same time.

"Talk about what—" I tried again.

"Want to talk—" he continued.

I laced my fingers in my lap. "Go ahead," I said, staring down at my hands.

"I'd rather not talk about it," he told the floor.

"We need to. It would be good for both of us," I countered.

"No. No, I don't think it would," he replied more sharply. Then he actually looked at me. "You still look like he—rubbish," Henry told the floor again.

"Gee thanks, punk." I crossed my arms and let my gaze rest on my toes under the blanket. It was hard not to think about the residual redness all around my eyes or the hollows of my cheeks. "At least tell me how long I'm out of commission."

He shrugged. "I don't know," he answered. "I'm surprised you weren't healed too."

I didn't believe him about not knowing, but I didn't want to grill him about Gilchrist since I knew there were cameras in this room. Talking to him mind to mind was possible, except they'd notice and wonder at the silence. "Yeah well, I hadn't asked for it at the time. At least I don't think so. I don't remember much beyond being out in the storm, and waking at one point in here to find that you were in serious trouble." I shrugged.

I'm sorry I didn't do better, he apologized. *It was my first attempt at healing someone.*

He sounded uncomfortable, unsure, and honestly regretful, weird! *It's okay. I can roll with it. Thank you for trying. I don't remember any of that.*

Neither of us said anything.

"Answer me one question," Henry quipped.

"Why should I?"

He gave a side eye roll. "Don't be a child. Can you honestly handle going on this mission?"

My face closed down to my poker expression. After this many years, I had a really good one. "Yes, Agent Bradford. I can 'handle' the mission. My powers would tip off the mark, so I can't use them. I still have my mind, a team, lots of equipment, and half a mind to put my foot up your butt. So, yeah, I can return to duty, rookie."

The punk grimaced.

I frowned at him. "This isn't my first near death experience, kid," I added.

Lie.

Since when could you detect lies? Or even get past my shields to read me?

I can't, but the little voice in the back of my head said that was a lie; that you've never been that close to dying before.

We continued to frown at each other. I'd frown at Gilchrist later.

The door opened.

"I'm sorry, Henry. Headquarters had a question that of course couldn't wait, so they had to ask me now," Pippa chattered as she came in. "Okay, dear, any trouble sleeping? Vision? Balance? How did your cardio go?" She shined a light in each of his eyes.

"No. Fine. Fine. Just like normal. May I go? I was supposed to have a meeting right now," he said without looking at me.

"Yes, yes, off you go," she shooed him along and then turned to me.

He took his opportunity to escape.

Not over, punk. I stared at the closed door.

"Nemo? Eliora?"

"My name is Nemo, Phillipa," I retorted without looking at her.

"No need to get snippy," she huffed.

"That whole thing was a ploy," I said with a dawning realization. Okay, so maaaaaayyyyybe I was still a little slower on the uptake than was good. "Many birds—one stone. You three get to see if he and I can be in the same room without trying to kill each other, which wasn't likely considering the lengths I'd gone through to save him, but it did tell you whether you could trust him to behave around me.

"It also provided an opportunity to see if my answer about being ready for duty would change in a more private setting, talking to someone whom I've 'gone through something' with, rather than spouting the party line of being fine.

"Hate to break it to you, but he got the same answer you all did. I can do this. I will be fine. All I need is food, rest, and time. Though we're running a bit short on the latter two, we can make it work. Yes, it's going to take time for my extraordinary abilities to come online, but there's plenty I can do beyond that. Thank you very much.

"Gah! Tell Mylonas the next time he wants a guinea pig to grill me to come down here and play twenty questions with me himself," I snapped.

Pippa pursed her lips.

I wasn't sure which had her angrier, that I'd figured out what was going on, or that I'd so baldly called them out on it.

"It wasn't the Captain, though he agreed to it," she finally responded in quiet, terse tones. "The Commodore was the one who set this up because he wanted to make sure there wouldn't be problems."

The urge to jump from my bed and track him down was so strong I had to take a moment and close my eyes. "Pippa," I said with controlled softness because otherwise, I'd have started shouting, "I want to be moved back to my own quarters, not tomorrow, not tonight, now. I don't care what you have to do, but I'm out of here. One way, or another." I opened my eyes and stared her down with just Human hazel-green eyes. Eyes that screamed just how angry I was.

She swallowed. "But there's no way for us to make certain you're okay in your room—"

"I know," I enunciated, cutting her off. "That is the point."

Pippa drew herself up to her full height. "I'll see what I can do."

I gave her points for dignity.

She left the infirmary room.

There was a pad of regular-sized, lined paper and a pen in case I wanted to jot thoughts down, journal, make notes, maps, whatever. I turned it sideways and began writing in large block letters.

After finishing my message, I removed my leads and my IV without bleeding everywhere. Then I got out of bed and walked slowly around the room with the pad of paper held over my head like a boxing round babe.

The pad went sailing and hit what had been Henry's bed just as the door opened to admit Cooper. Then the pad hit the floor.

"Whoa!" he exclaimed. "What was that?" He walked over to the bed.

"Nothing," I sputtered, "Really, just me blowing off steam. I'm guessing you're here to take me back to my room?"

He got there before I did and picked up the pad. "This isn't over, William," he murmured, reading out loud. Cooper ripped the page off the pad, crumpled it, and three-point shot it into a garbage bin. "Ready?" He tossed the empty pad on the bed.

I walked over to him and grinned a mile wide. "Yes. Yes, I am, sir."

He held out his arm like a gentleman. "Let's go then. Unless you need me to carry you?"

My eye roll was a given. “Seriously? Not you too,” I complained. “I can manage to get to my room. Let’s go.”

22

I walked down the mostly dark hallway and knocked on Fisherman's door. It was last call late, long after everyone else had turned in for the night. Since my escape from the infirmary the day before yesterday, we'd all been busy. Though it didn't surprise me that he was still awake.

"Come in," Fisherman offered.

Curious. One would've had to have better than Human hearing to catch his response, which meant he didn't want anyone who wasn't either me or Junior to enter. I wondered yet again why he'd left a discreet note summoning me here.

Opening the door showed him sitting at his desk with only one of those green shaded brass desk lamps lit. A highball glass of amber liquid stood sentinel on his desk with roughly two fingers worth in it. His eyes flicked to mine, but then he went back to staring at his drink. "Have a seat."

Shadows haunted the underside of his eyes, his face scruffier than usual. A tired air hung about him, and it wasn't the dim lighting being unkind.

I sat down in one of the two chairs opposite him, closer to the door.

He got up and walked over to his bar. Fisherman poured me a matching drink before I could ask him not to.

The glass appeared in my hands.

He was back behind his desk. "We need to talk, just us."

"Okay," I replied, drawing the word out a little.

The Captain took a sip and watched his fingers flex on the blotter after he'd set the glass back down. "I worked my way up to Navy SEAL," he began. "I was very good at it. So good that Naval Intelligence recruited me. The blacker the op, the farther off the books, the more they wanted me to take care of it. I made problems go away." Fisherman took a sip of his drink.

So, definitely more than a 'captain'. Huh.

My eyes followed his movements, watching him closely. There was no mistaking what he'd meant. I'd seen warriors, military men, heck-a-doodle—I'd been here myself, dark memory-fed insomnia soaked in booze. So I waited.

"In between missions, I began picking up private contracts here and there. Bad people who either couldn't, or wouldn't, be brought to justice. It got to a point where someone decided to dish out a little payback. Supposedly it'd been a robbery gone wrong. Except the thieves had missed all my ex-wife's jewelry and the upstairs safe. Neither were particularly hidden. They killed my daughter. She was in college then and had come home on the spur of the moment, but they'd known. The ex had been away at a conference." He took a long pull, got up, and refilled his glass, all the while not looking at me.

"I tracked them down, each and every fucking one of them. Took a leave to do it. When I found the last one, I realized my mistake," he muttered, lifting the glass to his mouth, saying the next bit into his glass, "one that I'd make again with no qualms. Vengeance is bad for business, but at that point, I didn't care. Something just like Trouble had mostly burned out its host. It jumped into me with vicious glee. Oh it was as happy as a pig in shit to ride with me."

I caved. Took a swallow of my drink. Ellie and Edwards being on board suddenly made a whole lot more sense. It wasn't even in me to chide him about his language. He'd more than earned his right to swear.

He came back and sat down, still staring into space.

"The really fucked up thing was that I didn't really understand at first what'd happened. Thought I'd hallucinated the whole thing. A little bit at a time this voice whispered in the back of my head. Moments when I should've held back, I didn't. The bosses didn't care initially because the end goals were being accomplished. It had me amped up on those extra-sensory abilities. Ops that had no right to have succeeded, did.

"Right up until I tried going up against someone who was—well, I guess you'd call him a half-Infernal. A small team had gone in with me. Oh he fucked my shit up alright. Most of the rest of the team too. We'd made the newbie hold back." Fisherman stopped talking and took another sip. "If I hadn't made him stay back...wouldn't be here right now; that's for sure. He dragged my bleeding, broken ass out of that compound. They tell me that I died for a minute or two. I don't know. I don't remember. That thing jumped ship. Don't know where it went."

I took a deeper pull. A demon shard was potentially running around that knew Fisherman's Essence. On a scale of one to ten? Bad. Very, very bad.

"The closest friendly locale was a British Intelligence safe house. We borrowed it. Only, a team who'd planned on using it returned ahead of schedule. I was a mess. But this pain in my ass Commander wouldn't leave well enough alone and let me die in peace. He insisted on saving my life. He knew what was wrong with me even before I had any shot of getting it," Fisherman told me with a direct stare. "That was twenty years ago."

I swallowed a lump in my throat. Tried to wash it down with bourbon. No luck. By then, William would've known what he was looking at with Mylonas. I'd explained some basic things so he'd be prepared while he was out in the world.

"The half-Infernal's men came looking to finish what they'd started. Not sure why. They'd kicked our asses already," he mused.

"Because it wanted to absorb the power from that demon shard. Trust me when I say you are glad you got away before it could try," I interjected numbly.

"We barely got out with our lives. That was pretty much when he retired from the field. The kid was eight by then, and the Commander realized he couldn't risk his neck like that as often as he had been. Apparently, his son had only been with him for a couple of years, and it wasn't going well..."

"And throwing himself into work had always been his go to before," I finished for him.

He nodded. "Yep."

The amber liquid beckoned me. It was an old dance. "Who knows?" I asked instead.

"Harry, and now you."

"Why?" The question crawled from my throat in a hesitant whisper.

"Because I need you to trust me. I fucking get it—in spades. Having all those abilities and then losing them. The frustration. We've been going round and round because I'm worried you'll make calls reflexively, banking on having skills that aren't at your beck and call in the moment. The hard decisions are on my shoulders and it's critical that you trust me to make those."

"Why would I trust the former host of a demon shard who'd become so dark of heart that there hadn't been any real fight for control? Ellie fights that friggin' foghat horrible monster every minute of every day. She has to," I stopped and stood.

He let me come around to lean in so I could stare into him.

I pulled back abruptly.

Without a word, I went to his bar cart and poured more booze for myself. Drained it. Then poured another.

His soul was a patchwork quilt of both Dark and Light. Callister Mylonas wanted that power back, maybe not the crazy, evil rider that came along as the price, but he craved those abilities. Even if he had to pay that price, the fool thought he could control it. Ooooooh the hubris of that thought. But if it meant having the capability to keep Junior in line? To have a chance at finding those girls. To not have to rely on us, but be able to protect his ship and crew...he'd do it in a hot second.

My eyes scrunched closed. "Cold sea breeze, coarse long grasses, salt, dirt," I mumbled into the glass, focusing every ounce of my will on something else. A place out of time and space.

Finally, my breathing slowed. I turned back to him.

He hadn't moved a muscle, but his eyes flicked up to mine for a second. Fisherman sat motionless, waiting for me to pronounce judgment. To reject him.

"Of everyone on this blasted boat," I said in a hoarse whisper, "you have my trust." Thoughts of what I'd seen threatened to overwhelm me again. I slammed back the rest of my drink and put the glass on his desk. "This mission will happen. Those girls will come home."

I couldn't stay in there any longer, but my feet stopped me at the door. "Don't ever let the punk look into your eyes like that," I commanded the door. "It won't go well."

"Would he try to kill me?"

"No," I hedged, as I turned my head to the side and spoke to the floor, "but he won't understand what he sees. There would be questions. Lots of them. None that you want to answer."

"Are you going to try to kill me?"

The ghost of a smile flitted across my face. A gleam from the amber liquid called to me in my periphery as I watched that floor for all I was worth. Just two old warriors having a drink. Nothin' wrong with that.

Explosions echoed in my head. Gunfire rat-tat-tatted across my mind. Swords clanged. Lots of late nights and amber liquids. Dead bodies littered my head.

"No…"

We'd both stared into the abyss. It had watched us back and made us blink. He'd been right. Callister understood in a way that the punk didn't get yet. If he survived, he would.

"You gonna be able to work with them?" he asked his desk, but his eyes found mine.

"Not much choice. We need them, both of them," I muttered. "We've planned as well as possible. Time to put things in motion." I spun and walked out of his office.

Though I heard his voice through the door saying, "May God have mercy on us."

Yeah, about that…

23

For the next couple of days both William and the punk had managed to avoid me outside of meetings and meals. During those times, everyone played perfectly polite, which I think disturbed the others more than our fights had.

I wasn't about to stoop to using mind-to-mind harassment of Henry to get answers. My cold war with William over his high-handed tactics was at a stalemate. Sadly, that was an old dance we were familiar with since it had been how we'd dealt with each other in the past. Whenever we'd fought, we both retreated, focused on work, and then hashed it out later when there was time. Probably wasn't the healthiest of habits.

Everyone else had already figured out that where it concerned me and any of the Brits, the best policy was to leave well enough alone.

We had a job to focus on and innocent lives hung in the balance. Okay, so maaaayyybe I was a bit grumpier and grimmer than before, but I was still working out how I was going to respond to what had happened.

Gilchrist had done as I'd asked. He'd saved the punk, but he hadn't healed me. I could kind of see why he would've made Junior do it, but that was like having a first year resident do surgery to fix the chief surgeon. You didn't leave things like that. Unless the management wasn't happy with the chief surgeon...Squirrels of that nature continued to chase themselves around my mind. Since it was too big, it got boxed and shoved into the closet in the back of my head. The conversation with Fisherman hadn't helped either. It still haunted my sleep. Into the closet with that one too. Needless to say, the closet was getting a trifle crowded.

Fisherman had decided to stay onboard ship with Pippa to coordinate the evac should that become necessary. At first, I'd thought that odd considering what he'd carried inside of him, but then another thought occurred to me: he didn't want to be that close to anything Infernal again. Frankly, he was right. It was too dangerous.

Coop, unaware that I'd known, had taken me aside and had said that between William, Cooper, and myself, it seemed unnecessary for Mylonas to be there, too many cooks and all that. I'd agreed with Coop, easing his mind and privately easing my own. Too dangerous by half.

The crew had been ordered to dress in civvies so we'd actually seem more like the cargo vessel that we were pretending to be. Our ship had docked with the other commercial vessels. Apparently, we even had some shipping containers to deliver. William's military crew in disguise would function as an actual shipping crew while we dealt with business.

It made the most sense for us to leave the ship in smaller groups: passengers, company people, crew, etc., so we planned to meet up in a parking garage in two vehicles, one for the boss and one for the bait. Edwards, William, and Junior left together: the businessman, his muscle, and driver. Grace, Ellie, and Clarice had departed, playing the part of girls on a shopping trip. Ivy had discreetly slipped off the ship with her equipment; just a blue collar gal on her way to work. Dobrek disappeared like the semi-legitimate businessman he'd used to be. Cooper and I went out into Marseille together—the tourist couple on holiday.

With all the people in town for the Festival de Marseilles, it was easy for us to slip in amongst the tourists. The city was all a bustle, and despite being mid-June, it'd been cool enough that a long-sleeved blouse and blazer wasn't out of place. With my hair down, and a pretty gauzy scarf around my neck, my coms were basically hidden. Cooper had managed with a nice navy colored windbreaker and ballcap.

We moved from shop to shop, museums, and anywhere that drew large crowds.

"I'll be right back," I murmured to Coop.

It wasn't hard to slip away, not with these crowds and my short stature.

I slipped down an alley and came out onto a busy sidewalk.

The team's chatter murmured in my ear piece.

A quick glance both ways and fleet feet had me across the street.

My fingers fumbled but managed to put the other ear bud into my ear. Music filled my head.

Their chatter increased. Someone asked where I was. Someone else asked if anyone was hearing music. An older melody filled my heart as I walked toward an arched portico and up its steps. The open but shaded entryway let a breeze through. A chill raced down my back.

Tremors sluiced through my hands as I gripped the cold metal handle and heavy wood, pulling the door open.

Voices rose as someone replied that yes, there was music playing—piano now, something American. Clarice and Cooper got called out on it.

Denials poured into my ear. Coop sounded annoyed.

I winced.

Different people connected to the Divine differently. It was how Humanity had ended up with so many various paths to the Holy. Music had always been a personal tie to that part of myself. Over the centuries, my tastes and what connected me changed, which made sense since I grew and evolved over time, or at least I sure as shootin' hoped that I did.

I'd discovered a remake of an older American song when Ivy had gifted me with a tiny music storage device something-pod while I'd been recovering.

She'd shown me how to put music on it. Boy, were they in trouble because this was the best! No wonder I'd seen people with these on their heads for years. So, while strains of the original had gotten me across that street. The remake helped me to find the courage to open the door...of a church.

Holy ground vibrated beneath my feet. Not all places of worship were Holy places, just like pristine wilderness wasn't always Holy either. I hadn't found a pattern to it and probably never would. That was okay. But when I did find one, whew, I knew it. Even the small amount of Darkness within me made it *hurt*.

This beautiful old gothic, Catholic church echoed with the sound of silence. Rather fitting. A handful of elderly people in black prayed their rosaries in French.

I took a small glass vial from my pocket and filled it from the finger font. Some of it spilled onto my hand. I bit my lip, stashing the vial and my burned hand back into my pocket as I made my way down the center aisle.

Sweat formed on my forehead.

Apparently, I'd gone farther afield than I'd realized.

The scents of incense and wood polish filled my nose. Flickering candles teased my eyes.

With no powers to protect me, this was incredibly difficult. I was laid bare as Human with all my faults and failings. It didn't help that there were underlying, darker thoughts on my mind.

The team's chatter felt like unwanted flies near my head, but I didn't dare take the bud from my ear.

I genuflected to one knee and slid into a pew closer to the back. The wood smelled of soap and lemons.

My guts twisted and turned in a way that had nothing to do with the Holy ground on which I sat and everything to do with a certain amount of prescience that this op was going to go so bad. Call it experience. Call it a Divine hunch. Call me superstitious. Didn't matter. I knew it like I knew when that op went bad *thirty-one years* ago.

Tremors laced my body with pain.

"Miss, are you all right?" a cassocked older priest asked in French. "Should I call someone?"

I turned to tell him to please just leave me be when our eyes locked.

He throttled his sharp inhale and switched to Old French, like fifth century old. "What are you doing here? Self-destruction is not a good look on you." The priest sat in the pew in front of me but turned around so we could talk. His short salt and peppered hair softened his intense dark brown eyes and tawny-beige skin, especially considering the lean warrior's physique he hid under those robes. When he used to let himself look younger...well, let's just say that the cassock helped.

"I needed guidance."

"You could have called. I am mostly certain you know what telephones are, yes?" He added drily. "I would have come to you."

"I am flattered, Tumas. You do not generally leave your sanctuaries. To be honest, I had not expected to find you here."

His gaze dropped to my right hand on the back of the pew.

The fingers were red and raw. My knuckles held dribbled burn marks down them.

A tsking noise escaped his lips. "Why? Ma chérie, why would you do this? And what has happened to you? How are you with so little power? Why is this hurting you so much?" He frowned. "What have you done? Or should I say, are you going to do?"

I lowered my hands and slipped black leather gloves on, trying not to hiss. "I am on the Hunt again, was brutally attacked, have far too much baggage, and a very bad feeling," my truthful words tripped over themselves in a rush. "Wrath dogs my footsteps."

Tumas sighed. Wrath and Vengeance were my two greatest weaknesses. It was one thing to have just cause and genuinely protect those who could not protect themselves; it was something else entirely to wrathfully exact vengeance, even on the Dark Ones. Manon had nearly killed all of us. The Human traffickers were not helping my temperament. It had been a bad couple of weeks.

We both knew this dance of old. His face softened, then morphed into a worried frown as his gaze wandered to the pews. "I thought you had quit that. You are right to be worried. There are so many threads...This has the feel of a Nexus point."

Nooooo...I stared at him wide eyed. A Nexus point was an essentially immutable moment in time where the events were going to unfold on such a cosmically, statically large scale of probability that for all intents and purposes, there was no changing it.

Someone called me across the headset insistently. Ivy?

My old friend abruptly glanced over my shoulder.

"Je regret, Père," Cooper's voice apologized from behind me in French. "I need to speak with my friend." His anger was palpable, even in my broken state.

I didn't turn. My breath raced like a bunch of chariots chased it. Everything was poised to crash on the turn of a coin. Couldn't stay here much longer. Couldn't face leaving.

Tumas' eyes narrowed, misreading my anxiousness. This was a place of power for him. Cooper wouldn't stand a chance.

"It's okay," I interceded in modern French. "He is a good warrior...and a friend."

My old friend didn't say anything. He just stared.

A side glance showed me that Cooper had leaned forward, cap in hand, and had slid down his sunglasses. "Look all you want. I already know what you'll find." Guessing that my friend was like me. He was almost right.

Tumas stood stiffly.

I did too.

Cooper straightened.

"Dieu te garde, ma petite fleur," Tumas blessed me and kissed my forehead.

The tremors stopped, but I knew that it was only temporary.

"Merci, mon chat," I joked back and turned to leave.

They hadn't moved, so I paused and glanced back.

Tumas leaned forward and shook Cooper's hand in a warrior's forearm grasp as he whispered something to him.

Cooper nodded. He turned and slid his shades back onto his face.

We walked outside.

I paused on the stairs, my breath coming in gulps.

"Cooper?" Bradford's voice queried.

"All good sir, clownfish in hand, on our way," Cooper quietly replied as he put his ball cap back on his head. Then he turned off his mic. "Little flower huh? Who was that, another old flame? And had you forgotten we were on the clock? What were you thinking ditching me like that? Seriously, Dade." Ooooohhhhh he was ticked, and as much as I hated it, he had every right to be.

"I'm sorry," I murmured and glanced around, taking the music bud out of my ear. Putting on my own sunglasses against the afternoon brightness helped my head. "He's an old friend. I didn't know he'd be here, and no, I hadn't forgotten. It was a little off-beat info gathering."

"Then who was he?" my friend demanded to know.

"Look," I paused. "as much as I trust you, Josh, who he is, what he is, and where he is aren't secrets that belong to me to share. He is a good man whom I would trust like I trust you." It would have to suffice as an explanation. "Don't suppose you're gonna tell me what he said?"

"Nope. Gonna tell me what you two talked about before I got there?"

"Nope."

"Okay," he sighed. "Let's go then. We're late."

"That's it? You're really gonna let this go?"

"Really." He gave me a sideways glance. "Look, either I can trust you or I can't. Ball's in your court." He turned his mic back on.

"Huh."

"Yeah, huh."

I started walking.

He put an arm at the small of my back, guiding me. "Managed to find a parking spot up the street," he muttered. Yup. Still ticked.

With a sigh, I turned off my coms and motioned discreetly for him to do the same.

Coop didn't like it, but he obliged.

"He's not like me, similar, but different," I said. "We've known each other a long time. I went there to basically get a sense of the odds."

"And?"

"We are such melba toast," I whispered. My fingers trembled as I pulled hair out of my face.

Something he didn't miss. "Anything we can do about it? Anything concrete?"

"Unfortunately, no. If I had something useful, I'd be telling you," I complained. "And did you seriously call me a clownfish?"

"Maybe."

We walked in silence, deciding to let sleeping fish lie.

I'd deal with whomever gave me that code name later. If we survived this.

24

Everyone had left the ship at various points during the day, taking turns scoping the parking garage where the meet was going down in the evening, getting supplies, and obtaining the lay of the land. I hoped super hard that the others had had better luck than I'd had.

The sun hung low in the skies. It had nearly set as Cooper and I pulled into a different parking garage. We'd found someplace discreet to meet up, load up, and prepare to go for bear. Edwards, Junior, and William were already there waiting for us. We got out of the SUV, and I opened the backseat door on my side.

"What? You decided it was a good time to go off book sightseeing?" Junior questioned me the minute I got out of the vehicle. "Seriously Dade, you're supposed to know better."

I took off the blazer to put on my holster and checked the Glock 19 I'd been issued. A smart aleck retort died on my lips as my periphery told me the punk stood at my four o'clock. Perfect position for me to deck him and he knew it.

William and Edwards watched us avidly.

While indulging in an elbow to his jaw for giving me grief in front of the others tempted me, now was not the time to physically or verbally take the punk to the cleaners for being a pain.

My breathing stopped for a second as the burn on my hand flared.

Temptation...

I cleared my throat. “My apologies for worrying people,” I said instead, “but I was chasing down a possible lead for further information.”

Junior blinked.

Surprising him had almost made reining myself in worth it. I focused on getting my suit jacket back on and settled.

The shocked silence was telling.

“And did it yield anything?” William asked.

I put a Ruger .38 into a small holster at the back of my waist, and checked my leg sheaths. It gave me an excuse to not have to look at him. “No, it didn’t.”

Coop gave me a side-eyed glance, but said nothing.

Junior missed it, but William had not. Edwards theoretically wasn’t paying attention either but I knew that was a load of hooey. There would be questions.

Grace, Ellie, and Clarice arrived with their ‘shopping’ bags and our remaining supplies. Edwards, Junior, and Cooper talked quietly with them as the trackers and assorted toys were distributed.

I quickly pulled my hair into a bun and kept my attention focused the other way, through the SUV’s interior.

“Who did you go see?” William demanded quietly from right behind me.

“Doesn’t matter,” I murmured. “It was a bust anyway.”

“Then why are you wearing gloves? In summer? You weren’t wearing them when you left earlier.”

That got him a glare. “They help with weapons grip. No fingerprints. All that good stuff,” I informed him. “Have you really been out of the field for that long? It’s nothing.”

His hand snaked out and grabbed my right hand. He surprised an involuntarily sharp inhale from me. “What-did-you-do?”

“Sir, Ellie has a question for you,” the punk interrupted, standing just behind his father.

William walked away, but gave me a look that said the conversation wasn't done.

"So, what did you do?" *That got you burned by something Holy?* He asked, a steel gleam in his eyes. *And since when were you so far gone, shall we say, that the Holy could burn you? Should I be worried? Should I be telling someone, oh like* him*?*

"I went to Paroisse du Sacre-Coeur, Church of the Sacred Heart, for a speculative assessment," I mumbled. *Don't you worry about me, punk, see to it that your own house is in order,* I thought at him sourly. He was far too astute for my comfort. "And if you threaten to tattle on me again, I'll kick your butt all the way to Hadrian's Wall." My glare was purely Human, but we both knew that had I been able to flare my power at him in anger without drawing attention, I would have.

He rolled his eyes with a satisfied smirk, as if I'd answered a question he hadn't asked but had wanted an answer to all the same, and he walked away. Somehow it felt as though I'd lost that one.

Dobrek pulled up in a black sleek sedan. The driver's side window whizzed down some. "Your car, sir," he joked in a deadpan voice.

"Hey, that's my line," the punk joked back while Grace fixed his lapels.

I turned my face from the others and switched to one of the private frequencies. "Hey Valkyrie, how's things?" I asked Ivy in a murmur. She was getting settled in at the buy site to watch over us.

"What? You get lost out there in the ocean?" she teased.

"Ah huh. No, went and grabbed one last item," I replied drily.

"Really?" Ivy sounded surprised. "What could you possibly have needed that our resident genius hadn't considered?"

"What's the last thing you'd expect me to carry?"

A silent pause. "Oooooh clever fishy," she said, then lowered her voice, "but be careful. I heard what the Bard said, and now it makes sense."

"Yeah, got that." I glanced around the area. "Think it's time for us to bring the party to you."

"Copy that."

I cleared my throat, looking at my watch. "Time to saddle up, kids."

Junior got into the driver's seat of the sedan, his father got in behind him. Dobrek hustled around to the other side of the backseat, giving me a nod along the way. Edwards climbed in the front.

The ladies climbed into our backseat with zip ties in their hands.

I got into the front passenger seat and turned around to go over the plan with them.

Ellie glanced down at my gloved hands and then back up at me. However, it was Trouble I saw staring through those clever brown eyes. It smiled.

I grinned.

Trouble's smile faltered.

I'd confused it.

Feeling satisfied, it seemed time to move on. "Okay, there's two pistols under that seat," I explained. "However, if things get that bad? Duck and cover first. Get any wounded back to this vehicle. It's armor-plated with bulletproof glass." I glanced at Grace and Clarice. "If we run into a worst case scenario and it's a full Infernal, one of you two sedates Taz and Trouble. You made sure Mary Poppins gave you enough to take out Junior or I? Because if it all goes South Pole, then I expect Trouble to possibly get a power boost and that would be super bad."

Grace gave me a look, like I'd asked her if she'd remembered to brush her teeth this morning. "Of course I did," she replied drily.

"Hey, I'd rather ask you and feel a little foolish than to find out in the clinch that you're not prepared," I said a trifle testily, which got a side-eyed glance from Coop.

"We know the plan, and we're prepared, Nemo," Grace informed me.

I turned back around to stared out the window.

Eliora.

Yes? I thought back at William with an irritated sigh.

You need to be calmer. Snapping at the team is not going to do anyone any good. Especially picking fights with Grace or Henry. He paused. *It's a good plan. Are you sure you're going to be okay doing this? Is that why you seem so angry?*

It was on the tip of my tongue to yell at him that I was angry because my gut told me that we were walking into a krabby-patty crapstorm. But if I'd let that irritated thought off its leash, then it was really going to morph into something bigger, badder, and altogether nastier.

Eliora?

William, I responded in a tightly controlled thought with a heavy exhale, *I am fine. I can do this. I stopped not only to get information, which didn't tell me anything that I hadn't already known really, but I also picked up some Holy water. Please let it go. We need to focus, not argue.*

Eliora, that was only part of the truth. I can hear your lie and feel your anger. There are things you're not telling me—again. His own anger was all too evident.

Fine! You want to know what I'm not telling you? I went to that church for inspiration, insight, whatever you want to call it, and it turned out that an old friend was there. He warned me that the odds are not with us for this to go well, William, I snapped at him. My fear fueled anger was sliding down the slippery slope to something far worse. My hand made the armrest on my door groan. The burn marks flared again.

Cooper mumbled something quiet.

Then why in God's name did you not tell me this sooner?! He shouted in my head. His temper had slipped its leash.

Yeah well he could join the party.

We need to bloody well pull this op then.

LANGUAGE! I yelled back. Lightning streaked across the sky. *You know better! And no, we are not pulling the plug. Edwards' niece's life is on the line and so are many other girls' lives. We are doing this. If we don't, we are never going to get this good a chance again and you know it. We'll spook the target. He'll go underground and move his operation.*

"Sir, we're closing in on the location," Henry told his father across open coms.

You tap Braxton's shoulder in front of you and tell that man that we are not going to rescue his niece. Go on. I'll wait. You tell him.

William's silence was telling. The connection between us lay open enough for me to have heard the thought that he'd refused to give even mind voice to, knowing its impact.

Don't bother to protect me from your thoughts, William. I heard you, and you'll be gratified to know I'm probably already well on my way. Are you going to be able to do your part, Commodore?

Commander Guillebert, do shut up. His mental voice reined in to controlled curtness.

Wait? The thought pulled me up short. *Since when was I a commander?*

Since you were reinstated in her Majesty's Service on our team. Based on your previous rank, service, and experience...and my say so, you were promoted to full commander. Just like I had been, well, before the ship set sail and they made me Commodore.

But, but I'm not Eliora anymore, I reminded him in a small voice.

Our cars crawled down the alley street to the entrance of the garage.

A part of you will always be Eliora. He twisted in his seat enough to catch my eye for a moment and then turned back around to face front.

The armrest groaned again.

"Breathe," Coop whispered to me.

Nemo, breathe, the punk told me at the same time.

Apparently, I'd stopped doing that oh-so-normal inhale exhale thing.

Our vehicles pulled up to the entrance. A small kiosk stood in the middle behind the automated ticket machine with its rates posted on the side. Junior said something to him and passed the man a small envelope.

The man nodded, gave a swift furtive glance at both vehicles, and stepped back into his kiosk, closing the door.

As our car passed, I could see him with a cell phone in his hands. I pulled down the visor and checked my makeup.

"Did he?" Grace murmured.

"Yeah," I muttered.

"He did say that our party had already arrived and was waiting for us," Junior warned the group in quiet tones. "I'd like to know why Valkyrie didn't mention that."

"Valkyrie?" I switched frequencies to the one she and I had used earlier. "Valkyrie?" Changed it back. "No word from our eye in the sky. I don't like it." My hands began sweating inside the gloves.

"Stay sharp, people. We must assume the worst," William said.

"We don't know that," I countered. "I just checked in with her ten minutes ago."

"We must still be prepared to have lost her in the interim, though with that time frame, she wouldn't have had enough time to give them any real information."

"Provided she wasn't compromised when the clownfish spoke with her," Grace interjected, "in which case who knows how much they heard."

"No, I don't think so," I assessed and then added. "Even if she were, they wouldn't have gotten anything from our conversation. We were careful."

Are we considering the coms compromised? I asked William.

We should for now. Radio silence from here on out. I'll tell my team; you tell yours.

I made a cut radio motion for them. After they turned theirs off, I spoke quickly, "Okay, the Commodore and I are calling for radio silence. We have to assume the coms could be compromised. Junior or I can broadcast in your heads if it comes to it."

Henry? Do you know how to broadcast?

Yes...

Good. If things go completely sideways, you or I will have to broadcast to the others for directions.

Copy that.

Huh. Chips were down and he was not only civil but on task. Who knew?

Don't forget, we need that location where they're holding their 'stock'. I reminded William.

I haven't forgotten, Eliora.

***

Ivelisse Nazario and the Enemy

Ivy had been thrilled that she'd managed to score an installer's van with two rolls of carpet tied to the top. It had provided the perfect cover for her to lie in wait for their 'guests' to arrive. Prior to that point, all she'd had to do was hang out in the back of the van and make sure she'd be ready.

Buying some cassoulet and fresh bread for dinner had been a lovely treat, a little heavier than she normally would've gone with, but it had been so worth it. However, all those meats and beans sat like a brick in her stomach now.

She listened to Nemo's snappish exchanges with both Bradfords, which made her wonder what her friend had been up to. Ivy checked her watch. It was time to get into place.

"Hey Valkyrie, how's things?" Nemo asked across coms.

A fast glance showed her that Nemo had chosen a private frequency. "What? You get lost out there in the ocean?" she teased.

"Ah huh. No, went and grabbed one last item," her friend replied drily.

"Really?" Ivy wondered now, her mind racing. "What could you possibly have needed that our resident genius hadn't considered?"

"What's the last thing you'd expect me to carry?"

Ivy thought back to how the Commodore had tersely grilled Nemo about her hands, and how she'd hissed in pain when he presumably grabbed one. Ivy had heard the clapping whump of his hand clasping hers. If her friend had been at a church, there was only one thing that might've burned her. But why would holy water burn her? Question for another time.

However, if it burned Nemo that much, then it would do a serious number on their prey. Excellent. "Oooooh clever fishy," she said, then lowered her voice, "but be careful. I heard what the Bard said, and now it makes sense."

"Yeah, got that," Nemo replied. "Think it's time for us to bring the party to you."

"Copy that."

Ivy shook her head. Her mani was up to no good, or up to good that was going to get her in trouble. She climbed into the front seat, leaving the weapon case on the floor in between the seats. The nose of the van was pointed at the wall, which made it a bit harder to make sure the coast was clear, but having the double doors facing outward in case of emergency made it worth the risk.

Not seeing anyone, Ivy slipped outside gingerly. She turned around to reach into the van for her case. In pulling it out, she found herself case to chest up against a man only four or five inches taller than her.

He smiled. This man scared her. It wasn't his dark beige skin, black hair, and dark brown eyes that had her speculating that their quarry had just found her, it was his eyes bleeding to completely flat black, like a shark's. No whites, nothing but an absence of light.

Her breathing sped up tenfold.

"Ooh, aren't you fun?" he drawled with an accented voice. "This is not your first time seeing one of my kind, is it?"

Ivy gripped the case to her chest like a shield. She slowly shook her head once.

His smile broadened into a grin. He let her see his second self's sharp teeth.

All her years of training deserted her. Suddenly she was a young girl back in Puerto Rico again.

"Oh sweet Ivelisse, how fun it would be to spend hours," he teased as he ran his index finger down the side of her face, "getting to know each other better, finding out what exactly makes you wake in a cold sweat at night."

She stopped breathing.

"However, I have other things to attend to, as I am certain you realize. So, since I am feeling generous, and because, quite frankly I think it will be more entertaining, I will give you an opportunity. If you walk away from this, no talking, no thinking, no contact with your team especially you newest friend for the next twenty-four hours, I will let you live.

"It will be delicious to watch you struggle with the knowledge that you let them walk into a trap, but it would mean saving your own skin. You would escape intact and live to fight another day."

"And if I refuse?" Ivy asked with more bravado than she'd ever known that she owned.

He leaned in to whisper in her ear. "I promise you, Ivelisse Acindina Nazario, that you and I will get to know each other very, very well... for a truly long time." The demon pulled back and smiled coyly. "You will never see the light of day ever again. That I can promise you."

A series of images flashed through her mind of what he had in mind.

Ivy swallowed hard. Tears slid down her face. "Ho- how long do I have to pack my gear and leave?"

The demon snapped his wrist, pulling his suit coat and shirt sleeve back, and glanced at his watch. "You have ten minutes before they will be here, so I would say you have five minutes to get out of this garage," he informed her, "and I do not think I have to remind you that I will know if you have broken your side of the bargain. Do we have a deal then?"

"Yes," she told him. "Please, just let me go."

His mouth lifted in a half smile. "Dear little Ivelisse, the world is a much more entertaining place with you in it. We have a deal." He turned, shoved his hands in his pockets and walked away as if he didn't have a care in the world.

Ivy yanked open the side door of the van. She frantically grabbed all her gear, shoved everything into the backpack and duffel she'd brought. Stealing a car was out because then she'd have to go past the team and that-thing. She knew where the pedestrian emergency exit was that would lead her back to the surface.

She slid the door shut with a clang and bolted for the stairs.

There was no need to pick a lock since it was an emergency exit. She'd already disabled its alarm because they had wanted to make certain there'd be more than one egress point. Ivy pounded up those stairs like all the hounds of hell chased her, which it felt like they might be since she couldn't shake the feeling of his sickening, dark power pursuing her.

Bursting onto the street level, a soft breeze blew across her sweaty skin.

Her hand made short work of wiping the tears from her face.

"He did say that our party had already arrived and was waiting for us," Henry's voice came across the comms. "I'd like to know why Valkyrie didn't mention that."

She needed to put some distance between her and the demon.

"Valkyrie?" Nemo called her. "Valkyrie?" She could hear the worry in her voice. "No word from our eye in the sky. I don't like it." Her voice returned to a more businesslike tone.

There would be time to worry about the team later. They had Nemo and Henry to protect them. Those two could handle things. She hoped.

Ivy quickened her steps.

25

Our vehicles pulled into the lowest level. After two parked cars, there were open spots, one on each side, just before concrete pillars. Another set of three cars lay on each side beyond that with another set of concrete pillars. A last set of three and then there was a dark alcove/entryway where a foot exit for stairwells, presumably, stood just out of sight.

Two of the cars that started the last set of three flashed their lights on our approach.

Junior pulled into the right hand spot and we pulled into the left one. It made sense since it put the 'buyer' farthest away from danger.

Car doors opening echoed all over the semi dark garage. The white tile walls did little to lighten the place. Then again, it could've just been my mood. Naw...

I saw four men get out of the car on our side. Wasn't sure how many exited the other car though.

My mirror showed that Junior had gotten out and opened the door for William.

Dobrek had jumped out and sprinted in a mostly dignified fashion around to William's side of the car, buttoning the jacket of his suit. If I hadn't known better, I would've believed he was an actual European business man, someone's assistant at that.

Edwards stepped out of the car, surveyed the area, and exuded exactly what his appearance dictated, a militaristic bodyguard, complete with muscles straining across the suit's cloth through his shoulders and chest. Thankfully, they had no idea that muscular physique held an incredible mind. Though the intensity of his gaze had me a little concerned.

As William's eyes took in everything, he whispered to me, *stay put until we send for you.*

Now wait just a gosh dang diddily moment. That hadn't been a part of the plan!

Coop made like he was going to open the door.

"Wait," I murmured. "Commodore said to hold."

"But that wasn't part of the plan," Cooper said, his expression soured. "What'd you do?"

My eyes widened in incredulous irritation, but my words were for Grace. "Twinkle Toes, you got eyes on the guys in that second car?"

"Ummmm...yeah, three guys, looks like extra muscle, and they're carrying," she told us.

"Hmmmm...four in the primary car. My gut says four originally from the second. So, either Goon Four is hiding nearby to jump us, or Goon Four is off dealing with Valkyrie. Either way, not a fan. Keep looking," I said, "oh, and no, I didn't *do* anything."

A snort sounded from the backseat. Amazingly, it wasn't Grace. Miss Twinkle Toes was all business.

I chose to ignore it.

"Damn," Grace murmured.

I turned to say something when I saw she had compact binoculars to her eyes. "What?"

"I count two suits and five goons," she muttered, "pretty well spread. All the goons are definitely packing."

"Dang," Coop muttered.

"Taz," I redirected to Ellie, "your Spidey senses tingling?"

Grace passed her the binoculars so Ellie could get a better look.

"No," our hacker said with a frown. "Not that I can tell from here. Looks like they're talking."

I wanted so badly to eavesdrop but that would pull enough of an energy expenditure to alert any Infernal who was aware and knew what to watch for.

"One of the suits is walking to the Co—the Bard," Ellie told us.

"Gimmie that," Grace commanded. "Looks like their logistics guy, or money man as you thought. He's doing something with the Bard's phone. The Bard just pocketed it. Other man is walking back to their leader. Athos pulled something from his pocket."

Cooper's cell went off and made us all jump.

"Bring them," Dobrek ordered in English, but his voice was thick with a Polish accent. He hung up before Coop could respond.

"Why didn't he just use coms?" Ellie demanded.

"Because they don't know for sure that anyone beyond Strider, Junior, myself, and Clownfish have them," Coop explained, "and we want to keep it that way. Let's go."

Coop and I got out and shut our doors. I opened the backseat door for the girls, whose hands were now zip-tied in front of them. They were supposed to act a little woozy from the imaginary sedative we'd supposedly given them to keep them compliant.

Coop pulled Grace along, grabbed Ellie, and then brought Clarice out so I could shut the door. Pretty sure I saw him squeeze her arm in reassurance. Something to file away for later.

Grace and Clarice stumbled forward with their 'guard'. Ellie lagged back like we'd planned, so I could bring her along and shield Trouble's presence if needed.

A soft whisper of wind blew by me. What the—?

We got a little past Junior, who leaned against the concrete pillar at my back left, when Ellie stumbled more than had been planned.

I moved in to pull her up and help her along, good guard that I was.

Snick. Jab.

Ellie had stabbed me in the inner thigh with a syringe!

My eyes lowered as I grabbed her hair to yank her head up.

Trouble laughed at me. *Gotcha! One Nemo or Junior grade dose of sleepy juice, as requested*, it told me in a laughing snarl.

Power filled my eyes as I tried desperately to burn through the drug. My ears rang.

Nemo! Junior shouted in my head.

26

The world did its best to tilt sideways.

With discipline scrounged from who knew where, I swallowed my power and did my best to ride out the effects of the drugs. This was not going to be pretty, and the longer I couldn't deal with the drugs in my system, the more impairing it would become, the harder to get rid of them. Thank God I wasn't seeing doubles of everyone yet.

My anger surged to the fore. I backhanded Trouble to the ground.

That drew attention.

It wasn't hard to haul her to her feet. I'd split the corner of her lip though.

Trouble laughed a husky, stoned sounding chuckle.

A nasally, quiet male voice spoke up. "Is there a problem? We won't buy damaged goods."

I glanced over at the buyers. The money man, assistant-type had spoken and looked concerned about their 'goods' being damaged. His voice said Croat. Hmmmm...

William, Dobrek, and Edwards were watching.

Cooper had Clarice and Grace leaning against a car hood to the left of our guys, just a little in front of them, but not too far. See the goods, but no touching yet.

"There's nothin' wrong that a little discipline won't cure," I responded in a thick Irish accent I hadn't used in decades. "She's feisty, this one is." I hauled Trouble along roughly.

Trouble obliged with some judicious struggling.

I told them to knock it off in Korean.

"Do they speak English?" the nasally man spoke up again. His boss just watched us. I pegged that suit at costing at least ten grand. Fisherman and I had been correct. Brazda had sent a lieutenant. Had to be Vinko Harvat, the one in charge of their trafficking.

"Oh aye," I replied. "They're bilingual Americans. Her an' the other one. Heard them talkin' to each other in Korean when they thought we weren't paying attention."

"And you speak Korean? How convenient," the boss drawled.

Oh hossapples.

"Aye," I replied slower. "A tour of duty with UN peacekeeping forces put me in South Korea for a year." I gave him a look as if to say what's it to ya? A little Irish attitude went a long way.

Trouble snickered again.

My head swung around as I delivered a glare and raised my hand to backhand them again.

William cleared his throat.

I nodded my head at him like a good soldier and dropped my gaze, with a split second side glare at Trouble.

"Such well trained staff, Mr. Smith," the boss drawled in cultured tones, his Croatian accent subtle and exotic sounding.

William inclined his head. "Thank you."

The boss let his eyes travel over Cooper, the girls, and I. His arm crossed as he rested an elbow on it and stroked his goatee. "Very well," he mused aloud. "We'll take all three girls. It would be useful to have two bilinguals, and the other is quite stunning. However, we want your Irish guard too."

William's eyebrows climbed as he glanced at Dobrek.

Dobrek pulled out his phone, but gave a slight negative shake of his head.

"Oh yes, the wifi in this garage is turned off at oh," he snapped out his wrist and glanced at his watch, "about now."

The floor tried to tilt on me again.

"I'm sorry, but her services are not for sale," William intoned politely.

"Then the deal is off; we will find someone else with whom to do business," the boss man replied casually.

Hoary higgity heck a doodle. I cleared my throat. "What're payin'?"

Boss man smiled.

William gave me a look. *Eliora.*

"What? I'm on contract. I ken go where I like," I countered firmly, but politely...to my, ahem, boss.

"See? I love an adventurous, enterprising young woman," the boss said in delight. "We will gladly match what they were paying you, plus ten percent more as a signing bonus. How does that sound?"

I had my gaze on the floor, trying desperately to make it stop moving. With a deep breath, but working hard not to let anyone know just how hard I was working, I looked up and nodded. "Sounds jest fine."

"Excellent. Then bring the girls to the address we have provided your former employer and I will see you there, budala," he crooned. His mouth broke into a smile just for me.

I had seen that evil grin before. Though not in many, many decades. Okay, maybe a few centuries. It looked wrong though.

Then their boss let me see *its* eyes.

A full Infernal!

The Infernal pulled its weapon and shot William in the chest. No muss, no fuss.

"*No!*" Junior screamed.

It pulled the trigger for a second shot, but Dobrek had pulled William's collapsing body to himself.

The shot missed William and grazed Dobrek.

Edwards pulled his pistols and began shooting, trusting Dobrek to deal with William.

Cooper drew too and began shooting.

Grace pulled Clarice down.

I full out decked Trouble, but not hard enough to break Ellie's neck. Definitely hard enough to knock them unconscious.

A sting smacked my right upper arm as I pulled back afterwards.

The whole space echoed with all the gunfire.

Car alarms went off everywhere.

My vision was getting hazy. "Fall back!" I yelled. "Fall back!"

Grace, Clarice, get Ellie and Trouble to the truck.

Cooper, cover their retreat.

Dobrek, get William to the car.

Edwards, Henry—cover them. I'll try to help Dobrek.

Cooper pushed the girls back, his back to them as the firing continued.

That thrice blasted Infernal smiled at me before disappearing behind the wall and out the emergency exit.

Goon Four stepped out from behind that wall with some sort of portable Gatling gun. I couldn't see straight and some of the lights had been shot so they flickered. Then its rat-a-tat-tats began.

I dove for Dobrek and William, shielding the three of us.

Then there was no Gatling fire pelting my shield.

I stared stupidly in that direction, my nose bleeding.

"Junior took him out!" Dobrek shouted at me in Polish.

William grabbed my shirt with his fist. *Eli—*

I gave him what healing I could. There wasn't much energy left in the bucket. I turned away and threw up.

Gun fire still hurtled past us.

Car—now! I thought at Dobrek, unable to speak out loud.

Dobrek got himself under William's one shoulder while I got myself under the other. It was messy but with Junior and Edwards covering us, we got to the sedan.

Henry! Car! Now!

We shoved and pulled William into the backseat, me under his upper body, Dobrek under his legs.

Cooper backed out with the girls in the SUV.

Shots still fired.

Henry yanked open the driver's side door and started the car. He squealed the tires as he backed out.

Edwards ripped open the front passenger door while still shooting. He folded himself in, yelling, "Go! Go! Go!"

27

Our car careened down the streets at high speeds, following Cooper back to the docks.

Dobrek was on the horn, presumably talking to Fisherman.

I hugged William to me. His pulse grew weaker and weaker. It'd been a heart shot. I kept pumping power into him...and his heart kept pumping it out. For some reason, I couldn't heal the tear within him. I couldn't see straight. Maybe I was doing it wrong. Though I didn't think so. Dobrek and I had a compress going on his chest, but what we needed was a surgeon and a whole lotta blood.

William mind-whispered something but I couldn't catch it.

"Stay with me, stay with us, don't you dare leave now," I mumble-cried in Gaelic.

"Nemo!" Henry shouted at me.

"I'm doing the best I can!" I yelled back. "Get us to the ship. He needs a doctor!" And I needed to puke again because the punk's driving was atrocious. I managed to get a hand on the button and got the window to go down some. The fresh air helped.

William's hand held something hard, digging into my leg.

William, never mind that. Focus on healing. I told him sternly.

Phone...his voice felt more distant than it should've been.

I shoved his phone into an inner leg pocket that had a velcro closure for important things I didn't dare lose. If he'd used this much energy to pass his phone to me, there was something critical on it he wanted me to have.

It was late enough that the docks were mostly deserted. Our men poured down from the ship bringing multiple backboards.

"Sir, you have two GSWs that we can see," a waiting medic said to Edwards as he climbed from the car.

"Doesn't matter," the warrior snarled, took a step, and collapsed.

"GSW to the chest," I told one medic about William. "He's lost a lot of blood. Pulse is thready—"

"Ma'am, you've been shot," another said to me.

"I'm fine," I tried to shrug him off, but ruined it as the world tilted again. I threw up once more, falling to my knees.

Time slowed down, essentially stopping. To my senses, it felt very similar to how it's pictured in the movies. Things moved in slow motion. Sounds became distorted. Everything began to freeze, or came so close to it that there was little difference.

I knew.

My head lifted in its own macabre slow motion and saw what I most dreaded.

William's Soul and the Archangel of Death herself stood just a few feet behind all of us watching the chaos.

Different cultures over the centuries had called her by many different names, the Morrígan, Azrael, Kali, but that the Lady had come personally to collect William was a message—to me.

There would be no cursing, at least not any productive kind. No helpful battle rage. No storming the castle. No take backs. No do overs. No mulligans. His time in the Mortal world was done. He was moving on to the other side. Forever beyond my reach because as far as any of us knew, Nephilim didn't go to the Heavens.

Her voice hissed in my mind. *You may speak...*

"William," I whispered, my eyes filling.

Eliora, all will be well. I understand that now. You and he need to take care of each other. Try not to do anything too stupid, either of you. I love you both. They disappeared.

He had left between one second and the next, between one moment and the next, to somewhere only Celestials, Infernals, and the Dead may go. A place I had never seen, nor ever would. He'd crossed to the far second of Eternity.

Time resumed.

"William!" I croaked a scream, but no one paid me any mind. Or rather, the others took it as my due.

The medic picked me up and carried me onto the ship.

I fought to stay conscious. It wasn't easy. More puke went over the side of the gangplank.

William...

***

Lonesome Agent, Long Shadows – Ivelisse

Ivy moved briskly down the sidewalks as if she had somewhere to be. She did. Anywhere but near that garage.

Her shoulders tensed yet again and she hitched the backpack higher. Ivy's left hand tightened its grip on her duffel. Her right hand sweated all over the rifle case's handle. The case had been disguised as a viola case, complete with assorted ratty stickers from around the world.

She was an agent; she could do this. Ivy glanced over her shoulder again and picked up her pace, unable to shake the feeling of being followed. Would he have bothered? It didn't make sense because he had other business to attend to very soon.

She needed someplace safe.

"I went to Paroisse du Sacre-Coeur, Church of the Sacred Heart, for a speculative assessment..." her hermana had said. She'd met up with someone she knew, so that meant there was most likely someone there who knew about such things.

It had to be nearby. Ivy veered to where the mouth of a small alley met the sidewalk. Setting her duffel and case down, she pulled out her phone and searched. There! Barely a klick away from where she was.

Short work to memorize the map. Phone went back into her pocket as she hefted her gear and got moving.

Ivy used every pavement artist maneuver she'd ever learned. She blended. She checked reflections everywhere. She stopped to shift her gear.

No one seemed to be paying her any particular attention. There were musicians and artists aplenty here for the festival. She must've heard eight different languages being spoken in the last two blocks.

Yet she couldn't shake the feeling that someone, or something, still stalked her.

She hustled up her pace.

The streets were beginning to empty out as the hour grew later.

Finally, Ivy noticed a shaded portico across the street. There were a couple of steps leading up to it. The church!

With a fast glance in both directions, Ivy darted across the street. She dashed up the couple of brick steps into the portico with its ivory stucco archways open to the night air, except the one ahead of her that contained two massive wooden doors with twisted iron handles.

A dim, overhead fixture cast little light.

Ivy set her case down and yanked on the metal door handle.

The door didn't budge.

"No!" she whispered tersely and yanked harder.

Nothing.

Tears threatened.

She had her back to the road. Her muscles itched.

It felt as though something were coming.

"Please," she murmured to the air, "please, I beg sanctuary."

A tall, dark shadow appeared to her right under the arched opening. Night air blew from behind him.

She got scents of incense and cedar.

"Why? Why should I grant you sanctuary? You reek of sulfur." His accent said French, but she couldn't make out his features.

"Please," Ivy choked out, "it's coming for me. I can feel it."

He took a step forward as his head tilted upward. Almost as if he were sniffing the air. "Oui, c'est possible."

"Please help me," she cried, tears streaming down her face. "She will need me. If I'm dead, I can't help her."

The shadowy figure stepped forward, his cassock snapping in the night breeze. He was taller than the dark one, a priest, but like no priest she had ever seen before. His dark, angry stare frightened her. She felt utterly bare in his scrutiny.

Those angry brown eyes narrowed as he loomed over her. "You allowed it to contaminate you, Ioudas. Tell me, truly, why I should rescue you?"

Ivy sobbed. "Por favor Padre, perdóneme. She and the young one are more than a match for it. I am one small Human. I do not wish to die." She dropped the duffel and threw her arms around the priest. "Perdóneme..."

***

Tumas stiffened and went still. His gaze drilled through the portico's ceiling with an arched, long suffering stare. His arms awkwardly went around the woman. "Estar en paz," he crooned, offering her peace. "I absolve you of your sins, child, but you must go. Return to your ship."

"Could I not stay here?" she asked, sniffling and pulling back. The woman worked hard to regain some composure.

He put his hands on her upper arms and gave her a tired, but indulgent look. "No, mi querido. You must be brave. Here." He reached into his pocket and pulled out a worn, wooden beaded rosary. "Take this with you. It should protect you until you are able to reach the others."

Her head nodded like one of those ridiculous bobble heads the shops sold to tourists.

She sniffed. "Todo bien," the woman murmured and gathered her gear.

"If you go left along the street, there should be some drivers willing to drop you off at the pier," he offered. There were a couple of watering holes that way, but no one would bother her. He knew that much.

The woman nodded and began to leave.

"Oh and Ivelisse."

She paused and half turned, her eyes wide.

"Fear is understandable. It may keep one alive. Then again, it may also lead one to fall," he warned. "Lest you forget, even Humans may Fall."

He could see her chewing the inside of her lower lip as she nodded again. "Gracias, Padre."

When she was out of sight, he sighed. *This was not what I signed up for*, he grumbled to the Ether.

A tall, lean man with dark curly hair and close cropped beard stepped from the gloom to stand next to him. His kaleidoscope eyes flickered rapidly. "No, but it is what we needed of you."

"You have altered the deal," he muttered.

"Pray that it is not altered further," the other growled, obviously unhappy with the direction things were moving. He disappeared.

"Your sense of humor leaves much to be desired, mon frère." He frowned at the air. "And it is now abundantly clear where she got hers." Father Tumas turned around and went back into his church to pray for strength for what he sensed was to come.

28

Me watched. She waited.

I hung by my fingernails. And it seemed that the cosmos was very intent on doing a flamenco dance on my fingers.

Due to all of our injuries, they'd set up the lounge as a general triage area.

The gunshot to my right upper arm had at least been a through and through so there was that. Not that I had even a whisper of juice to deal with it.

Everything kept trying to get up and run away from my vision. It left me blinking a lot.

Grace wasn't here. Someone'd said she was waiting with Fisherman in the hall outside where they were doing surgery on Edwards. He'd taken slugs to the lower abdomen, left shoulder, and his left thigh.

Dobrek had some cuts and a graze on his right upper arm, but nothing too horrible.

Cooper had taken a through and through to his left arm, though nothing worse. Clarice stood hovering over him regardless.

Trouble and Ellie were still out cold. They'd been placed on part of the sectional. The medics had me in one of the card table chairs while they finished sewing up my arm and annoying me with flashing lights. "Ow, stop that," I groused.

"Commander, we have to see if you have a concussion," the medic informed me. "Dr. Weatherford has concerns that you'll relapse."

"Mmmm...yes, Dr. Weatherford," I retorted drily. Pippa could go eat donkey dung.

He sighed. "We at least need to make sure you don't have any further injuries." His glance covered all of me, which was covered in blood.

"It's not mine," I whispered.

"No, it's the Commodore's," Clarice declared angrily.

"Leece," Cooper cautioned, gently grabbing her upper arm.

She shook him off. "No! This is her fault," she railed at me. "How did you not know? How could you have led us into a trap like that? When Ivy dropped out of coms, that should've been a big red flag!"

I stood up on shaky legs, drawing angry noises from the medic. "Because I got stabbed by your cousin with a syringe full of knockout juice!" I yelled back, voice building up steam. "How did you not know that Trouble was driving the fucking bus?!!"

They all paused, waiting for the thunder.

"Yeah! See? I am standing on sheer force of will right now," I snarled. "I'm just as Human as the rest of you."

"You will always be more than Human," Junior said quietly from the doorway, echoing his father's words from earlier.

I turned away from him.

The world spun.

My body stumbled back towards the chair I'd been sitting in a moment ago. A shaking hand went to my forehead trying to make things stop spinning.

"*FUCK!*" I screamed and threw the chair.

Henry strode over to me and got in my face. "I don't care what it takes. I don't care what you have to do to me," he sniffled, "just bring him back. Fix this. You did it once before. You have to do it again, you need—"

"I can't," I tried to explain.

His head bobbed in a shocky nod. "Yes, yes you can. You've done it before and you can do it again."

"Why do you even think I can do it?"

He paused, dropped his gaze, and then stared over my shoulder. "Because I heard the two of you arguing in your room."

The others glanced away in awkward silence.

"You were eavesdropping on us?!" I demanded. That couldn't be right. Didn't sound right. The punk was a lot of things, but so invasively stupid couldn't possibly be one of them. That was low, even for him.

"My mother had said I wasn't to leave you two alone unsupervised, so yeah, I listened," he said to the wall, "and I know you brought him back to life. So, please," he put his hands on my upper arms. Ugly tears mottled his face. "*Save him.*"

I shook my head in the negative.

The world spun some more.

My stomach heaved more. "I am so sorry, Henry," my words choked me as pain, both of ours, twisted my gut. "I can't. He's beyond my reach."

"Fix this!" Henry snarled at me.

Thunder rumbled in the distance. Oh sure, he had juice left.

His eyes widened, and he spun around to take off at a run.

"Oh hecatate hogwarts hairy harlots no!" I sputtered, realizing what he was thinking. A painful lunge that surprised him, let me grab Henry by the arm and spin him back. "You are not trying that. Hell no."

"THEN DO SOMETHING! FIX IT!" he screamed.

"I WOULD FUCKING FIX IT IF I THOUGHT BURNING THE WORLD TO THE GROUND WOULD MAKE IT WORK BUT IT WON'T, YOU PEA BRAINED MORON!"

Thunder clapped and lighting streaked across the skies.

Now we were both ugly crying.

"I have the power to shape Reality itself to my Will but he has gone beyond this world's Reality, beyond where I can reach him. His Soul stood on that pier with an honest to goodness Archangel and said goodbye to both of us. You weren't listening!"

Thoughts of that moment pierced me. I heaved gasping sobs. "*I loved him more than I have loved any being in over two thousand years and he is gone!*" All that remained was a yawning chasm of grief as I sank to my knees. "There is nothing left but you. You who hates my very being with every breath he takes."

The weight of his anger smothered me, riding the pulse of his power. Even in my state, I could tell his rage was putting him at risk. "Damn you, Nemo," he swore.

Thunder rolled again.

"Damn you to Hell."

The lights flickered.

I gasped in pain, curling in on myself, as his Wrath sucker-punched me. The weight of his condemnation broke my will.

He tore out of the room.

I crawled into the hallway on hands and knees and sank to the floor, sobbing as quietly as I could manage.

Dobrek came into the hallway with a box of tissues. He said not a word, but let himself sink down so he was sitting next to me. His arm went around my shoulders and pulled me into his chest.

I gave up and cried.

Tears slid down Dobrek's face too.

It poured out until there was nothing.

29

We stood.

Aleksander's head rested against the wall, his eyes closed.

Some things we could not fix.

However, some things we could fix. We would fix.

It was easy to get to the kitchen and demand a container of salt. No one was going to argue with us. Not today.

We made it back to where we had left the others.

"Nemo?" Aleksander asked while rubbing his eyes.

Nothing said seemed like a better course of action, so we walked past him into the room.

The demon shard and girl still lay on the furniture.

We set the salt down on the table and walked over to them.

It was surprisingly easy to drag her off the furniture and across the floor to an open space. The Nemo/Eliora personas had gratifyingly already cleared the space earlier.

We paused and considered how problematic the situation had become. The Eliora persona was supposed to have been dead, but the emotional connection between her and the Beloved had brought her back, impeding the Nemo persona's ability to think, to function. Their broken transition also impeded their connections to Energy. We were not so hampered. Maybe a good thing from the Beloved's death would be that one could pass and the other move forward now. We would watch and we would wait, then we could decide how to proceed.

Joshua came running up the stairs into the room. The host's kin followed him closely.

Ivelisse appeared in the hallway door where she stood slightly behind Aleksander. That was gratifying. She lived. *It is good to see you alive, Ivelisse. Nemo will be pleased*, we thought.

"Me," Joshua said gently, getting our attention, "what are you doing? Why are you here?"

"We are fixing what we can. The youngling broke the Nemo persona," we paused as our anger flared. "Too much has happened—this one betrayed us, the Beloved passed on where we will never go, the young one called down judgment, her body was broken to start. I am...what is it she says? I am driving the bus now."

They all had varying expressions of concern and fear. For now, that was acceptable.

We began pouring the salt circle. "This has gone on for far too long," we murmured. "It ends now."

Ivelisse disappeared, running down the hall. That was probably for the best. We did not need her for this, though her faith would have been helpful, but if she were that scared, then it was good for her not to be present. The fear would draw the little demon's attention.

This was a demon shard, a splintering of a more powerful demon's psyche. Infernals lost their power for Creation when they fell. They could not have children per se, save maybe the Lightbringer. What did happen, though, was some very powerful Infernals fractured in not only their personalities, but their powers as well, creating side personalities with a certain amount of consciousness. They were skewed, limited. Not very bright generally speaking. Mostly, they were echoes of the original Infernal. If there was anything left of the original, that Infernal tended to spend eons hunting down the broken pieces of power.

We started a prayer of sanctification in our old Gaelic mother tongue.

The two on the floor cried out as their backs bowed.

Chun Hei Clarice stepped forward, but Joshua held her back. "She's hurting her!" she exclaimed.

"This will hurt her, " we agreed, "but when we are done, she will be free."

"How do you have any..." Joshua paused, seeming to search for a word.

"Power? Energy?"

"Yeah," he said and nodded.

"We *are* Energy," we breathed as the circle closed. A limited amount of our true nature manifested.

The little demon did not like that, not at all. It writhed and shook and made the Human, Hyun Ellie, flop like a fish while speaking in languages these Humans could not even guess.

We continued with blessing Hyun Ellie, then paused. "Toss me that ointment," we directed Aleksander, who had just come and joined us in the room.

He did, thankfully, without question.

Blessings and a piece of our Holy light infused the oil, making it Holy. We made a sign on the top of Hyun Ellie's head, her forehead, her throat, her heart, her solar plexus—

The little demon bucked and snarled, trying hard to throw us off what we were doing. It swore. Then begged Chun Hei Clarice, "Help me! Help us! She's killing us! Sure, we'll be saved, but we'll be dead too." It made Hyun Ellie cry.

Her kin lunged forward again, but Joshua held on to her, tucking her into his chest and turning her away from what was happening.

We finished the blessings of the final two energy points. "In the old Sanskrit tongue, these were called chakras," we told the others.

"They still are," Aleksander said quietly, his eyes riveted to the two on the floor.

"But I thought you were a Christian, a—a—Catholic being," Chun Hei Clarice accused as she turned her head to face us. She was apparently still angry.

"There are many roads to the Great Divine," we replied gently.

It spat at us and then did something unexpected. "Neeeeemmmmoooo, Nemo Dade, wake," it called by name and by power.

We felt the Nemo persona stir. So did the Eliora one. That was not good. They had become tied together, confused and broken.

The little demon used Hyun Ellie's voice. "Nemo! Help! Me is killing me to stop Trouble!" it screamed.

Consciousness rose. Gathered speed and awareness.

"We will not let you stop this," we informed them.

I'm going to help, but we will—

Wrench!

"Do it my way, you overgrown, draconic butterfly!" I shouted, breathing hard, hands on my thighs.

Trouble grinned at me. That couldn't be good.

"Yes," Cooper cheered in a fervent whisper.

Dobrek nodded.

Clarice stared at me uncertainly.

The world tilted a little. I had to hurry. My current state of power was a limited time offer courtesy of Me.

"Hyun Ellie Kang, sleep dear Holy child, sleep in the Light of Grace, and be at Peace," I intoned.

Their eyelids fluttered. Ellie's eyes finally closed. She sank back against the floor. Now we could all see Trouble's gangly, misshapen body superimposed, lying face up above Ellie's.

Clarice gasped a scream.

Coop shielded her, trying to get Ellie's cousin to turn away from the sight.

She refused to though.

A noise caught my attention. Ivy stood in the doorway, a little behind Dobrek. She had a gun in her hands, trembling, safety off, prepared to shoot.

"Eassssy, Iv," I cautioned.

"How'd you get back? When did you get back? How did you survive?" Dobrek shot questions at her. "We thought you were dead." Apparently, he hadn't been paying attention earlier. I think we were all a little shell shocked.

"I escaped," Ivy mumbled, refusing to look at anyone but the creature.

"Why not tell us though?" Josh demanded.

"Couldn't use my coms. Someone came after me, but I got away. Had to wait and make sure it was safe to come back," she explained.

In my heightened state, I could tell she was leaving things out. "Ivy..."

"You don't know," her hoarse voice mumbled in Spanish.

Oooooh I had a guess, or two.

Trouble took advantage of my inattention and clawed at my ankle with its mismade hands. One had two fingers and a thumb. The other had five and a thumb. Guess which one it used? "Burn," it commanded.

I yelped, hard. A growl left my lips as the skin on my right ankle sizzled and smoked. Thoughts whirred in my head. Trouble shouldn't have had this much power. So, how?

It yanked hard and I went down on the floor, my head bouncing off the tiles. Thankfully, the circle remained intact.

"Damn you, Nemo," it whispered in Henry's voice.

My gut seized and my eyes shut tight, trying to push Trouble out of my head.

Then the stench of sulfur, rot, and body odor filled my nostrils.

My hand shot out as the base of my palm hit where its nose should've been.

Its teeth grazed my wrist.

I shoved harder to push it away.

WHAT are you doing?

Oh no. Henry...*Ahhhhhh...trying to exorcize Trouble from Ellie. Um, hi, how are you doing? We're fine here. Really*. I stopped talking. No time for conversation anyway.

Trouble was trying to bite me again.

No response came, which wasn't surprising.

Time to swallow some humble pie and hope—a lot. I shielded harder so Trouble wouldn't know what I was doing. *Henry Galahad, I call you. I summon you as a fellow Nephilim, bound by our ties, and as your commanding officer.*

Seriously? His extra surly, incredulous thought came back at me.

Oh that wasn't good.

"Nemo!" Cooper shouted.

Trouble tried to bite my leg this time.

"Nemo," Dobrek called and threw a water bottle at me.

"Genius," I muttered with a smile and blessed the water with everything that I'd borrowed from Me's holiness.

No time for niceties. I squeezed hard to make the cap pop off, but the seams split too, spilling lots of now Holy water on both of us.

The water sizzled on it.

Trouble howled.

Sadly, it didn't feel great to me either, which was really bad. I tried not to think about whether I could in fact get the job done.

Henry pushed past Ivy, striding into the room. He stopped, turned, and snatched the gun from her hands, put the safety on, and chucked it onto the sectional. "Invite me in," he growled.

I did my best to get Trouble in a choke hold. "Henry Galahad Bradford, you are welcome in this Holy place. Come into this circle."

He pushed through a membrane of light green power, and the three of us felt it like a pop in our ears.

Trouble grabbed me in those clawed hands and threw me over its head.

I hit the barrier upside down with my back. My body landed with a crunch and a thud. Eh, I didn't need that shoulder anyway.

My watering eyes begged to differ.

Henry reached through Trouble and pulled up Ellie's shirt. She had a belly button ring. Something silver and iridescent blue-green.

A series of very dark thoughts began rolling in my head.

"Stop," Henry commanded me. "Stop right there or I walk out of this circle and let you two hash this out without me."

Scrabbling to get on my feet, I muttered, "Fine." My nasty thoughts would keep.

Henry tried to dislodge the piercing. "It's been spelled to stay in place," he snapped. "I'm sorry Ellie." His eyes shifted to a swirl of blue-green and white. He tore the ring from her navel.

Ellie and Trouble screamed.

"Ellie!" Clarice screamed too.

Either the damage of removing the power item, or the scent of fresh blood, distracted Trouble enough to stop it moving.

Henry put the ring under his shoe and crushed it while speaking in Fae.

The ring exploded in a burst of dark, sickly green power.

A stench of burnt flesh filled the circle.

Dobrek flinched.

I stared.

The punk grabbed my right hand, my busted shoulder's right hand. I cried out in pain.

His power crashed into me hard.

I couldn't breathe. Panic crowded out thought.

Then something more Ethereal, more familiar, soothed and held—us.

No, no, no, no, no, no!

I shoved Me back down, but at least I knew why his power felt familiar in a good sense. They'd worked together to save the ship.

It was rough, but I released my own power, what was left, and joined with his.

An explosion of sparks!

I couldn't see.

Galahad was so bright, so...good-hearted.

A gasp escaped me.

This, this was the persona I'd agreed to safeguard, to train, to care for until there was no more.

My Energy encircled his. Guided his power without dominating.

We found balance. Our Ethereal selves.

Together we sang. We blessed Hyun Ellie Kang and cast out the Infernal, back to the depths of Hell. "Damn you to Hell for all Eternity, never to return to the Mortal World," Henry Galahad and I commanded Trouble. Together, we were too powerful for it to stop us from sending it back where it'd come from in the first place. This wasn't its home plane, which was why it had needed a Human host.

Ellie's eyelids fluttered as she struggled to sit upright.

I broke the circle with my Will and foot.

Clarice rushed in, sinking to the floor and hugging her cousin.

My glance caught Fisherman standing in the entryway.

He nodded.

I switched to watching the girls hugging and crying in the broken circle. As beautiful as it was to see them reunited properly, my heart hurt. This victory had cost us far too much. And the war wasn't over yet.

Pushing back sweat-soaked hair, I stared out over the stairwell. Wasn't gonna look over at him. Nope. No way.

Everyone seemed to have stalled. Unsure what to do or where to look.

I glanced over at Fisherman. "Yer gonna need a bigger boat."

Cooper barked a laugh.

Dobrek glared at him.

"What? She's right. And da—dangit, that was funny."

We all laughed in our various ways and various states of mind.

Then I realized two somethings. Henry was still holding my hand. And that my brain thought of him immediately as 'Henry', not the punk or Junior.

"Excuse me," I mumbled. "I need some air." It wasn't hard to burst from the room past Fisherman and race to my spot on the upper deck. What had been hard was letting go of Hen-the punk's hand. I frowned harder.

Once I was on the upper deck, I crashed onto hands and knees, stuck my head in between the rails, and puked again and again.

Fingers gently pulled back my hair.

"Go away please," I croaked. There. See? I asked nicely.

"He used to talk to you, you know," Henry said softly.

"What?"

"No really, he did it, all the time," he added. "My father would sit and drink his scotch and talk to this little framed photograph of you. Mind you, he kept it hidden in a drawer most of the time."

I gave him an unfriendly sidelong glance.

"Yeah, I know." He shrugged. "He did his best to hide it from me."

I sighed, not knowing what to say to that.

"He loved you," Henry murmured, "very much."

"Yeah...but he loved you more," I countered. "You know how I know that?"

He risked a glance at me.

I stood up on shaky legs and wiped my mouth on a bloody dress shirt sleeve. “Because he gave up me to have you in his life.”

I walked away. I had to. If I’d stayed, I would’ve said something that we were both going to regret.

He didn’t move.

Smart punk. He was learning.

30

I walked into my quarters. The first thing that hit me was that the Monet over my bed was missing. My hands were on the radio before I'd even realized that I'd crossed the room. "Get me Mylonas."

"Ms. Dade? Where are you?" Fisherman's voice crackled on the radio.

"I'm in my quarters. Where is the Monet?" I barked.

"Ah, I'm sorry, but we had to give it back," he responded cautiously.

My imagination put Pippa there and the two of them sorting and discarding syringe options full of knock out juice.

"Anyone touches the San Giorgio Maggiore and I will tear that person's arms off with my bare hands. Am I clear?" As far as threats went, I figured that was pretty solid. It was well within my abilities, and I knew there had to be staff nearby hearing this. Witnesses were oh so useful sometimes. "I would like dinner in my room and not to be disturbed until at least mid-morning."

"Understood, Ms. Dade," he responded slowly. "Debriefing then at eleven hundred hours, my office? Just us."

"Fine." I turned the radio off and threw it onto the bed.

Peeling the disgusting blouse that I'd put on at the beginning of the day proved harder than I'd planned. A busted shoulder did that sort of thing. Extending my senses, I realized that it was only dislocated. My head dropped.

A knock sounded at the door.

"Go away."

The sounds of a key in the lock drew a sigh from me.

Dobrek let himself in and shoved the keys back in his pocket. He too was wearing the same clothes. "Broken or dislocated?"

"Dislocated," I muttered.

He walked over to me and nodded at the ruined shirt.

I shoved it in my mouth and sat on the edge of the bed.

Dobrek slipped his foot out of his shoe and put it along my side so his toes were almost in my armpit and grabbed my arm. "Ready?"

I nodded.

He carefully yanked and shifted his weight as my shoulder popped back into place.

Several screams flew into the cloth in rapid succession.

Gingerly pulling back, he slipped his shoe on and went into my bathroom. Dobrek returned with a cup of water. "Here. Don't tell on me that I let you have some," he said gruffly while handing over a prescription bottle. "They're for pain, but they won't knock you out like whatever that stuff is that she keeps hitting you with...unless you want to knock yourself out?"

"No," I answered, hoarse, but emphatic. "Thanks. I need to eat first."

He gave me a nod and headed for the door.

"Hey," I called. My voice cracked. "Whose keys?" Because as far as I knew, Dobrek didn't have that many keys to this place, let alone one to my room.

Dobrek half turned. A brief smile flitted across his face, but it was sad. "Commodore's." He tossed me the key ring.

I missed with my left hand. They hit the floor.

He rolled his eyes and smiled. His face grew somber. "You've got until your eleven a.m. briefing." Before I could say anything, he left the room.

How'd he know? Mulling it over, I surmised that it was because he would've planned on doing the same thing. The jury was still out on whether Dobrek getting to know me well enough to anticipate my moves was a good thing or a bad one.

I took two of the pills he'd given me. My shower was woefully brief and much harder than I would've thought. Getting dressed was tough, but not undoable. When I checked the hallway, there wasn't a guard, but a full cart of food waited for me.

Loading up on calories helped some. What I needed was sleep, but that was about as likely as a flood in the desert. Provided I could stay a step ahead of Dr. Stabhappy. I stopped. It suddenly occurred to me that overall, I was upright and moving much better than I should've been, everything considered. How? Why? My mind rewound the last twelve hours.

Galahad...Henry's Ethereal core self. Something he hadn't actively had when I'd first come on board the ship. It made me wonder what Me had done to him while I'd slept because that's where the healing to keep me upright had come from earlier when he'd overwhelmed me with his power. What the higgity hollowed hairy harpy heckadoddles was that about? He hadn't been that capable before, so how had he done it? My brain switched to more gibberish, shying away from the whole thing as I pushed the cart back into the hallway and locked the door.

Needed to turn my mind to more productive things.

I searched the room. He had to have left it somewhere. William hadn't gone to this much trouble in setting up this room without providing me the one thing that I'd shared with him that my living spaces always had. In the wee hours one night, early into our relationship, I'd explained to him about where the hidden fighting equipment was in my place. So if we'd ever gotten jumped at my home, he'd know where to find things. Yeah, we'd lived that dangerously. He'd been torn between being worried about my practicality and being impressed by it. Apparently, approval had won.

My fingers found it. A push-in spring latch where a leg would've been at the head of the bed, hidden in between the couch side nightstand and the bed frame. However, it wasn't really a leg because the 'under the bed' area was one giant piece. No hiding underneath for me, but that was okay, because William's forethought had come up with something better.

There was a warm tingle under my fingers. Touch sensor release! Probably set to his and my fingerprints. I flipped up the covers as a drawer slid forward, sharing its goodies with me.

Inside, on the top tray, lay my old tactical outfits. Underneath was my own personal armory: guns, holsters, knives, sheaths, scopes, even a Celtic short sword. Everything a growing girl needed to go kick some traffickers' butts. A paper note rested on top.

As far as apologies go, this seemed better than flowers.

There was more writing on the back.

If you're reading this, then you've found the drawer, which probably means things are very bad otherwise you wouldn't have gone looking. Please, please, don't do anything utterly foolish that we will all regret. For me.

I couldn't swallow past the boulder in my throat.

Tear drops hit my legs. I swiped my eyes as best I could and sniffed. My brain refused to think further about his words, or the fact that he'd anticipated things going pear-shaped before I'd even stepped on board this stupid boat.

Putting on the tactical outfit hadn't hurt nearly as much as it should've, which was both good and bad. Pistols, scope, silencer, goggles, knives...I geared up and pondered grenades. Naw, those would draw too much attention and risk me as much as they might piss off the Infernal. Taking out the Humans shouldn't require that much firepower. The idea was to be quiet, sneaky and unseen. Slide into home without *it* knowing I'd left third base.

Physical pain teased the edges of my senses, so I took a couple more of Dobrek's pills. They were working fantastically, which probably meant that I would end up doing more harm to myself than was good. Though as long as I managed to save Edwards' niece and those other girls, then it was worth it. I did my best not to pay attention to how much risk to myself had suddenly become acceptable.

The plan was to scope out their warehouse complex, find the girls, free them, take out some normal Human baddies, and avoid that Infernal because it could clean my clock in a hot second. I was half Celestial. It was *all* Infernal. Though it did have some limitations while taking a physical form. Just like my mentor, Gilchrist, had had some limitations while in physical form in the Mortal world despite being an Archangel.

Regardless of the rumors, I had never taken down an actual Infernal. Half ones, like the opposite of me, yeah, but a full throttle, no holds barred, real one? Naw. As Tumas had said, that was self-destruction on a whole other level. So, put on the big spy pants, free the girls, and avoid the big bad. How hard could that be?

I pulled William's phone from the inner pants pocket of what I'd worn earlier. Sadly, after the day those pants had been through, they were toast. Figuring out the password for William's phone wasn't hard—Eliora's birthday. It was easy work to take the information off his phone and put it on the burner Fisherman had issued to me before we'd set out on the mission. A quick lift and shove put the burner under my pillow. That would give me enough of a head start.

"I am so sorry, William," I whispered standing in the doorway, his keys in my hand and his phone in my pocket. That blasted Infernal had provided clear instructions on where to drop and view the girls. It was an invitation for me sure as I was breathing. Nothing like fighting out of one's weight class to keep life interesting. Hopefully, it wouldn't think I was so stupid as to come alone.

31

Luck was with me. It was still dark out, which meant minimal staff and half the lights were turned off. That, and it was four in the morning. Couldn't ping to see everyone's location, but it was a good guess that Grace, Pippa, Fisherman, and Henry were probably in the infirmary area. Then again, Clarice and Ellie probably were too, which made it a safe bet that Cooper would be down there too.

These boots were supple and lightly soled, so I made no noise slinking down corridors. Most of the station operators were tired and glassy eyed. It had been a bad day for all of us. This had been *his* crew. Knowing him, they'd probably all been handpicked.

I slipped past the night operators and steered clear of the lounge.

Got to the exterior door that led to the gangplank.

A light breeze blew across my face. It felt good. I pulled a hood up to hide my hair, braided and secured in a bun. Never give the enemy a free handhold.

No one seemed to be patrolling the gang plank. I pulled a pair of night vision goggles and checked. Nope. No one in sight. Maybe it was a shift change.

I wasn't going to waste the opportunity. A brisk walk had me on the docks. I turned to the left around some stacked crates since I'd seen some vehicles in that direction.

"Ma'am?" A male British voice asked.

Dagnabbit. I stopped and turned.

He was one of ours, dressed in civvies like a cargo ship worker, but there was no missing that keen stare, awake and alert, just like he ought to be, even at this nutty hour.

I couldn't summon the gumption to knock him unconscious. "I am leaving on a recon mission."

"Ah, all due respect ma'am, but I thought Captain Mylonas had said that everyone was bunking down for the night, all things considered..." he trailed off into an awkward silence.

"Well yes, but this is on a need-to-know basis, and most everyone doesn't need to know."

He stared at me consideringly.

"I am a Commander," Nemo informed him.

The guard snorted slightly but turned it into a cough.

Time to change tactics. "You do realize, to some degree, who and what I am, yes?"

"Yes?" he responded cautiously.

"I served with the Commodore for years, many years ago, and when he brought me on this little boat, the Foreign Office reinstated me as a full Commander with all the rights and privileges, so as your senior officer, I am ordering you not to tell anyone where I am going, what I am doing, or that I have left the ship."

His eyes darted to the radio on his waist.

The thought danced across his face to wonder if he could radio Mylonas before I would stop him.

A sigh escaped. "All right. I'm going to lay this all out for you. I have intel. I'm going to go take out the creature that killed the Commodore. No lies, this is vengeance, and I will not do that by putting any of the rest of our team or crew in danger. Not risking anyone else's necks. Not again. It should've just been me the first time. The Commodore's son is good, but he's not me. I won't risk his neck, especially not now."

The guardsman's face changed, grew more stalwart. He stood straighter. In respectful silence, he saluted me. "Ma'am, yes ma'am," he replied with all that beautiful British gravitas.

I smiled faintly and saluted him back. "Carry on, Sergeant Barnes."

That got me a smile.

An idea hit me. "There wouldn't by chance be any cars here that we've co-opted?"

He frowned in thought. "Mmmm...yes, ma'am, those three over there." The good sergeant pointed out the ones I'd noticed before. "But the keys are back on the ship. I can get a set for you right quick."

My mouth quirked a wry half grin. "That won't be necessary, but thanks." I started to turn away.

Barnes nodded as his face grew solemn. "Godspeed, Commander."

A nod back and I was on my way.

***

I had managed to find a decent spot to ditch the car about a quarter mile southeast of the first warehouse in this section of the commercial docks. Darkness and the early hour covered me as I'd crept along its perimeter, sneaking in between all the shipping containers. Thank God they were tall, stacked, and I was short.

Taking a wide berth, closer to the service road on the east side, I made it to a large row of containers on the far northwest edge of a second staging lot north of that first warehouse. The row made it possible to get closer to the second warehouse right on the water's edge. It was only a long rectangle, not as big as the first one, barely two stories, whereas the other stood more than three.

There were more people here. Nighttime dock workers called out to each other in French. I managed to climb on top of one of the shipping containers for a better angle not too far off from the loading dock. My quivering right shoulder forced me to pause for a moment. I got out my thermal scope and slowly panned around for something holding lots of warm bodies in a confined space.

Bingo! In the far right corner, inside the building, a sizable heat bloom ebbed and flowed. Everything in me wanted to unfurl just a little bit of power to reach out and make sure I was right, but I didn't dare. Couldn't risk hurting myself by trying to use juice I didn't have, and there was no telling if the Bigbad Scary was in the vicinity. It all had to be done the mundane way. Hadn't done things 'the mundane way' in more than half a century. Ugh.

"Time's a wasting," I whispered to myself on a heavy exhale. It was hard to take the extra time to people watch, but I needed to get some sense of the pattern of the workers and/or any guards' movements. As best I could tell, there were four workers and two guards on patrol. Easy peasy.

The workers were thankfully keeping to themselves. Guards one and two were discreet about their gun toting status, nothing worse than some sort of short AK variant.

They walked a fifteen minute patrol in and out of the warehouse.

I waited for the guards to leave the loading zone.

Two of the workers went back inside for an espresso break.

It wasn't going to get any better than this.

Lining up the scope, I took the shot.

Dropped one.

The other came back towards him, face in his clipboard.

Just as he realized his buddy was on the ground, I pulled the trigger.

Number two dropped.

I scrambled down off my shipping container and raced for the elevated loading zone. It was higher up to accommodate the semis that came for their loads. Four giant truck sized garage doors loomed across the loading zone with a person sized metal door at the far right end. Both of the two garage doors, and the person sized door, on the right were closed.

The garage door beyond them stood open, which was where the bodies were.

Stairs on the very end of the right side gave me an easy way up onto the loading dock.

I hurried across and dragged one guy behind some crates. Came back and listened.

Didn't hear anyone moving.

Grabbing the second body, I dragged him over to the other one.

The person sized door on the end opened.

I dropped to one knee, took aim, and shot one to the chest, one to the head.

He must've been wearing body armor because the first shot made him stagger, but the second shot dropped him.

I scooted over to check the body. Dead-dead. No residual Energy. He wasn't linked to my nasty new enemy. Good.

He had a key ring. Even better!

Took that, his pistol and his AK. I pulled on the door handle. Locked.

With a grimace, I breathed in deep and moved the pins and tumblers with my mind.

Click.

My head throbbed painfully.

The keys jangled in my pocket.

Fisherman's words about reflex decisions echoed in my head. Know-it-all jerk. Wasn't going to be able to do that again even if I wanted to, sufferin' succotash.

Trying not to curse further, I slipped through the door and down a short hallway that spilled into the warehouse proper.

Before reaching the end of the walled portion, I crouched and used my thermal scope on the sporadically lit interior.

It wasn't easy. Heat blooms from the spaced out ceiling lights didn't help. But I kept it trained on the darker corner ahead of me where stacks of shipping containers stood waiting to be loaded onto ships.

Two guards stood near a container on the bottom that was lit up like a giant lava lamp.

I could handle two.

As I pulled out my normal binoculars, a better question popped up—if one of those two was the guy I'd seen walking patrol...

No go.

Okay, so I needed to keep him in the back of my mind.

I snuck from stack to stack, staying in the shadows.

Lined up around the edge of a shipping container. Paused to listen. Nothing.

Thwap. Thwap.

Two more down.

I ran for the container.

A sizable, shiny new padlock held it shut tight.

"Key, key, who's got the right key," I whispered to myself while scrolling through the keys on the guard's ring I'd stolen. "Maybe." Wrong one. Tried two more.

My hands sweated inside my gloves. "Yes!" Fourth one was the charm.

I made myself stop for a moment and listen. No sounds of the other guard, or the other two workers having discovered any of the bodies yet.

The door made a raspy grating sound as I opened the container.

Stench of unwashed bodies and other things assaulted my nose.

Soft feminine voices whimpered. Others shushed them.

"Hey!" I whispered as loudly as I dared. "Rescue! Up. Move. Let's go!"

"American?" one French accented voice asked.

"Yes!" More or less. My new persona's home at any rate.

This spurred the girls to pull each other up and grab the ones who were undoubtedly drugged.

"Eden!" I called. "Eden from New Zealand."

"Y—yes?" a quavering voice answered from behind some girls on the left. She stepped forward enough for me to see long wavy gold and light brown hair with big green eyes. No wonder they'd tagged her. I could see her uncle in that face, but more feminine.

"Uncle Brax sends his regards," I told her with a fleeting half smile. First he needed to survive his injuries.

Her face lit up like a signal bonfire. "Is he here?"

"No, but I'm going to take you to him. First we need to get everyone out of here," I explained. "Stay close, stay together! Help the drugged and wounded. I'm going to check first."

I pulled the automatic that I'd stolen around to my front in case it came down to spray tactics. A quick peek told me things were still quiet. My heart raced the bullet train of blood pressure because that wasn't going to last much longer.

"C'mon! Let's go! Eden, take the lead," I commanded.

She came forward with a petite girl's arm around her shoulders. The other girl's eyes couldn't seem to focus.

"Okay, head that way," I said, pointing at the direction I'd come. "There's a hallway. Everyone head for that hallway and wait behind the door until I get there. Do you know how to shoot one of these?" I showed her the pistol I'd taken.

Eden grinned. "Yes, ma'am."

I'd had a feeling. "There's one guard on the loose. He comes in, you shoot him. Understood?"

She nodded solemnly, but with a feral determination in her eyes that said more about her lineage than anything else.

I glanced around—now or never. "Go! Go go go!" I shooed the girls. The plan was for me to cover their six, count them, and make sure they all got out of that container.

"Fifteen, sixteen, seventeen," I mumbled and checked. All gone. Bit the inside of my cheek to not swear and cuss. These girls would never make it if I'd passed out from the power pull of damning these guys. Nor, if I were honest, was I sure that I could at this point.

With the pitter-patter of seventeen sets of feet sounding far too loud in my ears, we all ran for the side hallway.

I counted heads again as I picked my way to the door at the end.

Still had all my ducks. Now to see if I could safely get them down the row.

Eden and I locked eyes.

She had the safety off and a round chambered. Apparently, she'd given the petite girl to the next one in line so she was free to help me.

I gave her an encouraging smile and a nod. My hand moved to mimic opening the door slightly and looking for bad guys.

Edwards' niece nodded.

The door opened silently.

Missing guard and the two coffee break guys were all talking. My previous targets were now missed. Deep breath.

Head shot on the guard. Chest and head to worker one. Chest and head to worker two. All three dropped.

"Stairs," I commanded them in fierce quiet. "Run along the row of containers on your left until you get to the end. Hide in between the last two. Go."

Eden led the girls down the stairs.

A new guard showed up from within the warehouse at a run. "Hey! What the hell?!" He shouted in Croatian.

"Go!" I yelled at the girls who'd frozen in place behind me. "Go! Go! Go!" I added in French, German, and Turkish, some of the languages I'd heard in the container.

They didn't need to be told twice.

I took aim at my new friend.

Rather than aim back, he pulled something metal from within his shirt and blew it.

A piercing whistle split the air.

My ears rang from the sound.

I shot but it went wide. Okay, my head was ringing too.

Moving shadows caught my attention before my ears could confirm. More men. Dagnabbit!

Shots whizzed past me as I dove for the cover of the concrete stairs.

More shots cracked through the air as some of the mercenary guards dropped.

Wait. What?

I risked a glance off to my left, thinking Eden had found something more substantial.

Instead, I saw Junior and Cooper coming up the football field sized lot that was half full of parked containers, shooting and running cover. They were dressed in full tactical gear and looking like they were born to do what they were. A third silhouette appeared farther down the line. Dobrek!

Crack!

That was a sniper round.

Get those girls out of here! The punk shouted.

His words stopped the gaping. I hustled after the stragglers, whispering encouragement and commands to get moving.

Our group ran to the end of the row, ducking stray bullets, some whimpering, some crying, but a few were grim faced and determined to survive. I spread that last group out to help make sure they all kept together.

Once we got to the last two containers, I made them stay put while I ran for one of the smaller trucks I'd seen. Hot-wiring it took longer than I wanted, but faster than it felt.

I jumped in and drove it to the far side of the last two containers. Hopping out, I yanked open the back roll door. "Get in!" I shouted over the continued gun fire.

The girls stared at me fearfully.

It sucked. I understood why they were scared to get into another enclosed place like that, but this was the best we could do. *Grace! Ivy!* I yelled.

Ivy's not here, an out of breath Grace told me, *I'm coming*.

She burst out from between some of the containers parked in the middle of the lot in a full tilt run, her rifle case bouncing on her back.

Eden frowned at the approaching woman.

I liked this kid better and better.

"Go," Grace told me. "Go help them mop up while I get the girls to safety."

"Eden, this is Grace. She's part of the team. Go with her," I said. Couldn't bring myself to tell the kid to trust her because, honestly, I didn't fully trust her. Oh, I trusted Grace to get the girls out of here, but to leave me hanging for the authorities for this little party? Yeah, that was a different conversation.

Eden's eyes darted between us. "You sure?"

"Yeah, go. Get. Your uncle's waiting."

She surprised me with a hug.

I gave her a brief hug back and pulled away. Couldn't do mushy right now. Emotions were not my friend at the moment.

Grace cocked her head to the side, checking out my holsters. She handed me a couple of magazines. "Best go finish it."

"Yeah..." I turned and began running back to the fight. If I'd stayed, I wouldn't have gone back to the fight, because by now, we had probably caught someone else's attention. "Time to dance," I whispered into the night air.

32

Although it'd probably only been five, maybe seven, minutes since the firefight had started, it felt a whole lot longer than that. And sooner, rather than later, the sounds of sirens were going to arrive. We needed to get out of here.

My brain stopped as I ran, realizing that with as good as those three were, there was no way that things should still be going strong. There couldn't be that many bad guys, could there?

A spike of Junior's energy caught my attention.

No, no, no!

That was bad.

I got closer.

Mercenaries crouched along the loading dock and stood on the ground level shooting.

Junior, Cooper, and Dobrek shot in a good cross strafe pattern in controlled bursts, but their bullets weren't hitting.

Summoning a little juice, I *saw*.

Our worst nightmare had come out onto the loading zone and was shielding the mercenaries.

Another burst of Junior's energy preceded his bullets.

Down went the foot soldiers.

Oh hickory hossapple horsy hair! The punk had figured it out and no longer cared if he lit up the night.

Apparently, someone else realized why he was succeeding.

A throwing knife whizzed through the air nearly as fast as a bullet.

"Henry!" I screamed.

His body dropped to the ground.

The chaos continued all around me as I raced for him.

Couldn't hear a thing.

Music roared in my head as I dragged his body behind a container. I dropped to hands and knees next to his body, then ransacked his pockets for field dressings.

"Henry Galahad Bradford!" I yelled at him.

He didn't move.

The blade was cold iron. Poison for him. I yanked it out. Worse to leave it in there than to remove it. His blood flowed out from under my attempts at a pressure dressing.

It had hit him true.

Images of his father's fatal heart wound danced before my eyes.

"Don't you dare leave this world!" I commanded with everything within me.

The world tilted.

My vision sloshed sideways. Fluid slid down my face from my eyes.

There was no way I was going to fail William. If that punk brat was going to go down, I was darn well going to be the one to do it myself. Some nasty pansy demon bitch was *not* going to take him out. Not on my watch.

Power burst from me in shimmering waves and wrapped around, in, and through every particle of his being. "Henry Galahad Bradford, I call you forth, I call you back to this Mortal realm, by our Heavenly ties, by your father's dying wish, by my sworn Oath to protect you. You will breathe, and you will FUCKING LIVE, YOU MISERABLE SON OF A BITCH!" I cursed him to live again. "No cheating. No running away like a coward. If I have to live without your father, then by God so do you!"

Iridescent colored waves of Energy shimmered as they picked Henry off the ground. His wounds closed. Blood disappeared. Except for his uniform. Apparently, the heavens didn't do dry cleaning.

A small hysterical giggle escaped me.

Power put him back on his feet and his eyes opened. They glowed a flowing blue green. No pupil. No iris. No white.

His mother's gifts had risen within him.

As he settled on his feet though, his first conscious expression darkened that handsome face with the shadows of something very not good. There was no thread of pearl in his eyes.

I stood up with him. "Don't—"

"Get. Out. Of. My. Way. Nephilim." His voice echoed with power. He spared me a glare and moved past, away from the fight.

At first I couldn't understand why, but then I felt *it*. The nightmare had retreated to that first warehouse, and he was going after the blasted thing.

Sugar Daddies on popsicle sticks. Dangit! "Henry!" I called as I ran after him.

He paused between two containers.

This was going to be my only chance. I skirted around to get in front of him. "Henry, don't do this. You can't do this—well, I mean you might be able to but you can't because that is going to be really bad and I know because I'm talking from experience and that—"

"Stop!" he roared at me. "This is mine! I will kill it for killing my father. You will not deny me my vengeance!"

I nodded my head, a lot like a bobble head because things weren't working the way they ought to at the moment.

"You are crying blood and your nose is bleeding. Go to the others so they can take you back to the ship," he snarled.

Nope. Nothing doin', hoss. Someone's gotta save you, even if that means saving you from yourself.

A fresh spurt of blood slid down the sides of my eyes as I teleported the syringe I'd found in his pocket labeled "Nemo".

"Dose me? No, dose you." I stabbed him in the inner thigh.

He might be fast, but I was faster.

His fingers slid off my wrist as he collapsed to the ground.

I paused and leaned with one hand against a container.

There seemed to be less gunfire.

A thin wail could be heard in the distance.

With difficulty, I straightened. Had to go get Cooper and Dobrek 'cause there was no way I could carry the punk.

I turned.

"Hello my dear," the Infernal's deep cultured voice greeted me in delight.

Shite.

"Shite, indeed," it laughed.

33

The Infernal dragged me across the ground with preternatural speed to the first warehouse. It paused just outside the door.

I hit its hand with my last line of defense—the Blessed ring William had given back to me.

It screamed and shimmered from a tall, dark Eastern European man to an equally tall, beautiful woman with bottomless all black eyes and backhanded me.

Infernals, like members of the Higher Orders, could choose how they manifested. Apparently, its control was slipping if it couldn't manage to maintain its body shape.

Blood flew from my mouth as my body bounced off the ground.

That gorgeous, centuries old chain wasn't up to withstanding an Infernal's wrath. With a hard yank that sliced the sides of my neck, it was pulled from me.

I blinked.

I found myself inside the warehouse. That told me one of two things—either I was losing time, so not good, or the Infernal had teleported us, which could be good because teleporting cost all of us, good and bad, lots of Energy.

We were in a cavernous space, vaguely lit with the rising sun beginning to touch the upper windows. It held me with power in a standing position and began laughing.

I waited for a chance to break the bonds of power holding me. A sort of foolish plan, considering I had no juice left, my eyes and nose were bleeding, but hey, Human hope tended to spring eternal.

"You know what is the most delicious part of this?"

I gave it a flat look. "Is this where you give me the big Evil Villain Speech?" I drawled. If I was going down, I was going down swinging. Being an infuriating annoyance was almost as good as swinging.

"No, you poor pathetic fool. That Manon sends her regards," it whispered next to my head, where I couldn't see.

I froze.

The Infernal laughed.

"Oh yes," it continued, "Manon found out about her lover's little team that intended to curb the mischievous activities of non-Humans, so we worked out a deal where I took over here to entice your new friends to come play. It went splendidly.

"She started with making her lover swear that if he ever were to see you again, he could not have any congress with you, nothing, and he had been forbidden from telling you about their deal. That was her price for the child.

"Your enemy knew that sooner or later he would go looking for you in earnest. So when he and his team found you, she knew you would be wounded by him and not paying attention, especially with her whelp and the puny one causing you even more 'trouble'.

"The puny one had been feeding everyone all sorts of information, and you had no idea. Told the almighty Triad about the whelp by using someone's laptop. Provided us with your team's plans. Obtained extra power for more information once we were all here.

"It was a simple thing to kill your Human first. None of you ever saw it coming. Shame about the puny one though. She hadn't been sure if you would be able to banish it. However, now your altruistic nature has saved her whelp.

"She has won on all counts. The Human you loved is dead. His whelp hates you. Whispers have reached my ears that he even tried to Damn you. He'll be especially unhappy now that you've denied him his vengeance. Your team no longer trusts you since you abandoned them. They came with orders to bring you in, by whatever means necessary. You have nothing left."

It relaxed its power over my body.

My knees buckled as I dropped onto them.

The Infernal was right...I'd been a fool. How could I've been so blind? The enemy had led me by my nose the whole time. Mistakes and traitors at every turn.

...you've been a washed-up drunk for decades. His criticism echoed in my head.

Maybe it was time to hang up the sword once and for all. It'd been nearly a millennium and a half since Gilchrist had found me and sworn me into service. Time for someone else to take the blade. I obviously had lost my edge.

My gaze stared at the floor and splatters of my blood with unseeing eyes.

"That's a good girl," the Infernal crooned while caressing my cheek and then stood up straight, making its voice boom. "Behold! The Triad's favored Devadas! Nephilim warrior no more! She will be ours once we drag her down and break her on the rocks of her own misery! Hell's newest Infernal."

It stepped back and turned.

A sword flew out of the darkness, keen and reflective of all the misery and pain it had caused through the centuries. Even though we didn't run around Highlander style, swords were still the most effective way to kill one of us. Swords could hold some of our Energy. They could be Blessed or Damned.

My enemy stalked forward, letting the sword draw sparks off the ground while dragging the miserable thing behind itself. "Say goodbye to the Mortal world, Ne-mo." The sword was brought up for me to see all the tortured souls' pain trapped within its dark metal.

WHAM!

The door behind me slammed open.

I risked turning my head to glance back. My eyes watered at the bright light streaming into the darkness of the warehouse. Morning had dawned.

Henry?

Naw...

He marched forward as a halo of sunlight followed him. His tactical vest was gone. His uniform was dirty and torn. Cuts, blood, and slashes covered him, and he'd never looked stronger. He threw an automatic to one side. From the sound, it was empty. The punk thrust his right arm out to his side as if he expected a sword to be there.

A blazing one of sunlit fiery Energy appeared in his hand.

Sweet merciful Heavens! Please tell me I was hallucinating. If I wasn't—this changed the whole ballgame!

"No!" the Infernal snarled in an echoing shout as its physical manifestation slipped. "She is *ours*!" It got to me first and shoved that thrice blasted sword through my midsection.

A scream tore from my throat.

As I fell back, that brilliant fiery sword swooped past my head.

It slashed the enemy's off at the neck.

Everything shook.

A fissure opened in the floor.

My body got abruptly yanked backwards from the edge.

The Infernal's body parts turned to an oily substance lacking all light and slid down through the fissure.

Then it closed as if it had never been there.

I blinked.

The sword was gone.

Someone held me?

"Don't you dare die on me now," Henry commanded.

Oh, *he* was holding me. What?

I coughed up blood in response. More blood slid down the sides of my face from my eyes.

"Damnit Nemo, tell me how to save you!"

"Language...I think it's a little late, punk," I gasped as my vision narrowed. "Just do me a favor and stay out of trouble, eh? I promised your dad."

My vision went blurrier and darker.

"As I descend into the darkest realms, let me remember what it meant to hold the Light," I prayed in a slurred murmur.

"*NO!*" he screamed and hugged me to his body.

Odd, it sounded like he was crying. No way. He hated my guts. Had Damned me in no uncertain terms. Aw, crap.

"I Henry Galahad Bradford, son of William Harrison Bradford, child of the Heavens, beg You, please, please, save her. Do not let this all be in vain..."

He kept talking. I had no idea who he was talking to or why since I was mostly certain he had no idea how to swear any kind of Oath, and it wasn't like Gilchrist was around to help.

One of the Higher Order manifested in the sunlit doorway. Someone I'd never seen.

My spirit floated in that direction.

Chimes faintly tolled.

My head began to turn.

The Angelic One held up a hand, drawing my attention. *It has been settled. You will remain for now. There is much to be done and your journey is not finished.*

Have I not atoned enough?

Warmth and love filled me. *There is nothing to atone for, little sister. Simply continue as you have. Guard them well.*

My Spirit rushed back into my body. I gasped, or screamed, or both. Didn't know.

Henry nearly crushed my ribs.

I blinked.

Voices, so many voices. All talking at once. Rushing me somewhere. Telling me to stay with them. Where the higgity heck was I going to go? Sheesh.

Laughter.

Another pinch.
And sleep.

34

Sunset on the Mediterranean was nearly always spectacular, especially when one had only just come back to life earlier the day before.

The fact that my eyes were completely healed already had elicited deep thanks to whom I now suspected had a hand in my recovery. Vibrant hues of pink, orange, blue, and purple clouds danced across the skies.

I took a deep breath in and exhaled slowly.

A light breeze played with my hair as I stood on the deck. I'd snuck out of the infirmary. When Pippa realized what I'd done...whoo boy.

Dizziness filled my head momentarily, so I leaned on the railing with both arms. Okay, maybe being out of bed wasn't as good an idea as it had seemed. Though being fussed over so much was strange. Everyone wanted to talk to me. Ask me questions. Let me know that Edwards would be okay. Share their experiences. Make certain I was okay. Did I need anything? They just kept coming. I'd desperately needed some peace and quiet...and space, so here I was.

Arrangements needed to be made to get the higgity heck off this boat. That had to happen before anything else did. I couldn't do this. No more. Not again.

I'd saved him several times. I'd done my job. There were going to be more: more evil beings, more near death misses, more death.

I couldn't.

Sniff.

I was a washed-up drunk who'd nearly died far too much in such a short time. No way was I good enough anymore to keep him safe.

He was better off without me. They all were.

"And just what are you doing up here?"

His presence danced through me. It made me turn my head to look.

Wow.

A mantle of power had settled within him. He shone to my ethereal sight from the inside out for the first time. "Henry," I whispered.

He made a show of looking around himself. "Um, yes, unless you see someone else here that I can't."

I blinked, unsure of what to make of him.

The punk grinned wryly at me. "Yeah, I know...I'm still not sure how it's all going to work itself out, but I'm trying to be patient." There was humble shyness in his voice.

A pine needle would've knocked me over in that moment.

"Seriously," he said, putting his hand on my arm, "you look whiter than the clouds. Maybe we should get you back downstairs."

I put both hands on his face and stared deeply into his eyes.

It really was him, all of him, going straight back to his grandfather. He'd finally taken up the legacy his mother had rejected. Holy hotplates Batman! What had I agreed to safeguard?

Yup. Nope. See Plan A.

Celestial Energy suddenly zinged back and forth between us.

Each of us sharply inhaled as Energy sizzled down a strange new connection. We'd sworn Oaths to keep each other alive. I still wasn't sure what he'd sworn, but I knew that much. He still wasn't talking, but that was okay, since I had plans.

"Really? And how are you going to fulfill your Oath if you leave?"

I opened and closed my mouth. Nothing came out.

The punk was right. We were stuck with each other. It felt like Gilchrist's hand in this.

"I'm okay with it," he said quietly.

"Since when?"

He put an arm around me and turned us back to the railing. "It's a recent thing," he replied laconically, looking up to the sky. "We'll probably still fight. I'll make you angry. You'll annoy me. We'll call each other names. You'll teach me. I'll trounce you."

"You wish."

"You have no idea how much faster I've gotten at learning what you do," Henry replied with a dry sideward glance as he smiled.

My heart stopped and my throat closed.

He turned and tucked my head under his chin. "Yeah, I miss him too."

I didn't know what to say to that. For a split second there had been an echo of someone else's dry wit and warm smile. Yet, a part of me now rang with its connection to this Nephilim.

Someone completely different.

It was a connection I'd never had with any other of my kind. That I had never had with any other living being for that matter. I suppose that was the price we'd paid for making those Oaths. I needed Gilchrist to actually answer me so I could know for sure what was happening, and now that I'd noticed it, there wasn't a way to miss the thing. Yippee skippee. What the higgity heck did *that* mean? I poked at it.

Henry pulled back and glanced down at me in confusion—

Suddenly I saw something else within him.

I shut that door between us with the slamming strength of every cartoon character I had ever watched, heart pounding out of my chest as I leaned against it.

"Nemo?" he asked cautiously.

For once in my very long life, I honestly had no words.

"You do know that is a boy's name, right?" he commented drily, trying to distract me.

Didn't see him. Wouldn't let myself see him. Stared at the sky over his shoulder. I turned away and gripped the railing, feeling somewhat seasick.

"Okay, what'd I do?"

Holy Mother of Mercy, thank the heavens, he hadn't figured out how to read power to power or deeper mind to mind communications and emotions.

"Yes, yes, he has," he whispered. "Normally, your shielding is so strong I don't stand a chance, but you were just leaking everywhere, sort of. Something panicked you. I know that much, though I don't know what. It's a logical assumption that I did something." His voice trailed off into something sad and tired at the end. He'd rightly supposed, but not said aloud, that it had to do with his father...and with him.

I strengthened my shields. It took a moment or two of slow breathing and forcing my eyes to the horizon. "Henry, I will be disturbingly candid," I began. "Never, in all my life have I ever been connected to another being, Human or other, like I am with you. Not really sure what to do with it, or how it even works. Not sure any of the others have ever done anything like this."

His body tensed, like he was waiting for some sort of blow. Or the proverbial other shoe to drop.

It took all my courage. I glanced at him.

And promptly wished I hadn't.

His eyes gave it away. He expected me to reject him. To despise him. To leave him. He'd behaved horribly towards me, and now Henry thought that I would shove him away and jump overboard. The connection let me feel some of that fearful pain since he hadn't learned how to shield properly from me yet. His own mother had tried to kill him, more than once. His father was dead. Now I was going to leave too. He felt unworthy. All my vicious words had come home to roost.

I forgot what I'd been going to say. So instead I blurted the unvarnished truth, "I'm scared, Henry. This is uncharted territory. We've always been discouraged from this sort of closeness before, so I don't think any of us has ever been here."

He didn't say anything.

"I won't go anywhere...Promise," I said, testing the words as they came out of my mouth. Dagnabbit. I meant them. "You're right. I swore an Oath to protect you, so yeah, I guess you're stuck with me."

"You also promised the Captain that you'd stay," he replied quietly.

"I did? When was that?"

"When we brought you back on board. You promised to stay if he'd stop the Titans from wrestling in your head," he explained with a laugh and a shake of head.

Cue the eye roll. "Lovely."

He nodded a little. "I can stand being stuck with you. The better question is: are you going to be okay being stuck with me?" His gaze dropped to the deck. "I know that I haven't been the easiest person to deal with, or your biggest fan.... I am so sorry for that. For what I tried to do in the gym before. Truly. I'm sure there's lots of names you could add to that ever growing list of things you call me, but um, I want you to know that I promise to try to do better. To *be* better. Gil- Gilchrist–he- um, he showed me. All of my faults, all the terrible things I'd done." His voice dropped to a broken whisper.

Henry had gone to the place of Judgment. Wow...I knew that parade of pain. Now his expectation of me abandoning him made more sense as a flash of his memory of Gilchrist's displeasure leaked to me.

My heart sucker-punched me. "Yeah," I told him, my voice hoarse with too many messy emotions. "Yeah, I'm familiar with that feeling. He did it to me too. It's an experience like no other. And yeah, I can handle being stuck with you. We'll figure it out somehow." I tried to take a step and my left knee started to give way.

Henry instantly scooped me into his arms. "Right. Back to the infirmary with you."

"Punk," I muttered, feeling all too tired. Dizziness swamped me. My head fell to his shoulder.

"Seriously? Are you going to be all right?"

"Yeah, yeah," I mumbled, not entirely sure why I was suddenly in such rough shape. I'd been okay only a few moments ago.

As Henry turned with me to go back inside, I caught a glimpse of long, dark wavy hair disappearing from view on an upper balcony. Aw sugar daddies. That made no sense though; they'd always been like brother and sister. Trying to think was like my head trying to swim against a hard current.

"She's probably worried that we're going to kill each other," he murmured. "Or that you're going to leave, and none of the others want that."

My eyes narrowed as I lifted my head, trying as hard as a drunk on a three day bender to stare him down.

He chuckled. "I saw her too, and it wasn't hard to guess where your thoughts had gone."

I harrumphed. My head fell back onto his shoulder again.

"Try not to think too much, you're too far gone to do it well anyway," he commented.

"Just wait until I'm better," I tried to come back. It was lame, though.

"That was just pathetic," he said at the same time I thought it.

"Henry Bradford..." Pippa's displeased voice came floating out to us.

"Blo—"

He stopped and glanced at me. "Carries weight, huh?"

"Yes," I whispered and let my eyes close.

"Ah huh. I see that you're going to let me be the one to catch heck for this. Thanks."

"Learning by doing, punk," I murmured.

"You owe me one."

"Put it on my tab." My voice slurred a little. It seemed I was weaker than I'd thought.

No! Not safe! I jerked upright, opening my eyes. My heart raced. Danger!

"Hey, hey!" Henry crooned as I nearly upset us both onto the floor of a hallway. His power enveloped us both.

Hallway? When'd that happen?

The darkness had disappeared.

"Yeah, Pippa, we're going to need that," he said to someone out of my line of sight.

Pinch.

"Shhhhh...it's okay. You're safe. We're here. It's all right," Henry tried to reassure me.

"Hey, she okay?" Cooper's voice chimed in, but I couldn't see him. My eyes wouldn't stay open.

"She has a crew, a purpose, people who give a fig, and a much better base of operations," Fisherman stated. "She doesn't realize it yet, but she's *home*. Ms. Dade will be just fine."

Had I not been falling into unconsciousness, again, I would've argued with him...except that he was right. Great, now I was back in the World. So much for Plan A.

This was so going to bite me in the butt.

Tears seeped from my closed eyes. That just made me more upset.

Relax, I'm the only one here, and I promise, princess, you are safe, Henry whispered into my mind. A soft cloth wiped my face.

Princess? Seriously?

He chuckled. "I swear to guard your rest. Go to sleep, Nemo Aoife Dade."

I felt his compulsion as sleep pulled me under.

"Told you I was a fast learner."

"Punch," I slurred, absurdly relieved that I was safe and secure for the first time in a long while, so I let myself sink into a deep, healing sleep.

The End

Acknowledgements

An author's journey to create a story and see it finished as a book is so often presumed to be an isolated one. It's really not. While much of it can be solitary, writers need those human connections to bring truly creative endeavors to fruition. There are so many people who walk into and out of our lives during this process. A surprising number of them are so incredibly supportive either of us, or the work, or both. So, it's very important that they are acknowledged for all the wonderful things that they've done. Any missteps in this book are completely on my shoulders and not a reflection on the folks who helped. First, I'd like to express deepest thanks to my editor, Trenna—you are amazing! I also want to thank Michael, my publisher. Words, even my dynamic ones, don't do you justice. Thanks to everyone at Pepperback Press. You are terrific. Special thanks needs to go out to those who helped me with my research: Marc, Jim, Rachel, and Erik. You're a brilliant bunch. A sincere thanks to my readers: Katie, Dan, Steve, and Greg. To my fabulous writers' group, thank you so much for being so amazing, Dacia, Drea, Heather, Jess, Liz, Stacey, Stephanie, and Taylor. I would also like to extend tremendous gratitude to my family and friends for their love and support, particularly to my son, Xavier.

Keana Doyle is an Irish-American living with her teenage son, and their two feline queens, in Western New York. The "true" Upstate Region, a land of tall tales, taller trees, and the best pub fare in the North East.

When she's not writing, Keana teaches. However, life isn't all work. Gardening, trail walking, drawing, painting, and video games provide plenty entertainment.

Want more?

@pepperbackpress

Made in the USA
Middletown, DE
26 January 2024

48511623R00188